Hold on to your hats. What st
Wiebener masterfully spins into an Oklahoma tw...
ignored as this tale of espionage and politics moves powerfully from
one harrowing event to the next. If you like intrigue, *The Moriah
Ruse* should be your next read.

> —Ed Miles, Ph.D., Director of Psychology,
> University of North Texas Health Science Center

The Moriah Ruse is the best novel I've read about the world of
intrigue. Wiebener weaves a believable story that captures the
essence of how the spy trade works. This novel is gripping, full of
twists and turns while capturing the true side of human nature.

> —Kim Sardis, Division Director,
> Juvenile Services Division
> Office of Juvenile Affairs, State of Oklahoma

I was initially attracted to *The Moriah Ruse* because it features
female protagonists in a profession seemingly dominated by men.
Wiebener, however, has taken the 007 myth out of espionage and
replaced it—and Bond—with real people doing a thankless job
under impossible conditions. This is a great novel, one you'll want
to read twice.

> —Susan Damron Krug, Assistant Attorney General,
> Unit Chief, Victims Services, Oklahoma City, OK

I recently read *The Moriah Ruse* manuscript... and being a writer
myself, I flipped. It is a great read, holding my interest from pro-
logue to where "She took the tackle box from his overburdened
hand..."

> —Con Bliss, ex-Orange County Register staffer
> and political speech writer, Huntington Beach, CA

Wiebener's writing style is what I look for in a novel. Fast paced, well-researched, an ample supply of human nature with limited techno frills that tend to slow a story down, at least for me. *The Moriah Ruse* is intrigue at its best. You won't want to put it down.

—Roger Smith, CEO,
Valley Rehabilitation Services, Las Vegas, NV

Whether fiction or not, this story tells of the unknown, unsung heroes whose actions against forces that want to kill us, help keep America and the rest of the world out of utter chaos. A must read.

—John Wyckoff, computer consultant,
Oklahoma City, OK

THE
MORIAH
RUSE

MARVIN
WIEBENER

THE
MORIAH
RUSE

Tate Publishing & Enterprises

Published by Tate Publishing & Enterprises, LLC
127 E. Trade Center Terrace | Mustang, Oklahoma 73064 USA
1.888.361.9473 | www.tatepublishing.com

Tate Publishing is committed to excellence in the publishing industry. The company reflects the philosophy established by the founders, based on Psalm 68:11,
"The Lord gave the word and great was the company of those who published it."

Book design copyright © 2009 by Tate Publishing, LLC. All rights reserved.
Cover design by Kandi Evans
Interior design by Stephanie Woloszyn

Published in the United States of America

ISBN: 978-1-60799-956-0
1. Fiction / Political   2. Fiction / Espionage
09.08.14

DEDICATION

TO ERIK AND ERIN, TAMARA, AND TYLER
FOR YOUR LOVE AND KINDNESS; EACH OF
YOU BROUGHT HAPPINESS INTO MY LIFE
IN DIFFERENT WAYS. I AM GRATEFUL.

ACKNOWLEDGMENTS

A debt of gratitude to the many wise and dedicated staff at Tate Publishing who valued this project as much as me, and to Jerry Regier for pointing me in Tate's direction. To Lana Leist-Burkhart—the rancher, teacher, bartender, tombstone artist, world traveler, and friend since high school: for her encouragement and advice. To Leann Dykes, for her help when I had a quick grammar or computer question. To Cheryl Hutchison, for proofreading the manuscript and for all her astute suggestions. A special thanks to my gentle critic for her advice and patience, my wife, Peggy.

FOREWORD

Over twenty-five hundred years ago, the Chinese military strategist Sun Tzu wrote, "What enables the wise sovereign and the good general to strike and conquer, and achieve things beyond the reach of ordinary men is foreknowledge. Now this foreknowledge can not be elicited from spirits; it cannot be obtained inductively from experience, or by any deductive calculation. Knowledge of the enemy's disposition can only be obtained from other men." These simple truths set the stage for all intelligence operations. They are as true now as they were then. They apply equally to the movement of great armies or small cells—to a war of arms or a war of words—to the conduct of war or the decision to make war. The concept is the same: learn about the enemy (or a potential enemy) in order to defeat him.

Since its emergence as a world power, the United States has had to face enemies, both actual and potential. During the Cold War, the Soviet monolith posed a known threat with its legions of ground, air, and naval forces, backed by an arsenal of nuclear warheads. The simple principle of mutually assured destruction kept those forces in check and resulted in armed conflict with and among proxies—perceived or real.

The fall of the Soviet Union saw the rise of new

threats—some based on hold-over animus, some based on a resurgence of religious intolerance, some based on old fears rekindled.

The Moriah Ruse recounts a modern intelligence operation based on one of these new threats. It is more than a good yarn; it is a timely, believable story. In the tradition of the OSS during World War II, those involved include highly trained operatives and ordinary citizens called upon in extraordinary ways.

Marvin Wiebener does more than just describe the operation itself—how it was planned and how it was executed. In a very human way he relates how the personal strengths and weaknesses of those involved at all levels interplay to result in success or failure. Very realistically, he intertwines the kinds of unrelated, nonetheless real, political considerations that place in jeopardy those called upon to carry out the operation. In the end, he paints a very modern picture of the ancient principle so greatly described by Sun Tzu.

—Tom Walker
Brigadier General, retired
former intelligence agent

PROLOGUE

During the fall of Saddam Hussein's tyrannical ruling body of murderers and frightened puppets, and while the rest of the world was rejoicing, an event was taking place that many historians describe now as the property crime of the millennium. Lawlessness prevailed; opportunistic thieves ransacked the Iraq Museum International (IMI) in Baghdad, taking priceless Mesopotamian-era artifacts. By April of 2003, the United Nations, along with the US State Department, the CIA, and the FBI, were all working hand in hand in an attempt to retrieve as much of the stolen property as possible. Cooperating countries, the US included, passed laws making it a crime to buy, sell, or possess any item found to be on the museum's inventory. United States and coalition forces were warned not to be in personal possession of an artifact, and if something of historical or cultural significance was discovered during military operations, it was to be turned in immediately to the commanding officer. A special liaison from the UN was assigned an office within the green zone. All artifacts found in or around Baghdad were to be turned into that office for cataloguing and safekeeping.

In May of 2003, US Marines with a reconnaissance unit assigned an exploratory task discovered a cache of weapons, computers, and two crates of artifacts. The crates were marked, according to the translator, as belonging to the IMI. Three prisoners were taken in with the discovery, and by late that afternoon, an inventory had been taken and the IMI crates transferred to the UN liaison's office.

The US State Department contracted with three companies for the purpose of authenticating treasures found in Iraq. The contractors were also to authenticate any relevant cultural treasure seized outside the boarders of Iraq thought to belong to the IMI. One of those companies, Carlos Ramirez and Associates, LLC, was located near the Smithsonian complex not far from the National Mall in Washington, DC.

CHAPTER 1
NORMAN, OKLAHOMA
MONDAY, AUGUST 19

Dr. Lee Bethel and his wife hadn't been asleep long when the phone rang, Beverly, a light sleeper, awakened immediately and glanced at the clock; it was one thirty. A call at that time of the morning meant one of two things—a wrong number or an emergency of some kind. Her mother had been having recurring flashbacks of an assault that left her nearly dead during a robbery of their home several years earlier, and the anti-anxiety medication she was taking brought on side effects nearly as bad as the flashbacks. She just knew it was her mother, and at that hour, it had to be serious.

"Lee, wake up. It's the phone."

"Answer it," he said from beneath the pillow he had pulled over his head.

"It's on your side of the bed. Now answer it." Beverly was already out of bed, praying it wasn't a disaster.

Lee sat up and looked at the phone hoping it was a dream, but it wasn't. He fumbled nervously with the phone, realizing, in the fog of interrupted sleep that his wife's voice was full of urgency. Beverly pulled her robe sash tight and sat down on the bed next to her husband.

"Lee?"

"Yes. Who is this?"

The yet unidentified voice sounded eager. Lee couldn't tell if he was about to hear of an impending asteroid strike or that they'd just won the lottery. Beverly watched his expression for signs of relief or dread.

"Lee, this is Carlos Ramirez. I know it's late, but it's important."

"Carlos, what's going on at *this* hour of the night?"

Beverly let out a long breath of air and sighed, relieved it wasn't her mother.

"It's about our discussion at the Gray ranch—"

"Whoa, Carlos," Lee paused, trying to focus. "I can't remember what I had for dinner, much less our last conversation."

"I am sorry, Lee, but this is so important. Please forgive my inconsiderate manner." There was a brief accommodating pause.

"Okay, I think I'm awake enough to process elementary information, just speak slowly."

Ramirez obliged. "When I accompanied the Spanish Ambassador to the Gray ranch in July—"

"Yes," said Lee. The conversation was beginning to make sense. "You showed us photos of scrolls and several stone tablets allegedly taken from some museum in Iraq, right?"

"Exactly. Since then we've authenticated the tablets and determined they in fact were stolen from the Iraq Museum International in Baghdad. When we met in July, I had a translation of what was written on the tablets, but we hadn't confirmed their authenticity, so I didn't want to jump the gun and reveal the message without first knowing if they were the real deal."

"Carlos, I'm wide awake, my curiosity is in orbit, and I have two questions. First, what on earth did the tablets say that has you so excited, and second, what does any of this have to do with me?"

"I can't tell you what the tablets say, sorry."

"What? You wake me in the middle of the night, get my heart pumping, and you can't tell me what they say?"

"Lee, you've heard the expression used jokingly, 'If I tell you, I'd have to kill you'?"

Lee looked at his wife, the inquisitive sparkle in his eye slowly slipping away to a scowl. "Of course. Why?"

"All I can say, Lee, is that it wouldn't be a joke in this case. That's why I'm not going to tell you until the time is right."

Lee swung his legs off the bed and sat up straight, his senses alert to the conversations rapid slant in a direction he wasn't sure he wanted to go. The pause, since Ramirez's last comment had been long. Lee moved the phone to the other ear, hesitating another thoughtful minute while recalling his first encounter with the authentication expert earlier that year under very unusual circumstances in an equally unusual place. Bethel, a university professor and archaeologist, was working an ancient bison kill site on a ranch in northwest Oklahoma. The professor had used the kill site as an ongoing field lab experience for his graduate archaeology students. The box canyon was a treasure trove of ancient bison skulls, bones, butchering tools, as well as arrow and spear points dating back eleven thousand years. The field lab excavation was scheduled again this year, just as it had for the last five years, until the ranch owner, Fred Gray, discovered something on his land that not only brought the field excavation to a halt, but pulled the rancher's family into a dangerous state of affairs. Lee Bethel and his wife, Beverly, were deeply involved in the rancher's situation, much more than they ever expected to be, but in the end they were instrumental in helping to recover Fred and Helen Gray's kidnapped granddaughter.

Just before the Grays' lives turned impossibly torturous, Dr. Carlos Ramirez was called in to authenticate what the rancher had found on his property. Ramirez and Bethel formed a quick friendship and a trusting relationship during the turmoil that later surrounded the Gray family.

"Okay, Carlos, what the hell is going on?"

"I need you to help me with some archaeology details."

"What do you mean by *help* you? You just said you'd have to kill me if you told me what the tablets said. And, by the way, I'm none too pleased with that prospect." Lee looked over his shoulder at Beverly; he'd never seen her green eyes so large.

"I understand, and that will take some explaining on my part, which I don't have time to do right now."

"You know, Carlos, I'm no expert on biblical archaeology. I don't know how I can be helpful."

"I'll explain. First and foremost, I need someone on my team I can trust. Getting to know you this summer and seeing you and Beverly risking your lives to save Fred Gray's granddaughter said a lot about your character. Loyalty is the number one thing I need. I also need an archaeologist, not necessarily someone with expertise in Mesopotamian artifacts, but someone who knows how to excavate. You fit the bill just right."

A short pause ensued. "Lee, are you there?"

"Yeah, Carlos, I'm still here." Lee searched Beverly's eyes for a thoughtful sign, but he still had not wrapped his brain around what he was hearing, so how could she. "Where do you need me and for how long?"

"The DC area. I'll have you back in Norman by Sunday evening."

"Which Sunday, Carlos?" Lee was leery and wanted to nail down as many facts as possible.

"This Sunday."

"Give me time to sleep on it. I'll talk to Beverly and with my boss—"

"Forgive my rudeness, Lee, but I need to know now whether or not you can spend the next few days with me. And, before you say anything else, you have to know this is of national importance."

"National importance." Lee looked at his wife again, her wide-eyed expression still fixed on him, obvious signs of concern etching tight wrinkles across her forehead. "I don't suppose you can tell me why it's of national importance?"

"Sorry, no, I can't. At least not until after the vetting process."

"Hang on," Lee placed his hand over the phone mouthpiece and looked at his wife. "Says it's of national importance, but not why; says if he told me what this is about, he'd have to kill me." Lee forced a smile, hoping it would send the appropriate message. "Carlos says he needs me to come to Washington for the next few days and help him."

Beverly opened her mouth to speak, but Lee, anticipating the question, held his hand up. "I don't know, but I guess it must be important."

Beverly slumped forward, her reluctant nod barely discernible.

"Okay, Carlos, I'm in. First thing in the morning, I'll talk to my department head and make arrangements for someone to cover my classes. My secretary can make my flight arrangements, and—"

Ramirez interrupted. "It's all been taken care of—everything. You don't have to worry about any of it."

"How? What do you mean it's been taken care of? We've only been discussing this for twenty minutes, and I just now agreed."

"You wouldn't believe it if I told you."

"Try me; seems I've been gullible up to this point, what's one more wild story?"

Ramirez understood his friend's frustration, "I'll try to explain. The, I repeat, *the* vice president of the United States called your boss."

"Susan Randal, my department head?"

"No, your big boss, the university president. You do remember what he did before he became the university president don't you?"

"He was chairman of some senate committee, right?"

"To be exact, Lee, he was the longest serving chairman of the Senate Select Committee on Intelligence. Many considered him George Tennet's mentor. Anyway, those two talked, and now it's a done deal. All we were lacking was your voluntary agreement."

"Since you added the 'voluntary' piece, how can I refuse? So what's next?"

"You're on central daylight time, so it should be 2:12 a.m. in Oklahoma. At seven a.m. your time, a military vehicle will pick you up at your house. You'll board a military flight leaving Tinker Air Force Base at eight-thirty, arriving at Andrews Air Force Base at around noon. You will be met by two FBI agents and an agent from the Secret Service."

"Whoa, whoa. Why all the cloak-and-dagger stuff?" Lee asked, not expecting a straight answer.

"Before you and I get together and I share the information about the tablets, you have to endure about three days of intense vetting, that's why you'll be with the FBI."

"And the Secret Service agent, is he just along for the ride?"

"He'll be your bodyguard."

"Oh, wow, never had a bodyguard before. You think it's necessary?" Lee and Beverly were staring dumbfounded at each other. They both hoped after their summer experience a long period of rest was in order, but it didn't appear that was to be.

CHAPTER 2

Lee stuck the phone back in the charger and turned to his wife, both searching each other's eyes for a familiar look they could start an intelligent conversation over. Anything would do; a worried expression, a confused look, even fear, but nothing, just blank stares. Beverly shook her head to loosen her sleep-matted hair and stood up. "Don't go anywhere. When I get back from the bathroom, we need to talk."

"You mean I can't make a quick Wal-Mart run?"

She gave her husband a narrow-eyed glance as she rounded the foot of the bed. "Yeah right."

Six months earlier the Bethels were planning their summer activities, and for the first time in several years, Beverly planned on joining her husband at the summer excavation site. Lee was delighted, partially because of her background in paleontology; she could help teach as the students and

volunteers dug. He hated teaching, but loved the summer lab; between the two of them, she was the better teacher and could hold an audience spellbound for hours. But then something happened to change their plan. Lee received an urgent phone call from Fred Gray; owner of the ranch where the bison kill site excavation was to take place. Gray had found something in a cave, something his grandfather had stumbled across around the turn of the century. The rancher cautiously explained what his grandfather had told him about the discovery and about a family heirloom that had some kind of connection to the discovery. Lee listened to the old man; thoughts crossed his mind that maybe Fred was suffering from the early stages of dementia. Even though the rancher explained the events in an articulate way, paranoia was the first thought that popped into Lee's mind.

Beverly returned from the bathroom and sat down next to Lee. He was still staring at the floor. She lifted his chin and looked into his eyes. Her touch was gentle, loving, confirming. He looked at her. "Have I told you lately how very much I love you?"

"Yeah, about four hours ago. Now cut the crap and tell me what's going on."

"I'm hurt. All that lovey-dovey stuff was just manipulation to get me to talk."

"Yep, now talk." She smiled.

"Honestly, you know as much as I know."

"Except the details. Where are you going and for how long?"

"According to Ramirez, the vice president of the United States called the boss and arranged for me to be on loan to the government for a week."

"*The* US vice president?"

"That's what I said."

Beverly shook her head again, trying to organize thoughts that refused to fall into some kind of organized pattern. "What's next?"

"Someone from Tinker will pick me up at seven a.m…" Lee looked at the bedside clock, frowning. "That's only four hours from now."

"How long will you be gone?"

"Carlos assured me I'd be home by Sunday." Lee's answer tapered off with the sound of uncertainty.

━━━━━━━━━━━━━━━━━

At 0800 hours, the blue unmarked Ford Taurus pulled onto the tarmac at Tinker and drove to within ten feet of the ladder-way leading to the fuselage of the giant C-17 Globemaster. A master sergeant motioned Bethel aboard. Without trying to say anything over the din of the engine noise, he handed him communication headgear and pointed to a seat. As soon as he was seated, an airman plugged his headgear into a jack under the armrest. "Buckle up. We're taking off."

The plane was wheels up within ten minutes banking sharply to the left, headed east. The noise never subsided; Lee could see the fuselage wasn't insulated like a commercial aircraft. *Obviously not built with passenger satisfaction in mind,* he thought. The C-17 had one purpose, and that was to deliver cargo and soldiers to war zones as quickly and efficiently as possible. There were nine other passengers aboard, all in uniform, mostly officers sporting pilot wings. Some were trying to doze while others read. The loadmaster and one enlisted crewmember hurried about checking the cargo bay and mouthing words over their headphones to one another that Lee couldn't hear.

Bethel settled back in the semi-comfortable seat and thought about how his and Beverly's life had changed in the past few months. Fred Gray hadn't been paranoid or sliding into dementia as Lee had feared. The rancher, in fact, was on to something bigger than anyone could envision, a treasure of unimaginable value but at an unthinkable cost. *Who would've believed it?* Lee thought. He certainly hadn't.

CHAPTER 3

WASHINGTON DC
LATE MORNING, AUGUST 19

The two FBI agents were all business but friendly. They even made attempts to sound sociable. "How was the weather in Oklahoma this morning?" the older agent asked. On the other hand, the Secret Service woman was not friendly and made no attempt to engage in conversation. She was precisely what Bethel had pictured when Dr. Ramirez said he'd be accompanied by an agent from the Secret Service, except the agent was a woman. Her black hair was pulled tight to the back of her head and woven somehow into a braided bun, and even in stylish lace-up flats she was a bit taller than Bethel. The agent knew what her responsibilities were, and she was carrying them out as ordered. In an odd way Bethel felt more threatened in the car with three gun-toting professionals than he had all day. The realization that this was a national security issue began to sink in.

Within minutes Bethel and his escorts pulled into base housing at Andrews. *Officers' Quarters,* the sign read. They passed by stately homes with manicured lawns attractively land-scaped, making their way along a tree-lined street to a house set back from the rest. It looked more like an office building made to resemble a residential home. Lee noticed armed air force security vehicles in strategic positions around the building. He didn't ask why they were there—Lee was concerned he wouldn't like the answer. When the car stopped the driver turned, "This is it."

The Secret Service agent jumped out of the car. "Please wait, Dr. Bethel, for the all clear." She stood scanning the surrounding area. Without making eye contact with him she said, "Okay, you may exit."

Bethel got his bags out of the trunk, and the four entered the house. Inside he discovered a very homey, yet military-influenced setting. A chef was busy in a rather large galley just left of the foyer, and a uniformed attendant was setting the table. It was nearly lunch time. In the turmoil of the day, after Ramirez's early morning call, he'd had a granola bar and a cup of coffee. He was starved. Bethel was shown to his room and told lunch would be served in ten minutes. He stepped inside the small bedroom and started to close the door. The Secret Service agent reached in and stopped him. "Only partway, please," she said. "I'll be right outside your door."

He hung his cloths in a closet just off the bathroom and splashed cold water on his face. Bethel studied his expression in the mirror, dismayed he hadn't yet purged himself of the clueless schoolboy look.

"Lunch," the agent said.

He dried his hands and face; she didn't have to call twice. As he left his room, he stopped just outside the door; the agent turned to see why he wasn't following. "Mind if I ask a quick question?"

She looked up and down the hall then turned toward Lee. "No, ask."

"Is it okay if I talk to you? Maybe ask a few questions since we're going to be seeing a lot of each other for the next day or two?"

The agent looked down the hall again and over her shoulder.

"Yes, it's okay, but don't always expect an answer. No offense, but if I consider your conversation distracting, I won't be paying attention to what you're saying." She turned back toward the dining area and stopped. "Please understand, Dr. Bethel, it is only your body I'm interested in; rest assured I mean that in the purest sense."

Bethel was sure he caught the beginning of a smile as she turned away continuing down the hall in front of him, ever vigilant.

The only ones seated at the table were the two FBI agents and Bethel. The Secret Service agent looked out the window then entered the galley. She took up a position that allowed her to see the galley and dining room with just a slight turn of her head. *Like a lioness,* Bethel thought, *watching over her cub.*

"Is it okay with you if we go by first names?" the older agent asked.

"Yes, I'd prefer it," Lee said.

"Good. My name is Frank, and my partner is Erik." Special Agent Frank Ellison scooted his chair in closer and opened his briefcase, withdrawing three folders all marked with the FBI emblem and the word *confidential* in large block red letters across the top. He handed one to his partner. The Secret Service agent was not in the room, Bethel assumed she was prowling the hall and building perimeter. "Frank, I'm curious about the Secret Service agent; what's her name?"

"Limber Tapanga Crisp." Ellison looked up from the folder he was studying. "Her friends, both of them ..." He smiled to emphasize Crisp wasn't particularly sociable. "... her friends call her Tap; we call her LT."

"As in Lawrence Taylor the linebacker," Booker added. "She could play linebacker for my fantasy football team anytime."

"So if I've got to have a bodyguard, she's the one?" Bethel asked.

"She's not just a bodyguard, Lee, she's a one-man security force. She's the best. Five years on the president's detail, a Howard University Law School graduate, and a Muslim, by the way. She speaks four languages, including her native Somali."

"All that and she chose to be a federal agent." The statement slipped out before Bethel realized its implication.

"And what's wrong with being a federal agent?" Booker fired back.

"Sorry, uh, you know with a law degree and all, just thought she'd be practicing law."

"Gentlemen, now that we're all friends, we need to get down to business." Ellison motioned for his partner to open his file and begin. "By the way, me and the boy here both have law degrees."

"Oh, well, I should have known better; it wasn't meant as a put-down."

The young agent slid a thin stack of forms toward Bethel, saying, "These are all the documents you must sign before we can begin the background study. Essentially, they give us permission to look into your deepest, darkest secrets. Any questions?"

"Not at the moment."

"So you are sure there are no skeletons in your closet, your mother and father's closet, your wife's, or her parents' that would be detrimental to you if we proceed?"

"Maybe some things I'm ashamed of, like the DWI and a four-day stay in the San Clemente, California, jail twenty years ago, but nothing sinister or anything I can think of that would make me a security risk."

"Then read 'em, sign 'em, and we'll get this show on the road," Ellison said, refilling his cup. He held the pot up, but they shook their heads.

They moved into a small office just off the dining room as soon as lunch was over. A desk, phone, and three chairs were the only furnishings. There were no accoutrements, nothing to make the space look homey and inviting. The room reminded Bethel of the interrogation rooms he'd seen on cop shows. He wasn't uncomfortable in the small room with two agents who'd just told him he was

about to be turned inside out, but he was none to happy about what he'd allowed himself to get into, whatever that turned out to be. The one comforting thought was something Ramirez said on the phone early that morning. "At any point in this process, you regret agreeing to do this, feel free to stop, and we'll take you home." With those words in mind, Bethel felt some control over his destiny.

After all the documents were signed and witnessed by the agents, Ellison lifted his head and spoke as if to some invisible entity known only to him, "Let the record show that on this date at 1400 hours, Dr. Lee Bethel, professor of archaeology at the University of Oklahoma, has willingly signed all necessary paperwork to authorize Special Agent Frank Ellison and Agent Erik Booker to proceed with an investigation into Dr. Bethel's personal and professional background." Ellison looked at Bethel. "Would you affirm this statement by saying yes?"

Bethel looked around the room but didn't see any kind of taping apparatus, nothing. "Is this being recorded?"

"Voice and video. It will be archived, unless we need it for pattern analysis, or to see if we can detect any discrepancies in your reporting."

Bethel bristled at the thought of some analyst geek deciding, by viewing a tape, if he was lying. Ramirez's words were still a comfort, at least to this point, and he refrained from making the "big brother" comment sitting precariously on the end of his tongue. "Yes."

"Thank you. Now, Lee, would you tell Erik and me about the phone call you received from a Dr. Carlos Ramirez earlier this morning?"

The next three hours were grueling. He'd never been questioned as thoroughly—not even by Beverly—about his life as he was then. Every stone turned, twice in some cases. All the cans were opened and the worms dug out and dissected with the skill of a surgeon. The closets were persistently searched. Booker took Bethel's military discharge papers, his birth certificate, driver's license, marriage license, and was in another part of the building verifying their authenticity. When he returned to the office, he had copies of everything from Bethel's high school diploma to PhD confirmation documents.

Tuesday was a duplication of Monday afternoon. Some of the same question framed differently, Lee guessed that was the agents' way of trying to expose inconsistencies.

By Wednesday morning, the three men were behaving like old friends, exchanging war stories, talking about football and their favorite vacation spots. Bethel relaxed, knowing the background investigation process was about over. He'd either be with Ramirez the next day, learning about the national security issue, or he'd be on his way home.

"One last question before we wrap up here." Ellison pulled another file from his briefcase and studied a few pages.

Bethel sat up and rested his elbows on the desk top, "Guess I can handle one more question."

"Start from the beginning and tell us about the Gray family situation."

CHAPTER 4

Bethel tried to read the report Special Agent Ellison was looking at from his side of the desk. "What's that got to do with the background investigation?" He knew the answer, but acting naive seemed to elicit information from the agents he wouldn't get otherwise.

"Just routine," Booker interjected.

"Not exactly," Ellison glanced at the junior agent long enough for him to get the message. Bethel watched the crimson flush rise on Booker's face. "Nothing about what happened on the Gray ranch appears routine." Ellison continued, "As a matter of fact, the first time I read the complete FBI report, I didn't believe it—too fantastic. The thought of buried treasure being found in a cave on some ranch in the middle of nowhere was—"

Bethel cut in. "Unbelievable?"

"Exactly. Unbelievable. That's why I have to ask you to detail the event, day by day. I don't want to be responsible for putting the FBI stamp of approval on your background check if you're one brick short of a load." Ellison gazed at the report again and then looked at the archaeologist. "Frankly, if I hadn't spent the better part of the last three days with you, I'd think you were several bricks short of a load."

"Yeah, well, you and me both. I still don't believe it."

Throughout the rest of the morning and into the late afternoon, Bethel described his relationship with Fred Gray and how the old rancher had solved a long-standing family puzzle that resulted in finding treasure hidden in a cave by Coronado four hundred years earlier. "Unfortunately that discovery led to the abduction of Gray's granddaughter…"

The agents jotted notes. Ellison held his hand up, gesturing for him to slow down. "Okay, now, tell us about the kidnapping."

"The kidnappers demanded the treasure in exchange for the little girl. Beverly, my dear and sometimes adventurous wife, convinced FBI Agent Peter Miles to allow us to deliver the ransom, and we did. Miles told us to drop the ransom off at the place designated by the kidnapper and then get out of town."

Ellison thumbed through several pages in the report. "According-ing Miles' statements here, you and your wife don't follow orders very well." He kept reading. "Looks like you were almost charged with obstructing a federal investigation." Ellison slid his reading glasses down on his nose giving Bethel a dubious look. "Explain."

"Isn't the explanation in your report?"

Ellison nodded. "Indulge me. I have to compare your statement with that of Miles. Please, this will all be over soon."

Dr. Bethel's explanation of the events, following the ransom drop-off, seemed to satisfy the agents.

"Okay," Ellison said, still studying the report. "I think we have all we need."

Agent Booker cleared paperwork from the desk, stuffing it into his briefcase. Bethel got up and stretched.

"Wait." Ellison looked at Bethel. "I'm sorry, but I do have one more question. It's not official, you understand, so you don't have to answer it, but I'm curious, actually more than curious."

"What is it?" Lee said, lowering himself reluctantly back into the chair.

"What was that all about?" Lee asked. Thankful his question about the president hadn't been some kind of signal to the agents that he should be disposed of.

"Routine maneuver," she said.

"Why?"

"To see if someone is following us. Don't worry, no one is, it's just SOP."

Agent Crisp popped her phone open on the first buzz and looked quickly to see who the caller was. She answered, listened, and then said, "Agent Crisp. One ObCirc confirmed at 2200 hours." She shut her phone off and slid it back into the case on her belt just as quickly as she had answered it. Crisp caught the driver's eyes in the rearview mirror. "You get that?"

He nodded, "Yeah, One ObCirc at 2200 hundred hours, shouldn't be a problem if the traffic thins."

"What's One ObCirc?" Lee asked, guessing he wasn't apt to get an answer.

"One Observatory Circle. That's no secret, everyone knows who lives there."

"I don't—"

Before Bethel got his reply out completely, Crisp was on her phone again speaking English but in a mode he didn't understand. She finished the call and looked at her charge. "The VP."

"You mean the vice president?"

"Yes, beautiful home."

He decided a follow-up was in order, "So is the VP having a big powwow at ten?"

"Appears like it," the driver said.

"Routine?" Bethel asked.

"Absolutely," the driver quipped, sounding frustrated. "Happens all the time. Just as our assignment ends, just as we're expecting some down time, the VP decides to have some cronies over for poker, sour mash, and Cuban cigars—"

"Agent." Crisp cut in with the authority of a general and the precision of a diamond cutter.

The driver glanced quickly into the mirror and then back to the road. He was young, Lee could see, and he had made a serious disclosure error. Whether the meeting was for poker or something far more serious, it wasn't the job of the Secret Service to interpret its importance or its reason for being. He knew the inexperienced agent was destined for a severe chastising.

The three rode in an uncomfortable silence thick with tension the rest of the way to Annapolis. Crisp remained keyed on the environment surrounding the sedan, but Lee felt a cold distance forming between them. The driver remained fixed on his driving task, saying nothing, tiny beads of sweat forming at the base of his hairline glistened in the evening sunlight. The sedan made a right hand turn off the highway onto West Street and eventually back left passing the Maryland State Capitol building. Lee saw a sign indicating the Naval Academy was just up ahead. The agent turned the car onto a residential street coming to a stop in front of a small gated enclave of townhouses surrounded by stylishly designed landscaping. Beautiful trees, shrubs, and flower beds arranged around large, tastefully placed native stone gave the area a true forest appearance. All constructed with one purpose in mind—hiding the high security fence surrounding the property. The driver pulled up next to a keypad box and entered a code; the ornate iron gate began to slide open. A small building just inside the fence designed to architecturally blend with the landscaping stood in the center of the enclave entrance and exit streets. A uniformed security man stepped out of the building, and Agent Crisp flashed her credentials. The man reached for the wallet, but Crisp wouldn't let go. "I need to take a closer look, ma'am," he said.

"I understand, but I'm not turning loose of my credentials," Crisp said unambiguously.

The man bent down to get a closer look at the photo ID and motioned them through. Seconds later they parked in front of a door designated D4. Lee reached for the door handle, but it remained locked when he pulled.

slowly ebbing. The atmosphere in the room took on a relaxed air. "Never in my wildest imagination would I have thought we'd be where we are today. It's amazing."

"What's amazing, Jerry?" Unger asked.

"That the guy I used to have a beer with in that Georgetown bar would end up the national security advisor to the president."

"It's a wonder, isn't it? I mean, think about it: how do average folk get into jobs like these? Sometimes I think it was a comedy of errors." Unger smiled haplessly. "For me at least, certainly, it was not a planned, well-thought-out strategy on my part. If I'd put some intelligent thought behind it, I never would have voluntarily put my family and me through all this crap. And speaking of crap, we need to get to the business at hand."

The vice president explained that a discovery of significance was made recently in Baghdad. "The discovery is noteworthy in and of itself; however, it's given our illustrious CIA director an idea she briefed me on this morning."

James "Jim" Parker, the secretary of state, and other than Webster, the newest face in the group, moved his chair closer to the table. "If I may?"

"Certainly, Jim. What's on your mind?" Unger said.

"Is the president aware of what you're getting ready to tell us, and for that matter, what about the attorney general?"

"No, Jim, they don't know."

The secretary hadn't had time to learn the ropes yet. Parker, a Harvard graduate, former ambassador to Russia, and long-time personal friend of the president—as well as the oldest person in the room—was respected internationally as a statesman, but nonetheless naïve to government's backroom activities.

"With all due respect to you, sir, I have to ask, if this is so important, why the president wasn't informed at his morning intelligence meeting?"

"Very good question; I'll clarify. The president is aware of this situation we are about to discuss, acutely aware as a matter of fact, and—correct me if I'm wrong, Maggie—he has entrusted those of us around this table to solve the problem." Unger looked at Margaret Winters for assurance. Winters nodded.

Parker looked relieved. "So he does know what we're doing here?"

"No, Jim, he doesn't even know we're meeting."

"Then I'm still confused."

"The president must have wiggle room when it comes to controversial domestic and foreign affairs. He'll be briefed, in a general sense, as will the attorney general. He will know we are doing something about this issue; he just won't know the details."

Unger let his words settle in, hoping Parker would come to the realization on his own without further explanation. "Jim, we can't, just yet, put the president in a position where he'd have to take a stand, and we can't put the AG in that position either. His job is to make a legal judgment about the efficacy of all endeavors that come to his attention. At some point the president will have to say yay or nay to an operation with huge international consequences. And the AG will have to say whether or not he believes it's legal."

Parker looked around; it was obvious everyone else had already caught on to the slippery concept he was wrestling with. "Plausible deniability," he muttered as he slid back in his chair. No one said anything; no one confirmed his muttering, not even the vice president.

"If there are no other questions," Unger looked around the room. "I'll ask Maggie to take it from here."

CIA Director Margaret Winters explained the recent capture of the three al Qaeda insurgents who were in possession of a cache of arms and stolen artifacts from the Iraq Museum International. "The artifacts were turned over to the UN's special liaison office in Baghdad. Within a few days, the artifacts were taken to a neutral site and examined for authenticity. According to the analysts, the items were genuine and belonged to the IMI." She took photos from her briefcase and passed them around to the others. "These are the antiquities recovered by the military." A short lull followed while the group studied the photos. Jefferson poured his third cup and walked around the room, admiring the paintings depicting Revolutionary and Civil War battle scenes. Still standing, he asked, "So, Maggie, what have these antiquities to do with us?" The Secretary of Defense's tone was impatient, but his question was crafted respectfully.

"Promise not to laugh or roll your eyes?" she said.

"I promise but can't speak for the rest."

"It's the ark." Maggie allowed the word to sink in before continuing.

"The ark?" Parker asked, squinting at the very real possibility he'd misunderstood her.

"Yes, the ark of the covenant. Those tablets pictured there explain what happened when the Babylonians destroyed Solomon's Temple."

"The ark, Maggie, has been the most sought-after religious symbol in the world. As far as I know, there isn't evidence to support any of the various tales concerning its whereabouts." Norm smiled. "I know. I watch the Discovery Channel."

A round of gentle laughter followed.

"You're right. Until now there has only been rumor. But that's not the point. For the record, I don't even believe it exists."

Jefferson returned to his seat. "Then tell us, what's the point?"

Unger waved at Winters. "Maggie, can I say something before you go on?"

"Of course."

"Friends…we can't afford another Iraq. We can't afford the expense, too many lives and too much money, so we have to undertake this next operation Maggie is about to explain, when I shut up, in a much different way." The vice president paused, mulling his next remarks. "All the communications and human intelligence we've analyzed over the past eighteen months points to a southwest Asia, Middle East meltdown occurring in the very near future."

"But, Bill, that's nothing new. My gawd, the Kurds and Turks, Pakistan and India, China and Tibet, Israel and their legion of enemies, not to mention Iran, Afghanistan, just to name a few of the players." Jefferson leaned back in his chair, shaking his head.

"You're right, but here's the devil in these details, Russia's paranoia is back with a vengeance, and we've heard recently their unofficial government black market is negotiating a deal to sell Iran their newly re-designed MIRV."

"I'm sorry, Bill, a MIRV? What's that?" Parker asked.

"Very deadly," Jefferson said. "Multiple Independently Targeted Re-entry Vehicle, capable of carrying several nuclear warheads."

"I'm just guessing, from the name, that it's one delivery system that will strike several targets?"

"You guessed right, Jim. And of course we've queried the Russians, and they've denied it. We asked them to account for where all the MIRVs, are and they said they'd get back to us." Unger's voice rattled with cynicism.

"How does this tie in with the ark?" Webster asked.

The vice president gestured toward Winters. "Tell 'em Maggie."

"So, Jim, the answer to your question is no, they are not in bed together, but—"

Unger interrupted her again. "I agree, but they sure are thinking seriously about dating." The room fell quiet, everyone thinking about the complicated proposal and its frightening aftermath. The mantle clock chimed; it was four a.m.

"Maggie, I'm sorry," Unger said. "Please continue."

Winters explained while targeted factions were preoccupied with ark rumors a three-person team would be inserted into the port city of Chabahar to confirm signal intelligence regarding the MIRV shipments. From that point, the team would determine their next move based on what they find.

"What if the team doesn't find anything?" Webster asked.

"The Russians know we are watching, so we can expect them to perform their own razzle-dazzle. If we can't confirm they're shipping MIRVs to Iran through Chabahar our team will precede on to stage two."

"Stage two?" Parker sighed; concerned stage two would birth stage three, then four and so on, with no end in sight.

"Stage two, yes, the most important task for our team, eye-balling Iran's nuclear capabilities."

Unger tossed out more photos. "Remember these?"

Jefferson shook his head and scooted his photo back in Unger's direction. "One of our more embarrassing intelligence snafus. A sat photo of a couple of empty trucks we thought were mobile chemical warfare labs."

"Exactly, and that ain't gonna happen again. I don't mind us being wrong, that's human, but I won't be played for a sucker twice." Unger's color flushed crimson. Pointing angrily at the photo, he said, "We're not—I repeat—*not* going to send another marine or soldier to his death because of our misjudgment. We are going to be absolutely certain this time." Bill Unger pulled his glasses down lower on his nose to get a better look at the photo. "Maggie, finish up. I won't interrupt again," he said, trying to salvage some of his rapidly evaporating composure. "Tell us about this team of yours."

"Yes, sir, the team." Winters drew in more air than usual, she was apprehensive about how to sell the most important element of her plan to this particular group of men.

"As I see it, Carlos, you're thinking about how to get at the ark."

"Without disturbing the surface and in total secrecy," Ramirez said, easing back onto the couch, avoiding Bethel's wide-eye stare.

"What?"

"That's why you're here, to tell me how to do it."

"I'm an archaeologist, Carlos, not a magician. There's no way it could be done in secret."

"But it must, and here's the reason why."

Ramirez explained the fragile nature of the Arab and Israeli conflict from its origin with the birth of Ishmael to Abraham and Hagar.

"Carlos, with all due respect—"

"Sorry, I know you've read your Bible, and you know all this, but I want to emphasize the importance of understanding that this conflict didn't just start. It is the longest and most thoroughly dissected conflict between people ever known, and it will continue."

"And you're telling me this discovery, if in fact it's there, will provoke an all out war. At least that's what you're implying."

"I don't know that to be true, but I do know discovering the ark would validate ancient prophecy, and most likely, prevent reason and diplomacy from getting a foothold." Ramirez paused to anoint his burning red eyes with drops.

"I don't think reason and diplomacy have ever had a foothold, do you?"

"Frankly speaking, no, I don't think so, but regardless, the ark could bring the conflict to a devastating head." Ramirez held a finger up as though ready to make a proclamation; he hesitated. Bethel could see the drops weren't helping. His eyes still red, the freshly applied rinse running down Carlos's cheeks like tears.

Ramirez wiped his eyes with a bar napkin. "Lee...we must...absolutely must find out if the ark is there."

"And if it is?"

"I don't know, Lee. At this point it's one step at a time." Ramirez clicked another button on the laptop."

"The Western Wall?"

"Yes, the Western Wall, or what remains of the Jewish Temple destroyed by the Romans some years after the crucifixion of Christ."

Bethel studied the four photos displayed on the monitor. "And the wall's significance to the location of the ark?"

Ramirez pointed to a shadow near the north end of the wall. "That's a door, and we have permission to go inside."

"What's there?"

"Many passageways that meander through the huge subterranean vault directly below where Solomon's Temple stood."

"Okay, sounds easy enough," Bethel quipped. "Just march in there under the cover of darkness—I'd pick a moonless night—and take a look around."

"We have, but not at night, there is no such thing as night at the Wailing Wall."

"No night?"

"No. In the day, of course it's bathed in sunlight, and at night it's illuminated by large security lights and guarded by Israeli soldiers. So as a special favor to the president, we got a guided tour conducted by a renowned Israeli archaeologist and a renowned Arab archaeologist. It was a courtesy tour, a very rare one indeed."

"Did you inquire about the ark?"

"Absolutely not. We simply passed ourselves off as a temple study group employed by the Smithsonian."

"What did you see?"

"Mostly excavated rubble, huge stone used in the building of the first temple and the second. But many of those monoliths were arranged in what appeared to be a pattern that was obviously not part of the rubble."

"Did you ask about that?"

"Yes."

"And?"

"The guides' just shrugged. Foundation blocks, they said. I

Iran, and Afghanistan." The director stopped to allow the others to assimilate the information. Winters knew putting a team together with these skills and qualifications would be difficult, but her next requirement would cause the most conflict and narrow the field of candidates even more. "Gentlemen, to make this work...the two people must be brown eyed, and they must be women."

"Send two women into Iran to do, from what I can tell, a nearly impossible job. That's ridiculous, preposterous. What, on God's green earth are you thinking, Maggie?" Jefferson said, pounding his empty cup like a gavel on the hundred-year-old conference table.

"Whoa, August, take it easy on the table. You scar it up, and I'll have to pay for it." Unger was only partially kidding.

"August...I don't want to get into a war of the sexes with you. Just hear me out."

"I've heard about all I can stand, Maggie—"

"Excuse me, August. I promised myself I wouldn't play the gender card, but I'm breaking that promise with a question."

"By all means, Director, ask," his voice showing restraint.

"Would I get this kind of reaction from you if I were a man?"

"Friends," Bill Unger barked. "We've still got work to do and no time for petty spats. August...hear her out, please."

Agitated, but willing, the secretary of defense sat back in his chair, taking a deep breath; he didn't like what he was hearing. August Jefferson was old school, and he couldn't imagine putting a woman in danger.

"Gentlemen, a woman will be easier to disguise than a man, plus, women are virtually ignored as long as they are abiding by religious law, and part of the traditional law is covering. They will not be expected to converse, because they are women. Silence is a virtue in the region, at least when it comes to women." Winters looked at Jefferson as she explained. "The team will wear traditional clothing, which will afford them some ability to hide necessary tools of the spy trade."

"And how do we find two women that will fit within these parameters?" Parker asked.

"The CIA has already completed a computer profile search of women who either are or have been members of our agency, Secret Service, FBI, ATF, and DEA."

"How many?" Smith asked.

"Five." Winters passed the list of names around the room.

"Who else has seen these names?" Unger said.

"No one. All data regarding the members profile was encrypted and sent directly to my computer and mine alone."

"Any chance someone could hack in?"

"Not much, but I never say never. If someone tries though, we'll know."

Smith looked the list over and handed it to the FBI acting director. Webster sat up, tapping his finger on a name. "I know her."

"Which one?" Winters leaned in close to see what name he was pointing to.

"Crystal Stanton. She was my partner twenty years ago. If she'd stayed with the FBI, I think she would've become the first woman director." Webster paused, thinking. "She's really good at what she does, and she fits your requirements perfectly, although I didn't know she spoke Farsi, and the last time I saw her she was blond."

"According to her file, she participated in several undercover operations throughout the Middle East."

"Yeah, Maggie, and I wasn't privy to any of that. Coincidently, I had contact with her this past summer. Do you remember all the fuss about some rancher in Oklahoma finding Coronado's gold?"

"Yes. That made headlines for a month."

"She's the sheriff of the county where the treasure was found."

"What's a former FBI agent doing playing sheriff out there in the sticks?"

Webster shook his head, smiling. "It's a long story." He looked at the faces staring at him around the table. "Do you have the time?"

Unger quickly intervened. "No, we don't. I'm curious, but we must move on."

"Doesn't matter." Webster handed the list to Parker. "She wouldn't do it anyway."

"Why?" Winters asked.

"Another long story, but it involves a guy, and a strong desire to settle down and raise horses."

"That doesn't sound like a bad idea to me," Winters said. "But would you ask her as a favor to me?"

Webster nodded and, with a subtle sigh of reluctance to abide by Winters' request, knew he had to follow through; it was, after all, a national-security issue.

Parker looked the list over quickly and passed it to Unger. He gave it a cursory look and slid it back to Winters.

"My suggestion is that we consider Limber Crisp as the other team member, and we prep the other three as alternates in case we lose one or both members of the A team."

"Don't you mean D team?" Parker said somberly, surprised his thought was audible.

"D team...what do you mean?" Unger asked wiping his forehead with a once-white handkerchief.

"D for *dead*. This looks impossible to me; don't you have another plan?"

"I'll ask you the same thing I asked Mr. Jefferson, would it make a difference if the team were men?"

"I wish I could say I am politically and socially astute when it comes to gender equality, but in fact, I still see this as a man's job."

"I'm not stumping for Crys Stanton, as a matter of fact, I hate like hell asking her to do this, but when it comes to the skill it will take to pull this off, there is none better, and that includes both sexes," Webster said.

"I suppose you're right, but it's just counter to what I've believed all my life." Parker stared momentarily at the floor. "I just can't imagine sending my wife or daughter into that kind of danger. I guess that's why I'm a diplomat and not a general."

"Oh, believe me, Mr. Secretary...that thought crosses the general's mind too," Unger offered. "Okay, Maggie, tell us about Crisp."

The meeting went on until daybreak. Winters explained her reasons for suggesting Crisp be the second A team member, including the fact she was the only one who was a practicing Muslim. Although she was African, her skin was lighter than most from her tribe and only slightly darker than some Arab and Persian women.

The CIA director walked the others through the entire operation without the use of handouts or any other visual aids. "The less documentation the better," Winters said, describing the mission purpose. She explained the deception phase of the operation was already in operation, and they should expect to see news about the ark in the next few days. Winters suggested they be as curious about the news as they would've been without the knowledge they now had. The group nodded agreement.

Unger cleared his throat. "Okay, friends, let's wrap this up. I'll summarize. Maggie, you're in charge. All communications about Operation Moriah Ruse goes directly to you and no one else, correct?"

"Yes, sir."

"Webster, you'll approach your friend and encourage her to participate in this operation?"

"I will, but I'm sure she'll refuse."

"Well, we won't know until you ask her, will we?"

"No, sir."

"I'll call Richard at treasury and tell him to transfer Crisp to temporary duty as part of my security detail. I'll say I need someone with a Muslim background who speaks Arabic." The vice president studied his blank legal pad, "Now, Maggie . . . uh, I might sound hard-nosed about this operation, but you know I agree with Parker. If either of these women were my daughters, I'd put my foot down so hard it'd make the Mt. St. Helens eruption seem like a fart in a whirlwind. Pardon my disrespect."

"No disrespect taken, Mr. Vice President. As a matter of fact, I agree, but how you and I and the rest around this table feel is not the point. I hate this phrase, but I can't think of a better one—it is for the greater good."

The five men and Winters sat mulling the far-reaching effects of what was about to happen, a thoroughly discouraging set of circumstances and no alternatives. Certainly a plan that even smelled like a military operation was out of the question. Operation Moriah Ruse had to be carried out precisely and in a manner providing political deniability for the president.

Bill Unger stood, the others followed his lead. He raised his half-empty coffee cup. "Maggie, August, Jerry, Norm, Jim...a salute to you, may our endeavor tonight pay dividends far into the future. God bless our country, and God bless this team."

CHAPTER 11

ANNAPOLIS, MD
0730, AUGUST 23

The wind had picked up from the east, and the cool breeze passed briskly through the open window in Bethel's room. The sycamore leaves scratched against the side of the town-house, making a slap-crackle sound. The noise wasn't at all disrupting, soothing maybe, almost hypnotic.

Lee opened one eye; it was dawn. The fresh air and symphony of nature's ambient sounds were relaxing. He remembered where he was. His first thought was to call Beverly, but he knew the time difference would make it too early. Lee rolled over to check the time, and the next move he made was a leap from bed to floor. It was seven thirty-five a.m. He remembered Carlos saying to meet him for breakfast at seven, and he hadn't even showered. He sprinted across the hall to the bathroom, shouting, "Carlos, sorry, I overslept. I'll be down in five." Lee didn't wait for an answer. He rushed through the usual fifteen-minute toilet routine in record time and headed downstairs. A light was on in the kitchen and in the small foyer. No coffee had been made; there were no signs of activity. He went back to Ramirez's bedroom, the door was open, and the bed made. Lee checked the downstairs bathroom—nothing. He stepped to the front door and found it only partially closed; Bethel stood on the stoop looking around the parking lot. Ramirez's car was still parked in the D4 space. As the anxious moments passed, Lee felt the excitement of a few hours earlier giving way to fear and the prospect that his decision to join Ramirez was a monumental mistake. He instinctively reached for his phone to call Beverly but remembered in his haste to get down stairs he'd left it on the bedroom dresser. A storm of confusion was brewing, and standing on the walk next to Ramirez's car wasn't solving anything. He jogged the distance to the front gate and asked the security officer if he knew Dr. Ramirez.

"Yep," the twenty-something kid remarked without any helpful follow-up.

"Has he been through the gate this morning?"

The wannabe cop looked at his daily log and shook his head. "Nope."

"Well, umm, he isn't at his townhouse either, and he was earlier this morning. You have any idea where he might have gone?"

The officer shrugged, adjusted his badge, donned his iPod ear phones, and blew a pink bubble.

Lee hurried away cognizant of the fact he was seconds from an assault and battery charge. He stepped up his pace, hoping Carlos had returned in the meantime from a neighbor with borrowed coffee, sugar, toilet paper—anything. "He just couldn't have disappeared," he mumbled as his steps quickened.

Harper County Sheriff Crystal Stanton maneuvered her truck up a narrow gorge and onto the top of a small plateau about the size of a football field, her favorite spot on the fifteen hundred-acre spread. The prevailing south wind had died to a gust here and there, nothing strong enough to force the Oklahoma red dirt, sand, and cedar pollen through her clothes and into every crack and cranny that wasn't well-protected. The short buffalo grass was a dull, grayish-green this time of the year; it hadn't had a drink in two months, and there wasn't much rainfall predicted for the rest of the year. But it was hardy; no matter what Mother Nature came up with, the grass, sagebrush, and cedar seemed to thrive.

Stanton parked, opened her door, and took a long draw from her water bottle. A few deep breaths, it was like magic, stress melted away. No sound other than nature's music. She reached down and shut her police radio off and did the same with her cell phone. Stanton leaned her head back and closed her eyes; she had a lot on her mind, and the plateau was the best place to think undisturbed.

A case Sheriff Stanton worked on that summer brought her into close association with a local rancher by the name of Robert Gray. The Gray ranch was at the center of a media frenzy. Robert's father had discovered a valuable treasure that eventually led to the murder of one of Robert's ranch hands and the abduction of the elder Gray's granddaughter, Robert's niece. When the dust settled, Robert found himself enamored with the sheriff, and eventually invited her to attend a church service, then dinner with his folks; that was a couple of months earlier. In a rush of adolescent excitement, Robert purchased an engagement ring; all he had to do now was work up the courage.

Stanton had a feeling, the kind one usually attributes to a premonition but actually was no more than unconscious expectation born out of desire. She wanted to shed the badge and raise horses; most of all, Crys wanted the love of a good man. As far as she was concerned, the time, and man had all fallen into place, perfectly. She knew in her heart he was going to ask, and there was no question what her answer would be.

Stanton eased the truck over the embankment and into the gorge headed south to the county dirt road. Her brief respite worked wonders; she was refreshed, happy, and cautiously excited about Robert and the prospect of marriage. She dug through the truck's console and found her newest CD and stuck it into play.

Regardless of her future plans, she was still sheriff, and that meant responsibilities she couldn't ignore. If Robert asked her to be his wife, she'd consider resigning, but until then, she had duties to perform. She felt the retreat-inspired relaxed mood fading fast. Stanton reached down and turned her police radio on. There was an instant squawk from the radio.

"Unit one, do you copy?" The dispatcher sounded desperate.

"Unit one copy. Go ahead," the sheriff replied.

"Ten twenty-five HQ."

"Ten four. ETA ten minutes."

"Copy, unit one."

The terse conversation ended as abruptly as it began. A familiar chill locked around her neck like a noose. A thought pressed through her adrenaline-charged mind, maybe she was anxious to marry Robert for the wrong reason. Could it be she was looking for a reason to leave the life she'd immersed herself in for so many years, and Robert was only the vehicle and not the ultimate goal? She shook her head, hoping that would banish the thought.

Sheriff Stanton entered the old office complex housed in the aging county courthouse. The dispatcher nodded and pressed a button, releasing the magnetic lock on the bulletproof glass door. Stanton looked around the office for a clue as to why she'd been summoned. Other than the dispatcher—who was busy responding to calls—she saw nothing out of the ordinary. The dispatcher, still giving a cop direction to a local fender-bender, pointed to a message thumbtacked to the corkboard next to her office entrance. Stanton pulled the note off the board and sat down at her desk. Buffalo, Oklahoma, was a small town, located in the middle of farm and ranch country;

everyone knew one another. There were no secrets, and as a consequence, Stanton's age was well-known. To the casual observer, Stanton could pass for thirty-five. Locals took great pleasure in having their out-of-town quests try to guess her age. That was only part of the sideshow, however. Her beauty was nothing short of spectacular, which to Crys was more of an annoyance as apposed to an asset. Age was another reason she wanted out of law enforcement, she had a lot of life yet to live, but the aging process couldn't be denied. It was there, in some small way, constant reminders were everywhere.

She looked at the note, it was a blur, and she knew it wasn't the dispatcher's handwriting. Crys rifled through her lap drawer until she found her ten-dollar glasses and tried reading it again. The writing was clear; the message unambiguous. It was from her closest friend Jerry Webster. The status box on the message marked urgent, and beside the urgent mark the dispatcher had written *911*.

CHAPTER 12
ANNAPOLIS, MD
0842, AUGUST 23

Dr. Bethel swung the townhouse front door open hard. "Carlos," he yelled. The only place he hadn't looked for Ramirez was the upstairs living room; he took the stairs two at a time. The room was bathed in morning light but otherwise empty. As Bethel neared the hall leading to his bedroom where he'd left his cell phone earlier, he noticed the laptop was no longer on the coffee table. He remembered Carlos saying he would leave it there so they could pick up where they left off. Lee walked quickly back to where he'd slept and searched through his personal items until he found Agent Ellison's card. On the blank side of the card Ellison had written his cell number. "Just in case," Lee recalled the agent saying. Bethel keyed in the number and quickly downloaded it to his cell phone memory, then pressed send.

"Ellison," the agent barked.

"Frank, it's Lee Bethel." He held his tone down to avoid sounding alarmed, and steadied his voice to make sure Frank didn't miss anything he was about to say.

"Yeah, Lee. What's goin' on?"

"The man I came to see, after leaving Andrews yesterday."

"Yeah, Dr. Ramirez, what about him?"

"We talked late, and then went to bed with plans to continue our discussions early this morning. When I got up, he was gone."

"Gone. Gone how, where?"

"He's gone. The computer with classified information is gone. When I came downstairs this morning, his front door was open a few inches, and he wasn't anywhere around. I've checked with security at the front gate, and he says there is no record of him leaving the townhouse enclave this morning."

"So his car's still there?"

"Parked exactly where it was when I got here yesterday."

"Any sign of struggle?"

"No, as a matter of fact, with the exception of the front door being left open, the place actually looks cleaner than it did when I went to bed."

"Yeah, well … the only thing worse than a bloody, chaotic crime scene is a clean crime scene, that's assuming a crime has been committed, and that's a stretch at this point."

"So, what do—"

The agent anticipated Bethel's next question.

"Here's what I want you to do, Lee. Don't, and I mean *don't* touch anything. You've already contaminated some of the scene, but that's not your fault. I'd done the same thing. You can go outside or to the room you slept in last night. Stay out of the rest of the house. Do not leave; hear me."

"Yes, but, am I—"

"Hell yes, you're a suspect. For the record, I believe your story, but just the same, until we sort this out, you're the number one, as they say on all the cop shows, *person of interest.* So, as I said, don't go anywhere." A lengthy silence followed. Bethel had no idea what to say or ask next. "Lee. You still there?"

"Yeah."

"Listen…don't worry…I mean it. I'll be there in thirty minutes. Oh, yeah, if something goes wrong, anything…nine-one-one it."

"Don't worry."

"Lee?"

"Still here."

"Ramirez is probably at the nearest Starbucks loading up on stuff for your breakfast."

"Without a car?" Lee knew Ellison was trying to help settle his nerves.

"Starbuck's stores are everywhere; there's probably one across the street from the townhouse."

"Thanks, Frank, for trying, but something's up. I can feel it."

CHAPTER 13

Sheriff Stanton tossed the message in the waste can, a mix of feelings swirling, interfering with her usual calm and thoughtful reasoning ability. She knew her friend well and a nine-one-one call from him wasn't a good thing. Intuition told her not to return the call, but her sense of duty insisted otherwise. Stanton still had his number on speed dial.

"Crys, thanks for calling back." He recognized her number on his ID. "I've been trying to get you since this morning."

"Been busy, just got back in the office. What's with the nine-one-one?"

"First of all, Crys, I want you to take off your super patriot hat you wear so proudly and put on your *thinking of me only* hat."

"C'mon, Jerry, you're not making sense. First a nine-one-one call, now you're talking about hats. What's going on?"

"I know how you are, Crys, know what you think, and the second you hear what I've got to say, you'll hate me because you'll feel obligated, and I don't want that. I want you to say no to what I'm about to ask … understand?"

"It'll be a lot easier to say no if we don't go any further with this conversation, Jerry."

"I know ... I know, but they made me ask. Does that sound adolescent enough for you?"

Stanton laughed. She knew Jerry Webster was just as patriotic as she was, and the thought of someone making him do something was humorously absurd. "Oh Jerry, Jerry, now tell me who's making you do this."

"Sorry, can't tell you who—"

"Stop," she interrupted. "I'm on the verge of leaving all this crap behind me, Mr. Deputy Director, hoping to marry and enjoy the rest of my life." Webster held the phone away from his ear, thankful he was alone. She went on. "If I hear one more word that smacks of some super-secret lingo, I'm hanging up. Hear me?"

"Ah, umm ... yes, but—"

"But nothing. Now, before we go on, how are Marcia and the kids?"

"Great, I'll tell them you said hi."

"Good," Stanton's voice sounded pleasant. "Now, who asked?"

A lengthy pause followed while Webster mulled over the serious breach of confidentiality he was about to make. He knew it could mean his career at the very least, and the worst—well, he didn't want to think about that. "Maggie," he answered quietly.

"Maggie Winters?"

"Yes."

"So you've been rubbing shoulders with CIA."

"You could say that."

"Tell me why you called." A professional tone muscled its way back into the conversation.

FBI Deputy Director Jerry Webster described the operation without compromising parts that would not involve her if she chose to participate. He didn't sugarcoat anything; he knew his former partner too well. The respect he had for Stanton was extraordinary, and the least he could do was level with her even if it meant a confidentiality violation here and there; he was willing to risk the consequences. Stanton asked a few tactical questions that were of a general nature. At this stage of the conversation she realized the necessity for extreme secrecy. There was a lot more she wanted to ask but knew a phone call, particularly a cell phone, wasn't the most secure place to do it. "Jerry, I need to know more, and I need time to think. Can we meet on neutral ground day after tomorrow, say Dallas?"

"Listen to me, Crys. Maybe you didn't pick up on my cue; you are to say no to this operation. We'll simply bid each other a friendly good-bye and hang up. As Nancy Reagan so aptly put it, 'Just say no.' Now say it; I gotta go see a man about a dog."

"At least give me until tomorrow to think about it, Jerry."

"Crys, say no, please. I know what's going through that pretty head of yours. You're thinking the country needs you, and that isn't true, we've got lots of others willing to go," Webster lied, and he knew she knew he was lying.

"Tomorrow, Jerry. I'll call you before noon tomorrow." The following silence lasted longer than usual, prompting Stanton to think she'd lost signal. "Webster, you still there?"

"Yeah, Crys, still here."

"Well...what about it? Can I call tomorrow?"

"I'm going to tell Winters you said thanks, but no thanks, and Sheriff Stanton, the next time you're out this way, stop in an see us. I miss you." The phone was dead. Webster had hung up.

The sheriff looked at her cell display screen to make sure it wasn't a lost signal. She swiveled around and looked out her west window. Stanton gazed momentarily at the morning light reflecting off the leaves of a nearby grove of cottonwood trees. She watched as the usual traffic moved about at a relaxed pace. People leaving the Perculator Café bound for a hard days work; she took everything in knowing this moment might be her last peaceful interlude for a very long time. Her finger poised to call Webster back an emotional battle raging between duty and longing.

CHAPTER 14

Lee Bethel stood on the front step of Dr. Ramirez's townhouse watching neighbors leaving for work. Most were young professionals, attorneys, government officials, civilian Pentagon employees. Men in suits with ties, woman in business attire, all carrying leather satchels, a sure sign he was amongst a group of fast up-and-comers. No one looked suspicious or out of place. *A typical morning,* he thought.

Bethel spotted the trash dumpster partially hidden behind a privacy fence. He stepped off the walk on to the paved parking lot next to Ramirez's car and glanced inside, but saw nothing out of place. He remembered what Ellison said and didn't touch the Nissan Maxima; instead Lee walked the fifty feet to the dumpster and stood poised to open the door, he reached for the handle—caution pulling against his curiosity.

"Excuse me," a deep voice startled him. Bethel swung around, abruptly losing his balance and falling against the privacy fence. He stared for a second at the unshaven man dressed in a bathrobe and flip-flops carrying a large plastic bag of trash.

"You startled me," he said, hoping the honest explanation would justify his disproportionate reaction.

"Sorry. I just need to throw this in, and I'll be out of your way."

Bethel backed away from the door; the man discarded his bag of trash without looking inside and walked away. He'd watched his share of cop shows, and when someone was missing they always checked nearby dumpsters. In this case, however, all he saw was the usual assortment of black and white trash bags, a few grocery sacks, but nothing more. He shut and latched the door and walked to a bench bolted in concrete under a sycamore not far from Ramirez's townhouse.

Frank Ellison stopped at the enclave security post, not that he felt an obligation to stop, but he wanted to ask the guard a few questions himself before meeting Dr. Bethel. Ellison lowered his window and nodded at the blond knucklehead hip-hopping to whatever was screaming through his earphones. No response other than a jive butt movement that looked, to the agents, like some kind of disjointed convulsion. Ellison honked the horn. The security guard opened his eyes and took the earphones off. "Yeah, what's up." It wasn't a question, it wasn't even a greeting, and Ellison took it as a sign of disrespect. He stepped out of the car reached through the half-opened window separating him from the security guard and unlocked the door.

The guard stepped back, mustering the most authoritative voice he could manage. "Hey, you can't come in here."

Ellison reached for the landline phone attached to the electronic console and pushed the ear piece into the guard's stomach. "Call your supervisor right now."

"Why?" the guard whimpered.

"'Cause they need to get someone here to replace your fired ass."

"Who are you?"

Ellison moved in uncomfortably close to the guard. "Call 'em now."

The guard punched in a number, and the phone was answered immediately by the security company's local dispatcher. Ellison grabbed the phone. "My name is Frank Ellison, that's Special Agent Frank Ellison with the FBI…"

The guard listened wide-eyed as Ellison voiced his complaint. The conversation took no more than a minute. The agent returned the phone to its cradle and looked at the guard. "I'm going to ask you some simple questions, and I want quick, precise, and truthful answers, understand?"

The guard nodded, still wide-eyed, shaking.

Ellison wanted, more than anything else, to confirm Bethel's story. He knew the kid didn't have a clue, and observant he wasn't, but he had recorded the time Lee visited with him about Ramirez. Without saying anything else to the guard, Ellison and Booker drove on to the townhouse. As they turned the corner and negotiated the first of four speed bumps, Booker spotted Bethel waiting. "I'm beginning to really feel sorry for this guy."

"Yeah, me too. He tries to be a good citizen, and he ends up in a mess."

"You think this Dr. Ramirez is missing or just out, like you said, getting coffee?"

"Just trying to think positive, but in this case, I'm not so sure. Peculiar things happening that we're not in on…my gut tells me he's been abducted." The agents pulled to the curb in front of Ramirez's door. Bethel hurried over. "Glad you're here."

Ellison got out of the car, searching Bethel's face for an expression of relief. "Nothing?" he asked.

"Nothing." Lee explained in detail everything that had happened after the two Secret Service agents left the evening before.

"And you heard nothing?" Booker asked.

"I didn't hear a thing."

"Have you been back in the house since you called us?" Ellison asked.

"No, I've been out here."

Booker pointed to the car they'd parked next to. "That Maxima his?"

"Yes."

"You touch it or look in it?"

"Looked through the window is all, but I didn't touch anything."

Ellison squatted down on the grass near the front step to Ramirez's small portico and studied something partially hidden by a hosta leaf. "Erik, photograph that, but don't move it."

Bethel walked over and saw a syringe. "What do you think?" he asked, bending down for better look. Before Ellison could answer, Booker was there with a camera snapping photos. Dr. Bethel and Agent Ellison backed away to give Booker room.

"Lee, I need to make a call. I'll be back," Ellison said.

The meaning was clear, he wasn't to listen in. Bethel watched Ellison walk all the way to the dumpster to make his call. A minute later the agent returned, his probing eyes showing signs of worry. He motioned for Booker to join him. "Go around the property looking for anything that seems out of place. If you find anything, take pictures and leave an evidence marker. Don't go inside though; our forensic team is on the way. You just make sure no one goes in until they get here, okay?"

"Okay, but where are you going?"

Bethel listened, hoping his role would become apparent soon.

"I'm taking Lee back to Andrews."

"Why? Am I going home?"

"No, unfortunately."

"Where then?"

Ellison shook his head, looking apologetic. "I'm taking you into protective custody, Lee."

"What?"

"You may be in danger. My thinking is if Ramirez was taken against his will, whoever it was didn't realize you were upstairs. If they had, you probably wouldn't be here right now."

"This wasn't part of the deal, Agent Ellison. What's wrong with me just going home?"

"I can only imagine how pissed you are; I would be if I were in your shoes, but you're in to deep now for us to safely cut you loose." Ellison motioned for Lee to get in the car.

"I need to call my wife." Lee got in and flipped his phone open and punched a button.

Ellison reached over and covered the phone with his hand, "Wait, don't call her now."

"Why?"

"Because we don't know yet what we are dealing with."

Bethel's voice trembled, "What do you mean?"

Ellison pointed at the car door. "Shut it, I'll explain on the way." The agent backed up fast, paying no attention to the speed bumps on his way out. "If Ramirez is in trouble, and let me remind you we do not know that at this time, it stands to reason you might also be in trouble and if you are—"

Bethel had connected the dots; he didn't have to be spoon fed. "I get it. If I'm in trouble, she might be." His earlier apprehensions about his own involvement in this issue of *national importance* seemed petty compared to what he was thinking now. Through distorted visual images of something bad happening to Beverly, he was fashioning his demand to be allowed to return home. Just as he was about to make his case, Ellison continued, "As I was going to say, we have agents on the way to your house now, matter of fact their probably there. They'll let us know, and you can talk then. Okay?"

Relieved, Bethel nodded.

They drove past the guardhouse as they exited the enclave. An older man with short-cropped gray hair and an unmistakable military air waved a semi-salute. Bethel shook his head. "That's more like it," he said quietly as they moved into the street headed south.

"What?" Ellison asked.

"Just talking to myself."

"About?"

"The creep I talked with this morning when I was looking for

Carlos. The kid on duty was a real punk. The new guy looks like someone who takes their job seriously … wonder what happened to him?"

"Oh, probably just on coffee break." Ellison didn't elaborate; he was still angry with himself for allowing a fresh-faced, no-nothing twit to affect him in such a pernicious manner. He'd been trained to handle those kinds of circumstances professionally. Anyone with the authority granted by the badge he carried and a deadly sidearm holstered on his hip needed to be keenly aware how his own emotion could have a negative effect in a critical situation. *A sure indicator,* Ellison thought, *that I need to go fishing.* "Speaking of that, want some java before we hit the road?"

CHAPTER 15
BUFFALO, OKLAHOMA
MID-MORNING, AUGUST 23

Crys Stanton checked her watch, it was nearly ten a.m., and she had a decision to make and only minutes to make it. Not only would this situation be impossible to explain to Robert, it would also, most certainly, alter her plans in unimaginable ways. Webster had been right; as soon as Stanton realized the importance of Operation Moriah Ruse, her mind made an immediate adjustment, a neurological shift that somehow shut out her feelings for herself and drafted her into service for her country. She called the deputy director back. "Webster, you haven't called Winters back yet, have you?"

"No, Crys, just getting ready to."

"Look, I know you're trying to protect me, and I appreciate that, but this operation fits me to a T. Besides, you aren't being truthful with me about choices for the mission. I may have been out of circulation for a few years, but I still have my sources. There can't be more than six or seven women that meet those strict skill sets."

"Five."

"Okay, five. That's what I mean, Jerry. To put a team of two into the middle of that mess you'll need alternates if you expect this to work. Now, call Winters and tell her I'm in."

"You know, Crys, I feel like a traitor to you—"

"Jerry... stop it. You're not a traitor to me, and you're not my father, or my boss for that matter. Just call her."

"Crys."

"What?"

"I may not be your father or boss, but I am a friend, and friends don't do this to each other."

A long uncomfortable pause followed. Webster hoping the silence would give his former partner time to think rationally—and Stanton wishing for a crystal ball.

"Okay, Crys, I'll call her."

"Good. Where do you want me?"

"Quantico. There will be three days of orientation and two days of training."

"Then what?" Crys checked herself. "Never mind. I know you can't answer. I can be there tomorrow afternoon late. When does the training start?"

"Uh... yeah, that's another problem."

"Meaning?"

"The training starts at 0600 tomorrow."

"No. I can't get everything done here in time."

"Sorry, it's carved in stone. If you are still willing, I can have our jet pick you up at the nearest air force base at 1900 hours. That gives you six or seven hours to wrap up your business and get to the plane." Webster clung to the remote prospect that the time line he'd given Stanton would be insurmountable. "Typical government timing, Crys, they want everything done yesterday, so I understand if you're unable to get here that quick."

"Not so fast, Jerry, I'll be there at six. Now, have someone call me with the plane info. I'll see you in the morning."

Sheriff Stanton called her chief deputy and trusted administrative deputy Maude Bingham into her office and explained that she had been called to New York to testify against terrorists she helped arrest several years earlier.

Maude asked the obvious question. "If these guys went to prison years ago, why do you have to testify now?"

"These guys were tried in civilian court, not by a military tribunal; therefore, they have appeal rights."

"How long will you be gone?" the chief deputy asked.

"Really, there's no way to say for sure. Two weeks, a month."

"You'll stay in touch?" Maude Bingham sounded worried. All four of the deputies were young and inexperienced, and Bingham knew she'd have to ride herd over them during the sheriff's absence.

"Sorry, I can't promise that."

"Why?" Bingham and the chief deputy asked in unison.

"These terrorists are real bad guys, and they have a long reach outside their cell. My guess is the US Marshals will have me sequestered until after the appeal process. No outside contact at all."

The explanation seemed to satisfy the two deputies. Stanton excused the chief deputy from the meeting with congratulations on being named acting sheriff during her absence. As soon as the deputy left the sheriff's office, closing the door behind him, Bingham eyed Stanton with an intuitive stare. "This smells like a hog farm during a heat wave, Sheriff. What gives?"

"Oh, Maude … can't you, just for once, play along? All I can say is that's the word you are to leak around town. Trust me."

Sheriff Stanton was Maude Bingham's best friend. They didn't associate socially because of the boss-and-subordinate relationship both knew was essential for even a small sheriff's office to work effectively. "Of course, I'll get the word around, but young lady, you take care of your self and don't do anything dangerous. Promise?"

"Cross my heart." Stanton smiled.

Bingham left the sheriff's office with a list of to-dos. Stanton couldn't delay another minute, she called Robert Gray, but there was no answer. She called his folks who lived a short distance from Robert asking if he was there; neither had seen him in more than an hour. Time was passing quickly and the most important person in her life was no where to be found.

CHAPTER 17
NOON, AUGUST 23

Crys Stanton went through her mental checklist again; telling Robert was the last, and by far, the most difficult thing she had to do. A task that might alter her plans for the future, plans she'd been counting on. On the other hand, a separation of a few weeks might be just what she needed to make sure her intentions were based on genuine love of a man and not just love of the opportunity to have the life she'd imagined for so long. Crys knew she could be happy with Robert, they had so much in common, but she couldn't bear the thought of deceiving him, even in the smallest way.

As Stanton rose from her chair, there was a knock on her office door. "Yes?"

The door opened. "Hey, want to have lunch?" Robert said, smiling like a nervous teenager.

"Sure. Been looking for you, Mr. Gray."

"Really?" His smile widened.

"If it's okay with you, why don't we have lunch at my place and skip the restaurant crowd?"

"That's even better. You ready now?"

"I am. I'll meet you there in ten minutes."

Crys prepared a quick lunch, and Robert talked nervously about the cattle market. He could tell something was on her mind, but being a cattleman and not accustomed to social interaction, all Robert knew to do was talk of things he was familiar with. It didn't take long for him to cover his usual topics, and the closer he got to the end of his one-sided conversation, the more uneasy he became. She hadn't smiled or said much, and to Robert that wasn't a good sign. He breathed deeply trying to dissolve the lump that had formed in his throat in anticipation of bad news.

They sat in silence while Crys picked over her meal, distracted by her own thoughts and not hearing much of what Robert said. She hadn't noticed her guest finished lunch and was staring intently at her, the pained expression on his face wrapped in uncertainty. Gently and with some reluctance, Robert asked her what was wrong.

Stanton focused on the half-empty plate in front of her, afraid to look into his eyes. Finally she came around to Robert's side of the table and wrapped her arms tight around his neck. Neither said anything for what seemed, to Robert, like a long time. Having her close felt wonderful, yet he knew something was about to follow that would wipe the good away as quickly as it had come. "Crys, tell me ... what's wrong?"

She pulled back from their embrace and cupped his face with her hands and kissed him gently, passionately; the release was slow, teary. "Nothing is wrong," she said choking on tears and shallow sobs as she tried to explain.

"Sure looks and sounds like somethin's wrong."

"I've got to go away for a while, that's all."

Robert brushed her blonde hair away from what he considered the most beautiful brown eyes he'd ever seen. "Away? What do you mean, away?"

She handed him the fax Webster had sent as a compliment to her clandestine cover.

"What's this?" Robert asked, trying to make sense of the document.

"It's a subpoena, kind of." She gave Robert the same explanation she had given Bingham, explaining that due to the serious nature of the trial, she'd be in seclusion for a few weeks—maybe longer.

"So no contact between us at all?"

"None," she answered, embracing him again. "Hold me, Robert, please. I need to feel you against me. Tighter."

Stanton's cell phone rang; she was reluctant to give up the embrace but knew she couldn't ignore the call. "Stanton," she answered. Robert watched as Crys nodded and jotted notes. The conversation was one-sided and important, Robert surmised, still trying to arrange all the puzzle pieces in an informative pattern, a myriad of emotions disrupting his normally rational thought.

Stanton folded her phone shut and stared longingly at Robert, his face twisted by confusion. "I have to go, Robert." She stroked his face. He started to speak, but Crys placed her finger gently against his lips. "I'm on a very tight schedule. I wish I could explain. You have to trust me … okay?"

"Of course I trust you, but that doesn't stop me from wanting you to reconsider testifying. There has got to be someone else."

"I wish there was, but, no, there isn't." She took Robert's hand and led him to the door. "Robert." Her voice soft, encouraging. "I've had the most wonderful time of my life being with you these few months. Leaving is excruciatingly difficult; I don't want to go. I don't want to be away from you, but I must. You can make this much easier on me if you just turn and go."

She kissed him again, and he left.

Stanton watched as Robert walked to his truck, sad and confused with what had just happened. His usual squared shoulders and determined step were now nothing more than a stooped shuffle as he made his way down the sidewalk. Stanton turned away, no longer in control of her emotions. Deep sobs coming from unfamiliar places, unstoppable tears soaked tissue after tissue.

CHAPTER 18

William Unger arrived at work early everyday, including most Saturdays and Sundays, since becoming vice president of the United States. It was his firm belief the US deserved all he could do, all the time. He hated the public relations photo opportunities and canned propaganda sound bites his staff arranged for him non-stop since the inauguration. Unger ordered coffee and sat down at the large conference table where his assistant had arranged, in order of priority, the vice president's reading. The *Washington Post* lay folded on top of the stack with a note attached that read, *sec B pg 10*. He opened the paper to the article buried inside the *Post*, obscured intentionally to minimize its importance, but certain to be noticed by those it was intended for.

GOVERNMENT CONTRACTOR MISSING

Government officials confirmed late Friday that a Department of Defense contrac-

CHAPTER 20

Stanton didn't unpack; she laid out only the things she thought she'd need for the first day of briefing. The ex-agent learned years early to be prepared for the unexpected, and the best way to do that was to not let oneself get too comfortable. The dorm room was extremely small, a single angle-iron military-style bed in one corner with a pillow, sheets, and a blanket stacked on one end. The bathroom would accommodate one person. The occupant could operate the sink faucets, flush the stool, and turn on the shower water without doing anything other than twisting slightly to the right. The dorm, obviously for new agency recruits, had been added since the last time Special Agent Crystal Stanton visited the Quantico campus ten years earlier. On that occasion she was fresh from a counterterrorism assignment in Europe and was on campus to provide training as a temporary instructor.

Stanton sat on the side of the bed and opened an envelope left on the lamp stand. She pulled one sheet of paper out, that day's itinerary and briefing room location. Stanton shut the light off, glancing quickly at the clock's red numerals; it was 12:48 a.m. She tried to remember what day it was. .

"Reveille, reveille, breakfast at 0530, muster at 0600 in conference room A," a husky voice boomed in military fashion.

Stanton bolted upright in her bed and tried to focus on the shape standing in the doorway, light from the hall silhouetting the figure of a woman, her face obscured by darkness. By the time she had her feet on the floor, the door closed and the person was gone.

The mess hall was clean—sterile clean; stainless appliances ringed the room offering everything from coffee to soft-serve ice cream. The self-service steam table full of bacon, toast, potatoes, gravy, scrambled eggs, and a variety of fresh fruit adorned the refrigerated chest. *Enough food for an army,* Stanton thought, but the only people present were five other women and one man of obvious Middle Eastern extraction. She recognized Margaret Winters right away. Winters motioned for Stanton to fill a plate and join her. Name-only introductions made, the team ate in silence, knowing it wasn't the time or place for conversation.

Winters finished her breakfast, scooted back from the table, and looked at her watch, "Room A is just down the hall to your right. I'll see all of you there in ten minutes." She turned quickly and left.

In secure room A, Winters explained that everyone had been selected to participate in a mission of prime importance. "Each of you are uniquely qualified for this mission, as a matter of fact, the only people in the world qualified for this mission are right here in this room." Winters glanced around the room, looking for a hint of reluctance or insecurity in the women's eyes. She went on to explain the mission generalities, and the reason a two-woman team was chosen to carry out the mission. "If the US sends troops into Iran to force their hand, soldiers, marines, and innocent people will be killed, and that's not going to happen this time. I don't believe it is advisable to use a military special operations team or a CIA paramilitary team to accomplish this task. No matter how clever we think we are, somehow, someway information is leaked. Using any of those approaches would be tantamount to declaring war, so, in lieu of conventional forms of information gathering, we're going to try some slight of hand, cast an illusion into the mix, and pray for luck."

"What about the IAEA, the UN, diplomacy? Can't we find out what we need to know through those sources?" Aiya Baruch, the only Israeli and member of Mossad, asked.

"That's a strange question coming from you, of all people," Winters said.

"I suppose it is, but if this meeting is being recorded—"

Winters cut her off abruptly. "It isn't; I can assure you of that."

Baruch wasn't through, nor was she intimated by Winters. "Nevertheless, as I was saying, if this meeting is being recorded, I want my voice to be heard asking that question. I believe you Americans call it c-y-a."

The exchange between the two women seemed to relieve some of the tension that filled the small conference room like an over-inflated party balloon. There were some brief chuckles, and Winters even allowed a reticent smile to curl the edges of her mouth.

"Your concern and question have been duly noted, if not on a recording device, certainly in our collective brains."

"Thank you."

Winters uncased her laptop and pointed to the large wall-mounted monitor. She typed in a password, and the CIA emblem appeared. "Watch my presentation closely." She clicked a button, and the list of team member names appeared accompanied by a short résumé. "Do you see similarities?" Every one in the room studied the list. Winters noted the unanimous nod and scrolled to the next page showing a map of the Middle East. She turned to Isabella Franchetti, a fifteen-year DEA veteran and expert on

Asian heroin trafficking. "What university did Crys Stanton graduate from, Ms. Franchetti?"

"Wisconsin."

"Good. Now, Ms. Stanton, Limber Topanga Crisp's place of birth?"

"Somalia."

"Excellent…and her religious affiliation?"

"Muslim."

"Right again, Ms. Stanton." Winters faced the sheriff, her expression dead serious. "A two-part question for you, Ms. Stanton: what was the religious affiliation of those that perpetrated the attack on the US September 11, 2001, and do you have a problem with Ms. Crisp being a part of the team?"

Stanton thought better of slapping the rim-less bifocals off Winters' face and answered, "Muslim and no." She knew provocation was just part of the selection process and to react, in any manner, would have disqualified her on the spot.

Winters turned to the diminutive Lien Pham Carter, a Vietnamese orphan born in the midst of war to a village prostitute and an African-American soldier. She was abandoned at birth and taken in by a mission operated by the Catholic Church. A year later Lien was smuggled out of the country and adopted by Richard and Mary Ann Carter of suburban Spring Valley, California. "Ms. Carter, tell me Ms. Franchetti's agency affiliation and expertise."

"DEA and heroin trafficking in southwest Asia."

"Are you sure, Ms. Carter?"

"Yes."

"Ms. Baruch, tell us what you remember about Mr. Faxhir's background."

"Nadim Bin Faxhir is from Oman. A Shi'ite Muslim with current business interests in Islamabad, Tehran, and Kabul."

"Thank you, Ms. Baruch. Now, Ms. Crisp, tell us what you remember from Ms. Stanton's résumé."

Stanton watched as Crisp made her short but thorough presentation. She demonstrated a language precision superior to anyone else in the room, her English without error, her delivery strong and intelligent, almost robotic. Crisp's eyes looked cold, almost vacant. A *skill sharpened over the years as part of the president's protection detail,* Stanton thought.

"All right, Mr. Faxhir and ladies, the introductions have been made." Winters tapped another key, and a satellite photo of the port city of Muscat appeared. She maneuvered the pointer to a small building a few hundred yards from the shore and clicked again to enlarge the photo. "This is your staging area—"

Before she could finish her sentence, Aiya Baruch interrupted, "I'm sorry, Ms. Winters, but I am wondering why Mr. Faxhir wasn't called upon to demonstrate his powers of retention as the rest of us were?" Her inquiry was in earnest, although, being Jewish, she knew even in twenty-first century Israel patriarchal rule was still very much the way it was.

"Good question, and I can answer that easily. He is a man."

CHAPTER 21

Special Agent Frank Ellison pulled to the curb in front of the safe house at Andrews AFB and shut the engine off. He felt refreshed, a great night's sleep—all four hours of it. Friday was typically a day off. Webster suggested he use discretion when deciding an appropriate time to take a break, and this wasn't it. Booker was with his wife and kids, and Ellison didn't want to do anything to disrupt his partner's family time. Erik Booker was a gung-ho agent two years fresh out of the academy and very ambitious. Ellison saw himself in his partner and knew Booker looked to him as a mentor, enthusiastically following his every lead and command. Just another reason why the senior agent felt bad about the way he handled the security guard situation the day before.

Ellison called his partner earlier that morning, "Anything yet from forensics?"

"The place was clean, no prints other than Ramirez and Bethel."

"The syringe?"

"That's the only interesting piece about this. According to pre-liminary analysis there's neuroleptic residue in the syringe."

"Say again."

"N-e-u-r-o-l-e-p-t-i-c residue."

Ellison smiled to himself; Booker was using the big words for two reasons. He wanted to impress his senior partner, and he couldn't pass up a chance to say a word Ellison wouldn't under-stand—a sure sign of Booker's immaturity. "What's a, neuroleptic Erik?"

"A tranquilizer."

"Oh ... well, that's interesting, don't you think?"

"Yes, sir. By the way, where should I meet you?"

"Stay home today, Erik. Play with your kids, get a babysitter, and take your wife to dinner, just keep your phone on."

"Are you serious?"

"Yeah, I'm serious. I'll call you if something comes up. In the meantime, stay with the family."

"Great. And thanks, my seven-year-old has a soccer game this afternoon."

"Enjoy the day, Erik; this may not happen often."

Ellison handed his identification to the security person stand-ing post just outside the safe-house door. The heavily armed guard opened the door and motioned him through. Dr. Bethel, his wife, and mother-in-law were just finishing breakfast.

Lee waved. "Join us."

Ellison greeted Beverly and her mother and sat down. A stew-ard appeared. "May I get you something, sir?"

"Coffee."

"Any news on Dr. Ramirez?" Lee was anxious, his expression tense.

"Forensics hasn't revealed anything useful yet other than the syringe we found near Ramirez's door step. Apparently it had tran-quilizer residue in it."

Lee's eyes widened. "Tranquilizer...that'd make sense. That's the reason I didn't hear anything; they drugged him."

"That would be my guess. Two or three stout guys could surprise and overcome an unsuspecting soul quickly, dart and restrain him until the drug took effect. Problem I have is the scene. It should've been disturbed more than it was."

"What do you mean?" Beverly asked.

"A tuft of grass out of place, a mark from the sole of a shoe, a piece of fabric snagged on the handrail, something, some kind of evidence. But so far, nothing." Ellison looked down for a moment. The others could see he was in thought and didn't disturb him. He sipped his coffee and mumbled something.

"What?" Lee asked.

"Talking to myself," Ellison replied without lifting his eyes.

"Sounded like you said fake,'" Beverly said. Lee nodded.

The agent looked up. "Yeah...the scene looks contrived, like someone faked the abduction."

"Faked. I don't understand. How? Why?" Lee said.

"I don't know." Ellison's phone vibrated. He excused himself from the table stepped into the foyer and answered; it was his partner.

"Erik, thought you were at your son's soccer game."

"We're on the way, but before we left the house I noticed an article in the *Post* about Ramirez and thought you needed to know."

"An article about Ramirez and his disappearance?"

"It didn't use his name, just that a DOD contractor was missing and so were some very important photos."

"Who released the story?"

"An FBI spokesperson by the name of Hargrave. You know him?"

"Never heard of him. Erik, save the article for me, okay?"

"Sure thing."

Ellison stepped back into the dining room. "That's strange."

"The phone call?" Lee was returning from the galley with the coffee pot. He refilled the empty cups and set the pot on a warmer.

"Yes. That was Booker; he said there's an article about the abduction in this morning's *Post*. No names; the article just said some photos of rare tablets were missing."

"You said it was strange. Why? I would think it was newsworthy."

"Under ordinary circumstances, yes, but we kept the lid tight on this. We wanted to pull a few facts together before talking with the press."

"Maybe a reporter got wind of the account, and your public relations folks wanted to get ahead of the story by issuing a press release."

"Yeah, probably." Ellison nodded, but his expression didn't appear to agree wholeheartedly with his reply. He doubted Lee's theory, although it was a good place to bring the topic to a close. The agent stirred sugar into his coffee thinking about what had transpired over the last forty-eight hours, trying to piece the sequence of events together in some kind of organized fashion. Deep in thought, his mind wandered away from the small audience.

"Excuse me." Beverly's mother stood. "I'm going to freshen up, may take a nap. I'm still tired from all that happened yesterday." She smiled at Ellison and patted her daughter on the shoulder. Beverly wanted to do the same thing, but her curiosity was in full bloom, and she couldn't pull herself away from the conversation.

"So what's next?" Lee was up pacing.

"This is always the hard part, the part I've never gotten used to—"

Without her mother around cautioning her to be ladylike, Beverly interrupted, "What part, Agent Ellison?"

"Frank. I prefer Frank." He looked at Beverly. "The waiting. Waiting on forensics, waiting on some bit of information to surface, waiting on a victim or an unsub to make a move."

"Unsub? What's an unsub?"

"Unknown subject, a person of interest. A person we need to talk with who may or may not have information pertinent to the crime, if in fact there is a crime."

"What else do you wait for?" Beverly was no longer just asking questions, she was in interrogation mode, her green eyes focused hard on Ellison's.

"Mrs. Bethel, I don't mean to imply we all just sit around waiting for the phone to ring. Neighborhoods are being canvassed, known acquaintances of Ramirez are being contacted, abduction motives are being considered, art dealers are being notified about the missing document photos, and I'm here to ask you both more questions, looking for anything that might help us find Ramirez."

Beverly apologized, blaming her abrupt style on fatigue. "Okay, so maybe the right question to ask is what should Lee and I be doing to help out?"

"Nothing. If you venture outside the confines of this safe house, you might even complicate matters. The only thing you three can do is allow the air force to serve your needs. Movies, food, wine, books, whatever you want, but it has to be here."

"What you're saying is that we are being held captive for an undetermined amount of time." Beverly's sarcasm was back and distinctive.

"There are other more positive words you might use when framing that statement, such as safety, security, protection. Something a bit more palatable I'd think," Ellison said, knowing even those words weren't entirely accurate.

"Yes, I'm sure you're right. It just doesn't feel that way to me."

"I wish there was another way, but for now, this is the best we can do."

Lee stopped pacing long enough to work the tension out of his wife's neck. The massage gave him something useful to do while de-escalating Beverly's growing annoyance. She wasn't aware of how serious their situation was, and he hadn't been given the okay to tell her.

CHAPTER 22
QUANTICO, VA
FRIDAY MORNING, AUGUST 24

Aiya Baruch's question was as important as any asked that day. Everyone knew the answer, but it required a shift in an entrenched belief system that, if not made successfully, could end in disaster for the team; therefore, it had to be discussed in depth.

"It's imperative; I repeat…imperative for you to behave like a Muslim woman. You've all spent time on various missions in the Middle East; you know the customs, the culture, the religion, and the language. That's why you were selected for this mission, but that's not enough; you must be a Muslim woman. You must think like a Muslim, certainly not like a twenty-first-century American," Winters said.

Later that afternoon, the team was measured and fitted for clothing appropriate for the mission. Stanton was the only member that required a hair-color change; everyone else had light to dark brown hair along with the brown eyes. Although various eye colors could be found in Iran, brown was dominant. A loose-fitting beige tunic and matching hijab or head covering and veil were to be worn from that point on, and Farsi would be the only tongue spoken. Iran was still predominately patriarchal; women could not attend certain functions or ride in cars without being accompanied by a male relative.

"And it is this strong tradition that requires a man to lead the team from Oman into Iran," Winters explained. She motioned for Faxhir to continue the briefing and took a seat in the back of the small classroom. From that point on, Faxhir spoke various dialects of Arabic and Farsi, languages Stanton hadn't heard or practiced in years. He talked fast, intentionally throwing misleading remarks about Iranian culture and geography into the briefing in an effort to push the team to grasp linguistic nuances. All during the afternoon and late into the evening, Faxhir fired questions at the women and insulted them when the answer wasn't just right. At one point he berated Crisp for a language mistake; she remained calm. He pushed every button he knew to, but Crisp didn't react, bowing slightly instead, in an act of submission. Faxhir uttered a threat and rushed toward the Secret Service agent, grabbing her arm and pulling her out of her chair on to the floor. The others, including Winters, sat frozen, not knowing how far Faxhir was willing to go in an effort to prepare the women for what they might encounter in Iran. They knew Crisp was capable of protecting herself, but everything else, including Faxhir's next move, was a guess. He stood over the cowering women lying on the floor. She had drawn her knees in to her chest and covered her head. It was a pitiful and infuriating sight, yet no one moved or said anything.

Nadim Bin Faxhir stood over the fetal shape on the floor, his fists doubled-up and resting on his hips. He lifted his eyes from Crisp and stared coldly at each woman in the room, and as he did, each one dutifully bent forward in a sign of contrition. Faxhir returned to the front of the class, and Crisp to her seat. "You will not endure this treatment in Iran, and nowhere in the Qur'an will you find scripture to support this. However, herein lays the Muslim paradox—women are revered within this culture, as long as they behave according to very strict rules set forth by the male leadership. If a woman, in some Muslim cultures accidentally exposes her ankle in public, she can be stoned or beaten." He hesitated, searching eyes for telltale signs of fear or anger, signals that some astute observer might hone in on and question, but all he saw was confidence. "Any questions?"

Winters stood. "It's 2200. I know everyone is hungry and tired. You haven't eaten since noon, and you've been stressed a bit. Let's meet in the cafeteria and have dinner."

"I don't suppose we're having fried chicken and mashed potatoes, are we?" Stanton asked, knowing full well that cuisine was no longer an option.

"Sorry, from here on out, it's all Iranian food, and of course no more perfumes or scented makeup. If you're going to smell, your scent should be of saffron, not Chanel."

The next few days are grueling for the team—memorizing geographical locations, practicing the languages, physicals, and the toughest, most intense piece—learning about nuclear enrichment. Winters convened the group for the last time on Thursday morning, August 30. The seven lingered casually in the cafeteria after breakfast, engaging in small talk, knowing time was slipping away, inching closer to zero hour and the point of no return. Finally Winters rapped her empty coffee cup with her spoon. "Folks, this is launch day." Her voice was barely above a whisper, not because of the need for secrecy, but the influence of emotion she'd resisted until now. "This is a dangerous mission, but a necessary mission that hopefully will save lives. It is imperative we know absolutely what Iran's capabilities and intentions are, and I'm sorry to say, we don't." She sat pushing her cup around in circles, obviously in torment about the possibilities of failure and consequently death to some or all of the people sitting around her. The director of Central Intelligence had let her guard down, and her persona reflected that clearly. Margaret Winters had risen through the ranks of the agency, crashing through the glass ceiling with such knowledge and integrity that most of her competition could only stand in awe of. Today was different; she was one of a small group, a peer that was sending friends into harm's way. The thought tore at her heart, but she controlled the looming flow of tears and went on, "Now, let's go over this one more time. Stanton, lead off."

"The six-member team will be airlifted from Andrews at 1300 hours to Qatar. From there we will divide into three pairs, two members will leave at one-hour intervals in civilian vehicles for Oman."

Winters pointed at Carter. "Take it from there."

"We will arrive in staggered fashion at the staging house in Muscat beginning at 1700 hours, on thirty-one, August. Baruch and Franchetti will arrive first to set up and establish satellite communications with US Embassy personnel in Riyadh—"

Winters interrupted. "Who will you be communicating with at the embassy?"

"No one. Ours is a listening post only. We're interested only in periodic satellite and human intel transmissions regarding potential influences on the mission so that a replacement team can carry on should team one be compromised."

"And what about a rescue attempt if team one is compromised?" Winters pointed to Franchetti.

"The mission is priority—the only priority; no rescue attempts will be made." Her words rehearsed and perfunctory. One by one, over the past five days each of the team members had carefully wrapped their emotions tightly and stowed them somewhere cerebral in favor of the detached mentality required for such a mission. An emotionally drenched critical decision could very easily disrupt the mission resulting in death to one or all the team.

Faxhir explained again the route they would follow. To add authenticity to the mission he would have to make several stops. He explained, "I'll spend time with clients during these stops. To those

people, I am Faxhir, the gas and oil engineer expert from Oman. I've sold them equipment for their fuel processing plants, and they trust me. At each stop, I'll introduce Crisp as my wife, Zayna, and Stanton as my sister, Yasmeen, who I'm taking to visit relatives in Kashan. Of course I will do all the talking as is expected since these are business contacts and not social."

Stanton quivered slightly as the realization of what was about to take place settled through her body like flames through drought-stricken forest. Hot, caustic digestive juices poured into her stomach; she reached for her bag and found the bottle of acid relief tablets and chewed a handful.

Winters checked her watch. "In ten minutes, our escort will be here. This is it, ladies. If anyone has had second thoughts, this is the time to say so." She thumbed through a short stack of papers that lay in front of her, purposely avoiding eye contact. Winters knew that even a misunderstood expression on her part could send the wrong message, provoking a team member into a decision she'd later regret.

Stanton and the others had been in similar situations before. No one on the team was naïve or idealistic; they knew the risks. Oddly enough Stanton's major concern was whether or not Robert would be waiting when she returned; that is, if she returned. Obviously a mission that originally was to take weeks had now turned into more, how much more was impossible to predict. The uncertainties were plentiful, that fact everyone was sure of. Stanton caught Winters' attention, "I'm in, but may I go pee first?"

Laughter ended the sober moment, and one by one, each woman confirmed her participation.

"Okay, make a head call, grab your stuff, and be back here in five."

A scurry of activity followed, the team succumbing to the pent-up anxiety that had been building since being invited to participate in the mission. Doing something, even putting coffee cups on the cafeteria conveyor belt and cleaning the table of empty sugar packs was better than just sitting and thinking about what was in store for them. Winters stopped them before they reached the cafeteria exit. "This is where we part company, and I want to say two things. First, good luck. Second, you six very brave people have just fallen off the face of the earth."

CHAPTER 23

Vice President William Unger returned to his Washington office on Friday after four days of stumping on behalf of an incumbent Nevada senator running for a third term. The senator wasn't Unger's favorite, which made the entire time away from important matters that much worse. The president, however, liked the senator, but couldn't go himself, so the distasteful task fell to Unger.

The vice president entered his office through a secure private passageway, and as soon as he'd taken his seat, he pressed an intercom button to alert his assistant he was in. Two minutes later Charles came through the door bearing coffee, three nationally circulated newspapers, and his laptop. He laid the newspapers in front of Unger, each bore a sticky note with a section and page number written on it. "Welcome back, Mr. Vice President, I hope you enjoyed your trip west," he said, a detectable smirk forming on his customarily tempered face.

Unger rolled his eyes in response and picked up the *Washington Post,* turning to the section and page indicated on the note.

"Will there be anything else, sir?" He could tell his boss wanted some uninterrupted time.

"Give me a chance to read these articles first."

Charles left the office, closing the door behind him.

The second *Post* article about the missing DOD contractor had earned its way from deep inside the paper to page two of Section A. The headline and story suggested evidence found at the contractor's Annapolis residence supported the notion he was abducted. It didn't mention what the evidence was nor the contractor's name, but the article did state that an unnamed source said the content of the authenticated photos could play a definitive role in the already tenuous Arab and Israeli political future. Unger read the other articles and both reported the same information. The disinformation portion of the mission appeared to be working as Winters predicted. An accumulation of blurbs about an obscure government contractor fed strategically into the mainstream news outlets was growing in importance. The vice president estimated within twenty-four hours the abduction would be front page, and he was right.

By ten a.m. the next morning, all the major TV networks and print media had picked up the story, devoting airtime to the curious nature of the contractor's abduction. The *Journal Record* had scooped the story and identified the contractor, the neuroleptic laced syringe and the secret discovery the contractor was authenticating. Radio and TV talk shows were parading the usual array of religious and political experts before the public trying to persuade someone to utter a controversial remark and in turn boost ratings. Al-Jazeera News TV out of Qatar was the first to brandish the A word, and they did so shamelessly. Al Jazeera invited every articulate English-speaking radical Islamist they could find to talk about the apocalypse and what the concept meant to Christians and Jews. By the end of the day, Muslims worldwide were demanding the return of the tablets to the safekeeping of the IMI in Baghdad, promising reprisal if their demands weren't immediately met.

To quell the rising animosity between the religious factions,

Muslim and Jewish authorities ordered their government antiquities experts to meet and work out a plan of action, agreeable to both groups they hoped would prevent violence. The experts of both groups were moderates looking for a solution to the immediate problem, but the radicals on both sides demanded solutions that would, most likely, result in war. If the ark of the covenant was in fact locked in a chamber below what was formerly Solomon's Temple and now part of the land controlled by Muslims, the Israelis wanted access to it. This one single event would fulfill Jewish prophecy. This, of course, would provoke Muslims and their sympathizers into action.

When considering the consequences of propaganda baiting, Winters consulted with two CIA experts on the matter: an Israeli born and raised in Tel Aviv, educated at Princeton and Oxford, and the other, an Arab from Lebanon, educated at the American University in his homeland and Cornell in New York, both men authorities on the psychology of group behavior. Winters asked them for an assessment of potential risk of violence given the set of circumstances. Their combined theory was that some violence would be inevitable, but it would not result in an all-out war. Lives would be lost, and the agitation factor between the groups would mount temporarily, but in the end, assuming the authorities could reconcile, the turmoil would subside.

Winters could live with a few lives lost, especially if they weren't American lives, a tragic decision she hated to make, but someone had to. The marine's discovery came at the right time. Something was needed to distract the various Middle East factions in such a way their full attention would zero in on the outcome. The ark of the covenant was the perfect bait for the perfect ruse.

CHAPTER 24
MUSCAT ON THE GULF OF OMAN
SEPTEMBER 1

Nadim Bin Faxhir knocked twice on the door to the house where he and the five other team members were staying, a short pause followed while the women prepared themselves for an intruder. The two-knock signal was worked out in advance, but years of experience and thorough training taught the agents never to trust a prearranged alert by itself. A confirmation must be double-checked before accepting the signal as reliable. Carter asked who was at the door, and he answered, "Nadim Bin Faxhir, understand?"

Carter opened the door, and Faxhir hurried in. The keyword in the confirmation process, added if positive visual identification couldn't be made, was *understand* spoken in Farsi. Three of the women gathered at the small table to hear Faxhir's plan, Baruch and Franchetti watched the side streets through the only two windows in the house.

"I've rented a boat and crew to take us into the harbor at Chabahar. There is a lot of construction going on along the coast so we won't draw much curiosity. I have friends in the city that will put us up for the night."

eye on the crew. At this stage of the operation, he couldn't afford to trust anyone; they were moving out of the safety of a familiar environment into the unknown where the rules were different. One thing consistent about Iran was the certainty rules could change on a whim, as they often did. An ancient society and truly one of the most culturally developed on earth at one time, but a theocratic leadership bent on maintaining the status quo had successfully stifled the countries progress into the twentieth-first century. Growth and development knocked on Iran's door, and the religious leaders—seeing the corruption that was sure to follow—slammed it shut, rejecting modernization. No matter how hard the people of Iran worked to persuade the government to accept change the Ayatollahs would not budge. That absurdity, of course, resulted in modernization of the military with an array of new offensive weaponry while imposing antiquated religious idealism on the general public, all in all a very chaotic and fragile system making it impossible to predict leadership behavior. Nadim planned the teams itinerary with unpredictability in mind, each stop along the way to Natanz was for the purpose of gathering reliable intelligence to make the next leg of the trip as safe as possible. One mistake could cost them the mission and possibly their lives. Securing information from each of his business contacts would take time and patience.

The sun was beginning to set as the boat entered the port waters of Chabahar, Iran. Construction was going on all along the shore, huge cargo vessels flying the People's Republic of China flag were moored one after another, unloading materials and equipment. The PRC was providing the necessary building elements for the new port as well as the usual surreptitious shipment of silkworm missiles, most likely in exchange for oil. Armed security and military officials were everywhere, their attention devoted primarily to the unloading process suggesting the cargo wasn't entirely for construction.

Faxhir hurriedly climbed the short ladder to the wheelhouse, pointing to a ship bearing a neutral flag named *Bolivar.* "There," he shouted over the harbor noise. "Pull alongside the *Bolivar;* we'll get off there." The crew brought the vessel and its three passengers into a dilapidated pier next to the ship Winters said would be carrying the MIRVs. Satellite photos captured the name clearly, and according to US Naval intelligence, the *Bolivar* was a Venezuelan merchant ship with a dubious reputation. As soon as the mooring lines were secure, two uniformed men came aboard to check cargo and credentials, searching from bow to fantail. They were not rude, nor were they polite. Periodically they'd ask the boat's captain a question; eventually they seemed satisfied and left. As soon as the passengers stepped onto the pier, the fishing boat cast off and backed into the bay, disappearing in the darkness.

"This is the one in the photo," Zayna said. All three doing what economy-class tourists did, studying maps, looking over their passports, and digging through their bags. They couldn't take the risk of looking at the *Bolivar;* a guard might rightly assume they had an interest in the cargo beyond normal curiosity. The three walked slowly past the ship, Faxhir scolding wife Zayna for the benefit of the predominantly male port laborers, Yasmeen walking behind the couple watching the off-loading activity. She observed huge port cranes moving a system of augers back and forth siphoning wheat out of the ships hold into waiting trucks. This activity occupied the majority of the unloading zone. Nearing the front of the ship they saw the action change dramatically, military personnel were everywhere. Three trucks lined the pier as a number of crates the size of a midsize car were being carefully loaded and secured to trailers. The trio spotted a gate leading off the pier onto shore and headed for it. "I didn't see markings of any kind on the crates, did you?" Zayna said when she was certain they were out of hearing range.

"No, nothing, but we know what the MIRV crates look like, and that's them." Faxhir said.

"Orders were to be sure," Zayna said.

"Look, Zayna, those crates aren't full of rubber duckies. I'm confident they're MIRVs, we shouldn't jeopardize the rest of the mission just to crack open a crate," Yasmeen argued.

"I agree." Faxhir moved on toward the nearest street, ignoring Zayna's disagreement by waving at a passing cab. The small Datsun honked at oncoming traffic and made a U-turn, narrowly missing several pedestrians and one of the wheat trucks leaving the dock. The driver skidded to a stop at the curb near Faxhir's sandaled feet. They stowed their bags in the trunk and climbed in. The men talked fast, mostly about the weather and the new port; the women understood only a part of the exchange. The cabby spoke a dialect neither woman was familiar with. They remained quiet, taking a backseat literally to the male-dominated conversation, an attitude both women welcomed, knowing subservience was the perfect disguise.

Each stop along the way to Natanz was a carbon copy of the one before; each household welcomed the trio in festive fashion, a carryover from centuries of entertaining traders traveling from China to the Mediterranean and back. It was an insult if the guest didn't immerse himself in the tradition of the local host, usually resulting in the loss of a customer. You ate what the host provided and danced if the host invited you to do that. A businessman might spend valuable hours listening to endlessly boring stories about prominent sons and grandchildren, but in the end, it was the relationship built during these visits that assured a profitable journey. For the team, conversation around a plentiful meal was informative, paving the way closer to their destination. Usually by the third or fourth day, a contract had been signed and an order for updated gas-processing equipment was in hand.

It was five p.m. by the time the team arrived in Esfahan, their next to last stop before Natanz. The trip from Chabahar to Esfahan had taken ten days with stops in Zahedan and Kerman, the journey was so far uneventful, but at dinner that night with Faxhir's long-time friend and customer, the topic of conversation changed.

"Nadim, I fear a change in world politics is imminent."

"Ah … my friend, political changes are always occurring," Faxhir said, feigning disinterest in the topic.

"No, no, this time is different, and our illustrious leader is fanning the flames of discontent among our young people."

Although Faxhir continued to appear uninterested, he asked, "Amal, I do not keep up with such matters, what are you talking about?"

"You haven't been reading the papers?"

"No, I've devoted my time to business interests and getting these women to Kashan. That has taken all my energy, so what is going on?"

Amal handed Faxhir a five-day-old Tehran newspaper. Zayna and Yasmeen who were sitting on the floor behind Faxhir quietly watched as he silently read the article.

"Propaganda. That's all this is. I've lived in Europe and America; I can tell you with certainty, Amal, they're just trying to sell newspapers. Controversy sells, that's all there is to it. By next week, news people will tire of this story and move on to the next controversy."

"I would normally agree, my friend, but officials of several governments are involving themselves in this matter, and you can see there, in the article, what our president is saying about it."

"Doesn't he usually talk nonsense when he has the opportunity?"

"Yes, of course, but unlike Saddam, our president has the means to carry out his threat."

Faxhir didn't want to overplay his hand and seem more interested or knowledgeable than any other businessman. He listened to his friend's complaints without interjecting provocative questions. An hour later, the conversation turned to family—a more relaxing, less informative topic.

"I have a lot of work to do tomorrow, and the travel has been wearisome for the women. If you will permit me, I'll excuse myself, say my prayers, and get some sleep."

Amal stood, followed by other family members, and the two men embraced. Faxhir held the newspaper up. "May I take this to our room?"

"Of course."

Once in their room, Faxhir handed the paper to Yasmeen, and she quickly moved near a window where a nearby streetlamp cast just enough light for her to see. The article was long, a diatribe of hate, accusations, and warnings leveled mostly at Israel and the US. It was clear the Iranian president was using the ark of the covenant story to influence more radical denunciation of the West's attempt to democratize the world. A short article, picked up from UPI, accompanied the president's tirade on the front page. The journalist reported the body of a missing man believed to be an American was found beaten and disfigured in a Damascus hotel. The article went on to say the body might be that of man with close ties to the US government.

A few days earlier Vice President Unger arranged a meeting with Margaret Winters to discuss the progress of the mission. The group agreed not to talk of the mission while it was being carried out for obvious security reasons, but Unger was impatient and tension in the Middle East was building, he needed to know something.

"Good morning, Maggie," Unger turned to his aide. "Bring Ms. Winters whatever refreshment she wants, and Charles…"

"Yes, sir?"

"Absolutely no interruptions."

Charles nodded as he shut the door behind him.

"Sorry, Maggie, for violating our agreement, but I've got to know what's going on?"

"Mr. Vice President—"

Unger interrupted with a friendly smile. "Please, call me Bill."

"Bill, you know, you've been around the block a time or two, that when anyone—CIA, DEA, FBI—plans a clandestine operation there are always obscure and unknown variables that influence a missions progress."

"Yes, yes, I know, what I'm talking about is this thing about the ark and using it as a distraction. You read the papers, Maggie. Looks to me like this could build into something far more dangerous." He looked at the ceiling searching for the right words to express his thought without sounding regretful.

Winters scooted to the edge of her chair and leaned forward. "More dangerous than what?"

Unger removed his glasses, rubbing his eyes. His face reflecting the stress of his job; deep, tight lines permanently embedded over his brow, and the forced smile. Winters was tough—she had to be in her position—but instincts were impossible to deny and empathy edged professionalism to one side for the moment. "Bad day?" she said.

"Sometimes, Maggie, I think they're all bad…you do or say something and the next day millions of people want to cut your throat. Our government supports one regime and they murder a hundred thousand citizens; we support some other leader in their quest for democracy, and a month later find out his government is more corrupt than the one overthrown. The world is fragile, Maggie, too damned fragile."

"So, Bill, you're trying to balance all that on your shoulders?"

"Yeah, isn't that what you're supposed to do when you accept the political challenge? Isn't that what we promise to do? Isn't that what's expected?"

"Sure, some people expect you to save the world and make them rich in the process; some, on the other hand, just want you to do what's right."

"Maggie, I confess, I don't always know what's right." The vice president cleaned his glasses intently, as if he were scrubbing a distorting scum from his perspective on world affairs.

"I agree, sometimes our black and white lives fade to gray, but all we can do is what we believe to be in the best interest of the country."

"Okay, you're right, I know," Unger's brooding look turned agitated, "but you have to help me understand how millions of outraged Muslims and Jews is a good thing?"

"I'm sure you've heard about the syringe and its contents."

"Yes, thorazine I believe." Webster didn't want to explain what he knew until after the forty-eight-hour target Winters had set.

"Yup, or as my young, smartass partner would say—neuroleptic."

"Anything else from the lab or on-site forensics?"

"That's what I wanted to talk to you about, Jerry. There's nothing else. I've never seen a cleaner crime scene; it's too clean."

"And that leads you to what theory?"

"Based on my nearly thirty years of experience, I'd bet the farm it's bogus. Somebody's playing games with us, and I gotta pretty good notion who."

"Who?" Webster was reluctant to ask the question but realized if he didn't, Ellison would hone in on the omission; he had to play the conversation out to a satisfactory conclusion.

"Secret Service," Ellison explained his doubts about Limber Topanga Crisp and why he thought it odd an agent of the Secret Service would be assigned as Dr. Bethel's bodyguard.

Webster wanted to draw their discussion to a close as quickly as possible, it was evident Ellison was inching closer to a workable theory. "Frank, your assumption is interesting, and I'll take it into consideration, but right now I need you to focus on the crime as an abduction. Sort through the evidence again; see if you can find something you've missed; interview the neighbors and his associates again. And, Frank, I say this with all due respect—don't go off half-cocked on this Secret Service speculation. Hell, Frank, you may be right, but for now, work the abduction angle."

"You're the boss, Jerry, but I got a strange feeling we're barking up the wrong tree."

"Well, we'll see, in the meantime follow up, and I'll call you day after tomorrow to see where you're at."

Ellison didn't feel any better after the conversation with his boss. He'd hoped Webster would be more open to his theory and give him some latitude to work it from the bogus abduction perspective, but that didn't happen. Ellison was disappointed, he trusted his gut, and it wasn't leading him in the direction the FBI wanted to go. The agent put his Taurus in drive and headed back to Annapolis to do the only thing he could, and that was to follow Webster's orders.

Ellison and his partner spent the rest of the day going from door to door talking to Ramirez's neighbors, asking if anything had occurred to them since the last time they were interviewed. At six p.m., and with no more information than they had earlier, the agents returned to Ramirez's townhouse for another look around.

"Damn it, Booker," Ellison shouted from the upstairs living room. Erik Booker was downstairs in Ramirez's bedroom going through shoeboxes when he heard his partner; he dropped the Florsheim box on the bed and took the steps two at a time to the living room. He stood facing Ellison. "What?" he said, trying desperately to restore the oxygen he'd consumed responding to what he thought was an emergency.

"It's nearly 1900, Booker."

"Yeah, so?" Booker said uncoiling from his defensive stance.

"I've missed my pedicure appointment again." The senior agent smiled at his adrenaline-soaked partner. Ellison needed the comic relief, even if it had to be at Booker's expense, besides that it was harmless payback for his arrogant attitude when he explained what neuroleptic meant.

Booker stared at Ellison. "You've heard the story about the little boy that cried wolf too often?" he asked.

"Yup, but I'm not worried."

"Why?"

"'Cause I'm not that little boy."

"Okay, who the hell are you?"

"Make no mistake, grasshopper, I am the wolf."

"Oh, I would've never guessed." Booker rolled his eyes, a mix of exasperation and respect for his mentor. Ellison was tough and haggard looking in a suave sort of way, but nevertheless, the consummate agent and patriot. The animal metaphor fit the senior agent perfectly.

"Mr. Wolf?"

"Speak."

"It's late; can I go home and see my family?"

"Yes, go see the wife and kids. I'll pick you up at 0730."

Booker climbed in next to his partner yawning. "Morning, Mr. Wolf."

"Okay...it's early, enough with the names."

"You started it, remember?"

"No, Mr. Booker, I don't."

"You are getting old. You called me grasshopper, and you told me you were the wolf." The agent knew he was pressing his luck, but that was the way relationships—good relationships—were forged. Pushing here and there, violating a boundary from time to time, maybe even inadvertently stepping on your partner's toes just to see how they react, all principles Booker had learned in interrogation school.

"Booker, I'm in no mood for your fraternity shit this morning. Don't call me wolf, and I won't call you grasshopper."

"Agreed. So where we going?"

"Donut shop for a fritter and coffee then back to the townhouse, as ordered." Ellison's heart wasn't into the task, but for the time being he had no other options. His orders were to double-check the investigation, and double-check he would.

As the agents merged into interstate traffic headed for Annapolis, Ellison turned the radio to a morning talk show. Booker opened the paper and took a sip of coffee. They both sat occupied by their respective forms of media enlightenment until Booker shouted. Ellison's attention was on traffic and didn't look to see what provoked the outburst. "What happened?"

"Spilled hot coffee on my leg?"

"Why?"

"Pull over; you need to read this article."

"Read it to me," Ellison said reaching for the radio volume.

"No, you'll need your full attention on this article."

Ellison exited the interstate and pulled into a convenience store parking lot. Booker handed the paper to his partner. "While you read, I'm going in the bathroom to see if I can clean this mess up."

Ellison found the headline halfway down on the front page and began reading, a cold chill made him shudder. He adjusted his glasses and reread the headline—"Defense Contractor Found Murdered." The article went on to say the man believed to be the missing Department of Defense contractor was found brutally murdered in a hotel room in Damascus, Syria. According to the reporter, the contractor's body was being held by the Syrian government pending a complete autopsy and DNA analysis. Officials from the US Embassy were denied access to the body but were given his belongings that included the victim's wallet and passport. The reporter said Syrian officials have little doubt who the man was, and they are accusing the US of attempting to plant a spy in their midst. The article did not identify the victim by name, only that he had been working with government officials in an attempt to authenticate artifacts stolen from the IMI. A Syrian diplomat assigned to the UN in New York said, according to the article, their government had irrefutable evidence the US and Israel had hatched a secret plan to restore the Temple of the Lord where the Dome of the Rock, one of Islam's holiest sites, now stands. The diplomat said he had been authorized to announce that Syria would not idly stand by and watch such an irreverent, disgraceful, and foolhardy endeavor take place. When asked by the press what he meant when he said, "not idly stand by," the diplomat refused further comment.

Booker returned to the car, tiny shreds of paper towel covering his left trouser leg where he'd tried to blot the spilled coffee. His appearance was the least of his concerns as he slid in next to Ellison. "What do you think?"

"I think we turn around and head for Andrews."

"Get there before Dr. Bethel reads the morning paper?"

ment, and the boss wants to know what's going on in Jerusalem. Please forgive my poor telephone etiquette."

"You're forgiven, Jim. Guess you're between a rock and a hard place."

"You can say that again, skirting important information the president should have for the sake of plausible deniability is as close to impossible as anything I've ever done."

"I know … it feels a whole lot like lying, doesn't it?"

"Exactly, and I don't know how much longer I'm willing to keep up the charade."

"Just remember, Mr. Secretary, you are the president's best friend, and if anyone should feel the need to protect him, it should be his friends. I don't aim to be a hard nose about this, but one of the realities of these prestigious positions we hold is making sure the president stays out of the sewer. Frankly, Jim, you and I are expendable, but not the president."

"Don't you think I know all that?" Parker's state of mind made an important cognitive shift, at least as far as Unger was concerned. The secretary's voice, which had started out sounding desperate, was now angry.

"Of course I know you know, but sometimes we have to be reminded. Now, the advice I have for you, if in fact that's why you called, is to continue stalling him. You're a statesman, use some of that diplomacy." Unger's admonishment drew a lengthy silence from the secretary.

"Okay, I suppose you're right," Parker said. The secretary of state stood and moved to a window with a view of memorials to great leaders scattered across the manicured landscape. His thoughts drifted back decades earlier—a time he and his young friends were certain they had the answer. *Idealism has its place in the minds of the youth,* he thought, *but not now, not here.*

"Jim, are you all right?"

"Yeah, just thinking what I should do … listen to this. I'll make arrangements to meet with the Israelis; they've remodeled and added on to the Knesset, and they've invited me to address the parliament several times. Arrangements will take a few days; I'll tell the president the trip will give me an opportunity to assess the seriousness of the problem."

"You think that'll hold him off?"

"I don't know, but it's worth a try. You know, Bill, he's very interested in this whole prophecy fulfillment issue. He reads his Bible every day."

"I know, sometimes that scares me. Does he believe the US is to play a significant role in this Armageddon thing?"

"All I can tell you is he believes every word. I've known him thirty-five years, and his life revolves around that Bible, but ..." The secretary's voice trailed off.

Unger waited, fearing a question too soon would signal Parker he'd said more than he should have.

"I need to go, Bill, I'll keep you posted on my plan. Hopefully by the time I'm back from Israel the CIA mission will be over, and they'll have found something else to fuss over. In the meantime call the president and explain who this contractor that was found murdered in Damascus is; he's been bugging me about it ever since the first article came out."

"Will do, I have a meeting with him at four. If we don't talk again before you go to Israel, be careful. You are an important target to some of these freaks."

"Don't worry; I'll keep my head down."

Unger swiveled around, so that he could see out his window and leaned back in his tan and white executive chair. He had twenty minutes until his next appointment, time enough for a pinch of Skoal and a shot of Wild Turkey. The vice president sat enjoying a rare moment of solitude and his vices, trying to ward off the nagging feeling of impending doom.

Lee Bethel stood as the agents approached; it was obvious they had news he wasn't going to like. He felt muscles tightening around his chest, signaling a surge of adrenaline. Bethel forced a smile. "You guys look like you just saw a ghost."

Ellison did not return the smile or acknowledge the comment. "Let's go inside." The senior agent led the way to the interview room and motioned for Lee and Booker to take a seat. Agent Ellison picked up the wall phone and told whoever answered to shut the audio and video recorder off. "Have you seen this morning's paper?" he asked.

"Hadn't yet, why?"

"The front page article implies Ramirez has been found murdered."

Bethel could only stare, words refused to form while his mind sorted through the possibilities of what he'd just been told. Ellison allowed the cold, matter-of-fact statement to sink in, knowing it would take some time. He'd been in these situations often and hadn't found the perfect way of breaking bad news to someone yet. Finally Bethel took a breath. "You're not kidding, are you?"

"No, Lee, I'm not kidding."

"What did you mean *implies* he's been murdered?"

Ellison handed him the paper. Bethel was halfway through the article a second time when Ellison's phone vibrated. "Yes, sir," he answered after glancing at the caller ID. "Yes, sir, I can meet you any time you say." Ellison listened for further instructions and hung up.

"Important?" Booker asked, watching his partner carefully, anticipating a yes.

"That was Jerry Webster." Ellison turned to Bethel. "Webster is the acting director of the FBI, an old friend of mine. Says he wants to see us first thing in the morning."

"Us? You mean me too?" Bethel said quietly, sadness infecting his words.

"The three of us, FBI headquarters in DC at 0800."

"What about?" Booker asked.

Agent Ellison allowed his partner some room for inexperience and just plain ignorance, but not much room. "How long was I on the phone, Booker?"

"Ten seconds, maybe."

"Did you hear me ask him why he wanted to see us?" Ellison said, controlling the irritation in his voice for the sake of Dr. Bethel, who was still trying to make sense of the morning events.

Booker shook his head.

Ellison fixed a hard stare on his junior partner. "Think about this, Booker. Under what circumstances would you, an agent, ask the Director of the FBI why he wanted to see you? When you've come up with the answer please ... let me know."

"This is just unbelievable ... unbelievable. One minute you're working closely with someone, a friend ..." Bethel's voice trailed off into silence, oblivious of the exchange between the agents.

"I'm sorry. What were you saying?" Ellison asked.

"He was there one minute and gone the next ... it just happened so fast ... right under my nose. I don't understand how it could've happened without me hearing anything; now he's dead."

Ellison watched Bethel deal with his anguish, knowing anything he had to offer in the way of comfort would be negligible. He had to let Bethel grieve at his own pace and certainly not try to offer false hope. "Lee, are you all right?"

"I guess ... but, really I don't know ... confused perhaps and mad at myself. I just feel like I need to do something ... shoot somebody." Bethel's quiet, grieving voice was drifting noticeably toward rage.

"We're confused, too, and pissed, I might add. Here's my suggestion. Booker and I are going back to Annapolis; hopefully we'll find some clues—"

Bethel interrupted, "I want to go along."

"No, absolutely not. Without some formal training, you wouldn't want me on one of your excavation sites. Think about it,

I sure as hell don't need an amateur at a possible crime scene. Now, let me finish."

"Point taken, I see what you're saying, just thought that'd give me something to do."

The agents nodded. "You've got to stay here, at least until we pick you up in the morning. You may not fully understand this, so let me make it clear. A meeting with the director is unheard of, even if he is a long time friend of mine. There is, within the FBI, a well-defined management hierarchy, an agent just doesn't meet with the director without following protocol, and believe me, this ain't protocol."

"I'm still not following."

"I don't know what, but something's up. We're going to learn something in the morning."

Bethel lowered his head in thought, reluctant to voice any more questions or allow himself to contemplate the worst. "I hope it's good," he said.

"I certainly can't assure you it'll be good, but nevertheless it will be important."

Ellison drove into the underground parking garage at FBI headquarters at seven forty a.m. Even with photo identification, it took the agents and Bethel fifteen minutes to maneuver through all the security and finally to the director's office. Jerry Webster met them inside the director's alcove, several professionally dressed men and women were moving hurriedly around the complex of executive offices. A few recognized Ellison and made a point of greeting him before moving on to their own offices or meetings in various conference rooms. That particular floor was unlike any other in the building. Individual offices afforded more privacy, desks of cherry wood and matching furniture instead of gray or beige metal desks occupying small, glassed-in cubicles on floors below the executive level. Booker was enthralled with the plush surroundings. Thick taupe-colored carpet silenced the constant movement of people, walls adorned with art work and framed photos of past FBI leadership-lined walls and indirect lighting cast a soothing amber glow, a noticeable contrast to the bright fluorescent lighting found elsewhere.

Webster waved in the direction of his office door and followed his three guests, stopping briefly to tell his assistant he wanted no interruptions.

"Coffee, anyone?" Webster asked before he sat down.

Bethel and the two agents declined.

Acting FBI director Jerry Webster pulled his chair around from in back of the executive desk and sat down. The gesture—a signal the conversation they were about to have was semi-unofficial—was meant to relax his guests. "What I'm going to tell you will, I hope, offer the three of you some relief, but the level of secrecy here is the ultimate. In other words, prosecution to the extreme is possible if you do not maintain absolute silence." Webster paused long enough to entertain a question if one had been asked. The three sat silently, uneasy about what they were being told while mulling over what *prosecution to the extreme* really meant.

"Dr. Bethel, you have been part of a very important national security mission. Unknowingly, you and Carlos Ramirez have been active participants in the bait segment of this mission." He hesitated again.

Bethel looked at Ellison for confirmation but the senior agent appeared surprised too. "Did you know about this?" Bethel said.

"Hell no."

"Not many knew, only six people are privy to the entire mission."

Ellison was showing signs of agitation, behavior that was becoming more of a problem for the agent the older he got. "Mission, what mission? What's going on, Jerry... I'm sorry, Director Webster?"

"Apology not necessary, Frank. I know how you feel. You're a trusted, decorated, and experienced agent, and you've been left out of the loop, but in this case it was and still is necessary."

"You're saying you can't tell us more about the mission?" He looked sternly at his friend and boss.

"Right, I can't tell you." *For two reasons,* Webster thought. Other than the simple fact he'd been sworn to secrecy by the vice president himself, the element that concerned him the most was Ellison finding out Crystal Stanton was intimately involved in the operation side of the mission. He was aware of their history together and knew Ellison wouldn't take the news of his former fiancée's participation well.

"I'm confused then," Ellison said.

"About why you're here?"

"Yes ... why are we here?"

"So I can tell you Ramirez is alive."

Bethel's response was obvious, his education and training hadn't prepared him to control revealing body language like Ellison and Booker. Although the agent's pulse quickened, it did nothing to spark a noticeable reaction.

"What?" Bethel said.

"Ramirez is alive and well."

Ellison moved to the edge of his chair. "His bogus abduction and death was just part of this mission you can't tell us about?"

"Yes, it was contrived as a distraction, and unfortunately, that's all I can tell you. I felt the three of you should know—you were worried and behaving exactly like I wanted you to behave."

"You mean you wanted us to behave genuinely?" Ellison was trying hard to understand the need for deception between him and Webster; after all, they'd been friends a long time. He felt played, which wasn't squaring well with the whole FBI brotherhood crap he'd believed in most of his career.

"Of course, I wanted you to act like you would if Ramirez was abducted. I don't think anyone can persuade someone unless they believe it to be true. We couldn't take a chance; we had to make it appear real so that if the bad guys were watching they'd be convinced by your actions."

"I see your point. I don't like it, but I do see the relevance." Ellison studied the director's face for clues that might divulge details of the unknown mission, but nothing. "So, Director Webster, does that mean the three of us are released from this task?"

Bethel jumped on Ellison's question with his own before Webster could respond. "May I take my wife and mother-in-law home?"

"No to both your questions. I told you that Ramirez is alive to offer the three of you some relief, but you must continue to play out your role until the mission is complete."

"Any idea about when that'll occur?" Booker asked.

"Maybe a week, maybe a month or two, there is no way of telling."

Ellison's voice was calm. "And in the meantime we keep looking for Ramirez's abductors?"

"Yes, and to add validity to your investigation, I will reassign you both to bureau field headquarters in Damascus."

Booker raised his hand; Ellison winced at the prospect of what his partner was about to ask. Webster nodded. "Director, sir, I didn't realize we had bureau headquarters in Damascus?"

Ellison looked out the window, biting his lower lip, as Webster dutifully informed the young agent, "As in most hostile countries where the US has an embassy, the FBI has a room we rent from the State Department. I think, if memory serves me correctly, that room in Damascus is about ten by ten feet and occupied by two people plus desks and file cabinets. I believe there are two metal folding chairs where two people the size of a normal twelve-year-old can sit comfortably."

Ellison winked at the director. "Isn't that office in the basement?"

"Yes, it is."

Booker had heard enough and slid back in the chair thinking about his wife and how to tell her.

"And what do *we* do in the meantime?" Bethel asked.

"I've arranged for you, your wife, and mother-in-law to be

guage skills might be questioned, or maybe their papers wouldn't be in order. If a nuclear scientist questioned them extensively about uranium enrichment, their lack of real scientific knowledge would be easily detectable. Security at the site in Natanz would be tight—even recognized staff would be questioned randomly and documents checked and double-checked.

The mission up to this point had been simple; Nadim Bin Faxhir was known throughout the region. He'd worked closely over the years with Iranians consulting on various forms of fuel processing and escorting his wife and sister to visit relatives wouldn't seem unusual. The women had remained silent throughout the twelve-day trip. Keeping to themselves and studying the enrichment process when they could was a good thing about the long trek into northern Iran. When they left Amal's home, however, their previous identities of sister and wife came to a halt. Now, Zayna and Yasmeen must morph into professionals within a very sophisticated and elite fraternity. Discovering evidence to support the belief Iran is enriching uranium for military purposes or merely to operate the countries electrical power sources was to be a complex and well-choreographed ballet. A drama to be played out quickly requiring precise timing and every skill the women were capable of.

Faxhir pointed to a collection of odd-shaped buildings set a mile off the main road into Natanz. "That's it, our destination. As soon as we turn onto the access road, we will be monitored, and by the time we reach the administration building, their security team will have run the plates on this rental car."

"And that will tell them who you are?" Yasmeen asked.

"Yes, and although they are not expecting me, they will find my name on their list of people that have been given limited plant access."

The women were prepared, each had their credentials ready to turn over, and their responses rehearsed. Faxhir stopped at the first guard post; a very large, bearded man stepped from the small building and demanded identification. The guard looked closely at the papers and at the two women, not bothering with Faxhir, his gaze more leering than inquisitive. He knelt down to get a better look; a grizzly bear sizing up a lame deer for lunch did so more tactfully. The guard handed the papers back to Faxhir, still staring at the women. The two agents offered a sheepish expression, bowing their covered heads slightly in proper submissive form. He stood and motioned Faxhir through.

"We're approaching security gate two," Faxhir warned.

The next identification process took longer but was performed much more professionally. Eventually a well-dressed man approached smiling. "So sorry for the inconvenience we've caused you, Nadim, but we have our rules."

"We understand, and it is good to see you again."

"It is always good when old friends meet." The man turned to the women. "And the ladies?"

"Consultants from Pakistan University, Xerxes. Doctors Yasmeen Binte Mahir and Zayna Binte Sayyid, this is Xerxes Sattar."

The man turned briskly toward the women with a token nod.

"The last time I was here, Dr. Sherafat and I discussed some engineering problems. He needed expertise he didn't have, and I promised to broker an arrangement between the countries."

"But, Faxhir, they are far too beautiful for such an intellectual endeavor." He smiled.

"Yes, they are. I agree: it is a waste. They should be bearing children, but alas, nothing anymore is as it should be."

"Sad, my friend, but inevitable. I'm afraid the ways of Allah are being eroded in front of our very eyes. Nevertheless, ladies, you are here, and I'm sure our scientists will be pleased." He turned and beckoned the three to follow him, first through a metal detector and then an apparatus that displayed an image of their bodies, leaving nothing to the imagination. The escort led them through a series of concrete, windowless hallways to the cramped administrative complex and to an office door marked *Director of Science and Research*. Sattar knocked, opened the door, and stepped aside allowing the visitors to enter the small, cluttered office, and then disappeared into an adjoining office. Dr. Sherafat was engrossed in solving a mathematical problem on a large chalkboard fastened to one wall. Dust from constant erasing and Sherafat's cigarette smoke filled the air. Three Dell computers sat on individual tables arranged in a semi-circle to the left of his desk, the only decorations—the required eight-by-ten framed photo of the Ayatollah and slightly lower and to the left a five-by-seven photo of Iran's president—hung portentously on one bare wall. Although the team was sure Sherafat knew they were there, he made no effort to acknowledge their presence. They stood fixed on the grand disarray the physicist's office was in. The only two chairs were stacked high with journals and diagrams of equipment required in creating nuclear energy. Dr. Sherafat was obviously consumed by what he was doing, neglecting, as a result, his personal appearance as well as what minuscule amount of social skill he'd picked up over the years. Thick unruly reddish gray eyebrows nearly engulfed the top of his government-issue, black, rimmed bifocals, but they paled in comparison to Sherafat's mustache that hadn't seen the glimmer of scissor blades in months.

Faxhir stepped closer to the old man, trying to avoid the clutter of boxes and reams of copy paper. He cleared his throat and spoke softly. "Dr. Sherafat…sir." He paused hoping the man would turn around. Faxhir took another step closer, he was now close enough to touch the physicist, but knew better than to startle him, "Dr. Sherafat…sir."

"Yes, yes, I hear you, just take a seat…I'll be with you soon."

Soon turned out to be five minutes, and with nowhere to sit, the three stood quietly, waiting.

Sherafat wrote vigorously, making indecipherable mathematic squiggles until he ran out of chalkboard space, continuing the equation on the back of a brown paper sack. He dotted the last figure and whirled around to face his visitors for the first time. "There, it's done; now we can talk." He pulled his glasses off and studied Faxhir's face, his own twisted into a perplexed squint. "Who are you?"

"I am Nadim Bin Faxhir from Oman; I consult with your government concerning natural gas processing. We talked two months ago about the gas centrifuge issue you were having."

The old man smiled, looking around his office for somewhere his guests could sit. "Oh yes, of course, now I remember. You said you could help me."

"I did, sir."

Sherafat continued to direct his questions and his attention only to Faxhir. He cleared the two chairs and motioned for him to sit down. Zayna and Yasmeen stood in silence.

"Yes, you promised to bring me an engineer with cascading centrifuge experience."

"And I've done better than that, Dr. Sherafat."

The physicist turned his gaze for the first time to the women, "I see you've brought me two women engineers instead of one good male? Is this a joke?"

"No, sir, one woman is a nuclear engineer and the other a physicist like you. Both have extensive experience working inside Pakistan's nuclear weapons program." Faxhir watched the old man's face for a reaction and wasn't disappointed. As soon as he noticed Sherafat's left eyebrow rise slightly, he went on. "Of course I know you are not enriching uranium for military purposes, but Yasmeen's experience with U-235 will be helpful. The engineer, Zayna, requested her help. In essence, Dr. Sherafat, you're getting much more than I promised."

The two-for-one sales job Faxhir was promoting drew a scowl from the old man. The director of science and research looked from Faxhir to the women and back several times. Yasmeen and Zayna stood inhaling the acrid air trying to bend their knees slightly to compensate for the anxiety rush bombarding their nervous system. They knew even a shudder might tip the old man to ask questions neither could answer.

"Dr. Sherafat," Faxhir waited as long as he could, a distraction was the only thing he could think of.

"Yes."

"I've come a great distance, and I'm tired. I must find a hotel nearby. I am sorry I did not consult with you first regarding the women, and now I'm afraid I've wasted your valuable time."

"Nonsense, we have fine accommodations right here on site. We entertain many visitors and consultants, there is no need for you to endure the rigors of our security protocols each and every time you enter and leave." Before Faxhir could object Sherafat was on the phone making arrangements for their stay. "I have a very important meeting I must attend now. Someone will be here momentarily to escort you to your quarters; we will meet at five p.m."

Faxhir whispered, "There may be cameras and listening devices planted everywhere. Be cautious." He turned just long enough to assure himself they'd comprehended the gravity of what he'd said, and from their expression there was no doubt.

Shortly Xerxes Sattar reappeared. "I understand you are to be our guests for a few days."

Faxhir glanced at the women as Sattar opened the door for them to leave. "Yes, that is apparently Dr. Sherafat's wish."

"Follow me; the dorm is not far."

Sattar led them through a labyrinth of narrow passageways to an elevator that took them down to an area marked level three. The doors opened into an even narrower hallway. The only illumination emanating from light bulbs hung sporadically down the tunnel-like hall. Finally they came to a series of doors identified by the numbers one through ten. Sattar stopped at room two and unlocked the door. "This will be your room, Nadim. Ladies, please follow me." Their host skipped two rooms and unlocked number five. "One of you here." He reached in and turned the only light in the room on, and Yasmeen stepped in. Sattar skipped two more rooms and unlocked number seven, turning the light on for Zayna as well, and after setting their bags down, the team returned to the hall where Sattar was waiting. "At four forty-five someone will escort you to the meeting scheduled with Dr. Sherafat." He pointed to a set of double doors at the end of the hallway. "Those are the facilities. It's even equipped with a washer and dryer. The lights go out automatically at nine p.m. and come on again at five a.m." And then he added casually, "The same with the elevator."

"And the stairwell, where is the stairwell?" Faxhir asked.

Sattar pointed in the direction of the elevators. "On the other side of the lift shaft, however, for security reasons the doors are chained and locked."

"Do we get a key?"

"The key is on a hook just to the right of the fire alarm box."

Faxhir continued to push for information, his anxiety about their quarters still well masked, but growing as his confidence began to vanish. He knew he was treading on thin ice, caught between self-preservation and not wanting to appear suspicious of their host. "And you will be back for us at four forty-five?"

"Someone will take you to Dr. Sherafat's office at that time; I will be back in the morning to introduce you to the scientists you will be working with." Sattar looked in each of the rooms and mumbled something. "I'm sorry; no one has brought you fresh linens. I'll take care of that right now."

As soon as he was gone, Faxhir motioned for the women to join him. "Remember what I said about voice and video surveillance." He whispered, "Don't appear like you're looking for bugs or cameras."

Yasmeen moved in close to Faxhir; making it appear she was on her way to the bathroom at the end of the hall, as she passed by him, she said, "Have you noticed the deadbolt latches on the outside of our doors?" She kept walking, not waiting for an answer. Yasmeen stepped through a door marked *lavatory* in four languages, including English. The interior décor matched the rest of what she'd seen—austere, cold, unfinished concrete and stainless steel prison fixtures. Two stools without privacy dividers and two urinals along one wall and one shower with a thin mold-infested plastic curtain across the doorway. The two sinks bore remnants of the last occupants, a concoction Yasmeen thought resembling dried blood or vomit—possibly both. She tried to recall a place as filthy in her years of undercover work, but nothing came to mind. Her eyes drifted slowly to the washer and dryer at one end of the room, a hastily written sign taped to each appliance indicating they were out of order; two metal ventilator screens were welded to heavy steel plates embedded in the concrete ceiling. A glimmer emanating from in back of one of the screens indicated the possible presence of a camera lens. There were no soap or paper towels in the dispensers and no toilet paper anywhere. The lavatory was simply unusable, and Yasmeen had to go. Although she'd never consider changing genders, she thought under these conditions being male had its benefits. She walked over to the cleaner of the two stools and lifted the floor-length kameez to her waist, pulled her panties to her knees, and squatted to within an inch of the rim. The relief was worth the indignities she endured knowing a room full of security personnel were most likely enjoying the scene. As she left the lavatory, Zayna passed her on the way to freshen up. The hall was so narrow the women had to turn sideways to pass, and as Zayna got within whisper range, Yasmeen said, "Don't drink coffee, and pray for constipation."

At the scheduled time, a man none of the team had seen before arrived to escort them back to Dr. Sherafat's office. When they arrived, one of the computer tables had been cleared of equipment, and in its place were an assortment of Iranian fare.

"I'm sure you're hungry." Sherafat's demeanor was friendlier, a softer tone to his voice that no longer sounded distrustful, and although he directed all remarks only to Faxhir he at least smiled briefly at the two women. "My favorite is the pollo; the meat is lamb. The vegetables and fruit are fresh from our nearby garden. Eat, enjoy." The old man threw his hands up in a festive demonstration of his attitude change, clearly from one extreme to the other in a few short hours.

As they ate Sherafat asked questions that sounded friendly, but to the experienced agents they were carefully crafted open-ended inquiries intended to expose hidden motives. The next two hours was a chess game, strategist against strategist, Sherafat playing the role of shrewd interrogator, and Faxhir acting the part of a common sales representative from Oman. At just after seven p.m. Sherafat brought the conversation to a close. "Thank you for visiting with me tonight and sharing my table. In the morning, the women will be escorted to respective labs to meet the people they will be working with. I hope you enjoy your stay and the accommodations. Now if you will excuse me, I have much more work to do before turning in."

Zayna glanced at Faxhir as they all stood; the non-verbal coaxing reminded him to ask Sherafat for hand soap and toilet paper. The director of science and research scowled at the question, the inquiry clearly an insult to his status. He pointed toward the door herding his guest into the hall like a shepherd guiding goats into a pen. Sherafat rapped hard on the door next to his and stepped in and shouted to whoever was in the room to provide the proper necessities for their guest. He stepped back into the hall and disappeared into his own office without saying anything else to Faxhir. A second later Xerxes Sattar appeared. "I'm so sorry your accommodations were lacking the proper necessities. That is my fault. I believe you will find what you need in your quarters now." Sattar backed into his office, closing the door behind him without waiting for a response.

Faxhir glanced at the women; it was obvious they all shared the same suspicions of the two-hour encounter. Just then their escort arrived to guide them through the maze and back to their hideous lodging arrangements. When they reached level three, the escort opened the elevator door and murmured, "Lights out in one hour and fifteen minutes." The door shut, and team one was alone and totally at the mercy of Dr. Sherafat.

the midst of fear and darkness, a state of being she'd trained for but had never experienced to the horrifying degree she had this night. Yasmeen dressed in the dark—not knowing what time it was—and leaned back against the wall, and with her hand ready to lift the hem of her tunic, she fell asleep.

CHAPTER 30
CIA HEADQUARTERS, VA
0600 SEPTEMBER 15

Margaret Winters opened her office blinds although the sun hadn't yet made its appearance. It wasn't practical for the CIA boss to think in terms of long days compared to short ones; they were all long and getting longer. Friday, to most people, was the end of the workweek, but no such thing for Winters; it was just another day, a disaster—somewhere—was waiting to happen.

She'd received a call the evening before from the administrator of the Senate Select Committee on Intelligence informing her she was being summoned to discuss a recent spike in Middle Eastern hostilities. Winters knew the risks and penalties if she was caught lying to the committee, there was no tolerance for even vaguely misleading members. Losing her job was only a minor concern; federal prison loomed as the ugliest consequence she was sure to face, and for what? So the president of the United States could honestly tell the public he had no knowledge of the mission? "Regardless," she whispered, staring at the first

rays of light blossoming above the trees. "It was my plan. I sought permission from Unger; I put those people in harms way, and why?" The answer was clear in her mind, but she wanted to hear how it sounded out loud, it was imperative that she appear confident.

Winters had witnessed high-ranking officials give feeble testimony, and as soon as their weakness was exposed committee members behaved like a pack of half-starved hyenas. Falling on one's sword was bad enough, being picked apart by a bunch of naïve politicians was intolerable. She stood before a full-length mirror rehearsing answers to anticipated questions aloud and practicing her physical presence so she'd convey confidence. Body language was as important as the words coming from her mouth, and in some cases even more important. She just had to remember not to appear arrogant, a difficult task for her, since Winters knew more about international intelligence than all the committee members combined.

The committee administrator motioned to Winters and opened the door to the Capitol chamber where all intelligence meetings were conducted. The meeting—always closed to the media and the public—was just getting underway. The chairwoman announced Winters arrival and asked the members, who were still milling around, to take their seats. "Committee members," she said, rapping the gavel one time marking the official beginning of the meeting.

Winters knew the gavel sound was the signal to activate the recording system. She'd been before the committee numerous times and realized anything said after the introductory gavel rap was on the record, even audible whispers. The CIA chief kept her mouth shut until she was formally addressed—a practice the secretary of defense suggested during her vetting process. August Jefferson, a longtime friend of Winters' father, was a frequent house guest during her teen years and college days. He'd witnessed firsthand her drive to be the best at whatever she did, and her passionate desire to make the world a better place. Sometimes though, Margaret's drive and passion came forth in a string of sophisticated words laced graphically with expletives ending any chance of resolving the issue calmly with diplomacy. Winters recalled her friend's advice and sat dutifully at the long table quietly waiting for the hubbub to end, knowing the mic sitting just six inches away was on.

The chairwoman rapped the gavel again. "Director Winters," she began, "thank you for coming in on such short notice. The committee and I apologize, however, we have some concerns we need information and your advice about." She stopped talking, held her hand over the mic, and listened to an aide whisper something to her. "Sorry for the interruption, Director Winters."

Winters nodded.

The chairwoman read from a prepared statement concerning the escalating violence in the Middle East, and how authorities in the countries involved were growing increasingly concerned about citizen unrest. The fear of escalating conflict was looming again and the growing animosity seemed to be over the ark of the covenant. She stopped reading and peered over the top of her reading glasses at Winters. "Director Winters, before I go on, tell me … is there a smidgeon of truth in this report about this ark thing?"

"I have no idea—"

The committee member from Nevada interrupted. "You have no idea, Director Winters." He dabbed at the perspiration forming on his balding head. "What on earth do we pay you people for?"

The chairwoman returned the ball to Winters' side of the court with a scowl in the legislator's direction. "You were saying, Director."

"An artifact was found in Baghdad that had archaeological implications. A stone tablet taken from the Iraq Museum International during the war; we've had a team of experts working on its authenticity."

Another member held up a laminated news article. "Does this artifact have anything to do with this man's disappearance?"

Before Winters could answer, the chairwoman, aware some congressmen had an altogether different agenda, cut the question

the interpreter provided by the embassy, Ellison discovered the victim had been murdered somewhere else and his body moved to the hotel in an apparent attempt to make it look like the murder occurred there. The pathologist was almost sure the man had been dead at least twenty-four hours before he was discovered, but there had been very little decomposition.

Agent Ellison suspected what that meant but chose to appear ignorant in hopes of getting more information out of the pathologist. "What do you make of that doctor?" the interpreter asked the question in Arabic. Ellison's ploy worked, the pathologist slipped off his latex gloves and removed his glasses, turning to the interpreter, he spoke slowly about the decaying process and how the body would have to have been frozen soon after his death and then allowed to thaw on the hotel room floor. Ellison faked a curious look in the pathologist's direction and nodded, as if the thought had never occurred to him. "Please tell the doctor we respectfully request he not reveal that information to anyone yet. Tell him the information, if it could remain confidential, might help the police in their investigation." Ellison's orders were to make it appear as though a thorough prolonged investigation was taking place which wasn't difficult. The Syrian government ordered the police to cooperate fully with the FBI, but the government didn't stipulate how quickly they should cooperate. The passive foot dragging by the Syrians worked nicely with Ellison's orders to delay the investigations outcome as much as possible. Ellison thanked the pathologist and returned to his hotel to see what Booker had learned.

CHAPTER 31

WASHINGTON, D.C.
1100 HOURS, SEPTEMBER 15

Winters read the message several times then folded the missive, putting it in her jacket pocket. "Take me back to the office," she told the driver. He repeated the command over the mic attached to his headgear and the lead vehicle made a U-turn on the unusually empty thoroughfare. Winters' head was spinning on high alert and in full-rescue mode. Nothing mattered more than getting whatever team members were left back home safely. If the message was true, the mission had sustained a devastating blow and was destined for failure anyway. Getting team two out of Muscat was priority and relatively simple, that task could be handled with one or two phone calls, rescuing team one was another matter altogether. As the director of Central Intelligence and her entourage crossed the Potomac on their way to Virginia, her mind entertained briefly the fall she was about to take all in the name of preserving the president's and the vice president's anonymity. How hard the fall was anyone's guess. In the end, she thought, it didn't really matter, after all it was her plan, and it made perfect sense for the others to distance themselves from her. She'd respect that no matter what the consequences were. What frustrated Winters the most was that her detractors would have reason to revel in her failure, and there wouldn't be anything she could do about it.

The lead and follow-up vehicle in the director's caravan pulled away from the Escalade as soon as they entered the secure parking area below the headquarters building at Langley. Winters grabbed her briefcase and stepped out of the open door, her assistant remained seated watching her laptop screen.

"Director," she said.

Winters turned, agitated, her dark cropped hair flared slightly. Her assistant and former CIA analyst knew not to take her boss's behavior personally. She'd worked with Winters long enough to know her moods—knowledge necessary in her line of work when good mental health was essential.

"What?" Winters said.

"You're receiving a directive to meet with the vice president at 1400."

"Today?"

"Yes, ma'am."

Winters slammed her briefcase against the heavily reinforced concrete wall realizing security cameras were recording her reaction. She punched a button then positioned her hand over the handprint authentication screen and the elevator door opened. When they reached her office, Winters dismissed her assistant with an order to remind her when it was thirteen-thirty. After the door closed, she placed a call to August Jefferson.

"August."

"Maggie, what's going on?"

"I'm afraid the mission is going to hell in a hurry; I need your help, and I need it now."

"You know I'll do what I can, but there are limitations—"

"I know there are, August, I'm asking you to help if you can, and don't if you can't, it's that simple." Winters had a way of cutting through the Washington political maneuvering that sometimes cost her valuable legislative support.

"Okay, Maggie, I'm listening."

"I need to get support team two out of Muscat, now. The air force hauled them into Qatar and local drivers took them the rest of the way."

"Not a problem; we've got a good relationship with those gulf countries, as well as Qatar. Have team two packed and ready to go; someone from the embassy will pick them up. What else?"

"This is the big one."

"I'm still listening."

"Will you authorize DIA to assess the risk of extracting team one?"

"What's their location?"

"Natanz, Iran."

"Natanz."

"Yes."

"Oh shit. Pardon my Swahili, but that would be impossible, Maggie. I'm sorry."

"I'm just asking, August, that you assess it, not do it."

"Why, CIA have a mole?"

"Oh God, August, I hope not ... no, the reason I ask is my folks would have to share that intelligence with my lovely CIA enemies and in turn my *friends* would leak the information to the media, and I can't have that."

"Good point. Let me think, and I'll call you within the hour."

Winters waited, each passing moment stirring her anxiety higher. She mindlessly pulled document after document out of her in-basket giving each a cursory review before signing and returning them to the out-basket. She stopped long enough to down some antacid just as her private cell phone rang. It was August Jefferson with news.

"I can have an official risk assessment, including required assets

on your desk by in the morning, or I can have a rough summary in your hands by four p.m."

"I'll take the summary... August, thanks. I owe you big time."

"Excuse me, Director Winters, you wanted to be reminded of your appointment at 1330."

"Yeah, thanks, tell the guys I'll be down in ten minutes." Winters had one thought, and one only: getting team one out of Iran. At this point in the game, the pride she felt from doing a tough job well was fading. Her job was on the line, and more importantly, her reputation too. If the sky was truly going to fall on her getting the team out of Iran was her focus, and according to the message she'd received from the only asset working at the nuclear facility in Natanz the original plan was deteriorating rapidly. Juggling protocol, politics, diplomacy, and protecting the executive branch of the federal government while endeavoring to save lives was like trying to balance a bowling ball on the head of a pin in a hurricane. Being summoned to Unger's office couldn't have come at a worse time. Winters needed all her time and energy—what was left of it—devoted to a plan of action and waltzing around with the vice president was an interruption she couldn't afford. She would just have to make a quick assessment of Unger's concerns, tell him something that would satisfy his need for constant progress updates, and excuse herself. *Easier said than done,* she thought, as she fastened her seatbelt.

CHAPTER 32

NUCLEAR FACILITY
NATANZ, IRAN
0500 HOURS, SEPTEMBER 15

The overhead light flickered several seconds giving the small room an eerie torture chamber effect. The rapid flashing could very easily stir the inhabitant's mind to hallucinate. Yasmeen closed her eyes and felt for the knife, a natural instinct to protect her from whatever was about to happen. Finally the light blinked on and stayed that way. She moved her hand away from the knife hidden by the hem of her tunic and stretched; scanning the room for hidden cameras while she eased tension from every joint in her body. The door opened easily, and Yasmeen stepped into the hall and made her way to the lavatory. Zayna was already there and just stepping out of the shower; Yasmeen flushed the stool and turned on the faucet. "That was a weird night," she said splashing cold water on her face.

"What do you mean?"

Yasmeen turned slightly in order to see her teammate's

Yasmeen followed the men around the catwalk to a stairway identified by a large letter E attached to the handrail. She felt better, the room was air-conditioned, and the well-lighted openness allowed the claustrophobic sensation to momentarily retreat. There were ten white-coated scientists, all men, in the ceiling-less room. The glances in her direction were rapid, almost imperceptible; no one said anything, not even a nod. She looked around the catwalk making a mental note where each guard stood, looking for weaknesses in the security arrangement, but finding none. What Yasmeen did see was the piercing glare of the guards looking directly at her; another wave of apprehension settling around her like toxic smoke. At the far end of the room, partially hidden in the shadows, she could see the unmistakable outline of the immense man she'd now had two brief encounters with. Talavi stood looking even more menacing. He took a step forward, out of the shadow and stared directly at her, his appearance alone was enough to send an icy shiver down her spine. One of the scientists stepped in close and pointed at a computer monitor, whispering, "Watch that one ... he has a reputation. Some call him the eliminator."

Yasmeen turned away from Talavi and looked at the monitor. "And what does he eliminate?" she whispered back, knowing full well what he meant.

The scientist didn't answer her question directly; he simply smiled. "I'm sorry if our ways seem clumsy and aloof, but you have to understand the conditions we work under." He presented his hand. "I am Dr. Ansari, your personal contact during your stay." His extended hand was the first physical gesture Yasmeen had experienced since arriving in Iran, and she wasn't sure how to respond. Assuming Ansari was familiar with proper exchanges between non-relative male and female co-workers, she took his hand. His grip was firm, his hand warm, the dark eyes friendly. Ansari's demeanor had changed dramatically since they were in Sherafat's company twenty minutes earlier. He turned to the others and cleared his throat. "Gentlemen ... may I have your attention?"

After introductions, the men returned to their activities, and Ansari motioned for Yasmeen to follow him. For the next few hours, he escorted Yasmeen from room to room introducing her and explaining what was taking place in each of the labs. Fortunately no one asked her questions she couldn't answer. Most had been questions concerning fissile isotope uranium 235 and nothing about highly enriched uranium (HEU) required for military purposes. A sense of relief enveloped her as the day progressed, everything she saw pointed to the development of nuclear energy for domestic purposes. She reminded herself that while the situation might appear benign, there was a strong chance she was being intentionally deceived. A conflict raged within between a part of her that wanted to do a thorough job and not leave any stone unturned and the instinct to run as fast and as far as she could. The answer to that debate was clear; however, she was there to do the job right, no matter what the consequences happened to be.

Yasmeen glanced at a nearby clock, it was late, and she was anxious to see Zayna. Dr. Ansari saw the fleeting look. "We work until seven p.m.; guards won't allow us to leave earlier unless we have a pass signed by Sherafat."

"It has been a very long day, Dr. Ansari, and I am feeling a bit lightheaded."

"Can I get you some water?"

"No, that won't help. I am sorry; I should have told you earlier that I suffer from hypoglycemia. Are there vending machines nearby?" She knew there weren't and the complaint was a ploy to cover her obvious physical signs of confinement.

"There are no vending machines; food is not allowed in the lab. Come with me." Ansari climbed the stairway to the catwalk with Yasmeen following, and as they neared the guarded exit, Talavi stepped into their path.

Ansari stopped several feet away from the huge man, just out of reach of his massive hands. "Please, Dr. Mahir has need of medical attention; I must take her to the infirmary."

"No," Talavi said with all the authority necessary to persuade Ansari to step back. "I will escort Dr. Mahir." He tightened his grip on the Russian-made Kalashnikov.

Yasmeen could see her host had no alternative but to do as he was ordered. She stepped around him and followed Talavi through the exit and into the hall.

CHAPTER 33
CIA HEADQUARTERS
1535 HOURS, SEPTEMBER 15

"The office, as quick as you can," Winters told her driver. The meeting with Unger hadn't taken as long as she'd anticipated, but nevertheless it was an imposition at a moment when time was critical. The vice president wanted an update on the committee meeting, and to bring her up to speed concerning Secretary Parker's Middle East itinerary. The trip into DC and the forty-five-minute meeting with Unger was a waste, but it was done; now she could devote time to the crisis brewing in Iran.

Margaret Winters opened the cardboard envelope marked *TOP SECRET: For Director Winters' eyes only,* and quickly scanned the strategy assessment provided by the Pentagon through the secretary of defense. The report cited details beginning with diplomacy and ending with the physical extraction of the team carried out by US Special Forces. Winters ignored the diplomacy component, extraction

As Frank Ellison left the restaurant, he slipped his shaded sunglasses on so that he could watch the waiter without being obvious. He didn't know whether he and his partner were being followed, but he felt followed, and for a veteran of the FBI, that's all that mattered. His intuition had led him down some strange and dangerous paths, but he'd always trusted his gut, and, he was still alive. A state of being he grew less impressed with each time he thought about it.

The waiter scurried around to tables quickly filling with happy tourists, wearing happy tourist cloths, preparing for a happy and exciting day of sightseeing. Ellison thought about getting everyone's attention and telling them what life was really like; he wanted to explode their happy-mood balloon; he wanted them to feel like he did. The waiter wasn't paying any attention to him, which in a way was a relief and in another disappointing. If he could confirm someone was out to get him, he'd at least feel there was a purpose, but as it was, emptiness buoyed by his decaying self-esteem was all there was. Ellison returned to his hotel room to leave his blazer; heat was already building after a cool night, and he didn't need the extra burden. Syrian law prohibited anyone with diplomatic immunity from carrying a weapon. He had nothing to conceal, so having no purpose, the jacket was just in the way. Ellison stared at the bed, fatigue was another curse he could do without, but it remained nearby ready to envelop him at the slightest cue. He sat down in an overstuffed chair, leaned his head back, and fell asleep. A dream drew him deeper into his subconscious, at first pleasantly. Ocean waves crashing softly on a remote beach, palm leaves fluttering, but as comforting as the scene was, it turned bleak quickly. Images, first of someone partially concealed behind a coconut tree and then a horrifying vision of himself buried on the beach up to his neck in sand. He couldn't move and the pressure from the weight of the sand stifled his call for help. In reality Frank Ellison thrashed violently from side to side until he and the chair fell over. The agent struck his forehead on the metal bed leg, tearing a two-inch gash above his eye. The cut wasn't serious; nevertheless, the wound bled profusely. He grabbed a hand towel and held it against the cut. He got to his feet just as hotel officials and police, weapons drawn, rushed in.

It took the better part of an hour to convince the police he had only been the victim of a very bad dream. According to the hotel manager, guests on that floor could hear him yelling for help. Maid service cleaned the blood drops from the light-colored carpet, and as the last person left his room, his cell phone rang.

"Frank, this is Jerry Webster."

Ellison found a spot on the towel that wasn't bloody and held it hard to his head. "Yeah, Mr. Director … what's goin' on?"

"Frank, this is Jerry; don't throw that director stuff at me, and what's with you? You sound like you've been drinking."

"Just coffee … hang on, Jerry."

Webster heard the clatter of the phone being laid on a solid surface. He heard the agent cough hard, again and again. Ellison inhaled deeply; Webster could hear him wheeze, followed by a deep sigh. Finally Ellison picked up the phone. "Okay, I'm here."

"Man. What happened?"

"Long story, chief; really, I'm fine. You didn't call just to chat about the weather, did you?" Ellison hurried the conversation along, there wasn't a rational conclusion his boss could make out of his story other than the fact he was a knucklehead, so there was no point in trying to explain.

"Okay, I'll take your word, you can tell me some other time. Right now, Frank, I need you to listen very closely to what I'm saying. I don't want you to miss a point; I don't want you to misunderstand a word. Are you alone?"

"As usual."

"First, my friend, this is voluntary."

"Uh huh." The doubt and sarcasm in Ellison's voice was obvious.

Webster explained the side of the mission Ellison hadn't been privy to. "CI Chief Winters sent a team into Iran during the turmoil between Arabs and Israelis thinking the growing posturing and saber rattling would be a distraction."

"And it didn't work?"

"Yes and no."

"Okay, boss, I see I'm not going to get a straight answer, so just tell me the problem."

"We have reliable information that one team member has been murdered and the other two have been identified and are now cut off from original escape plans. We have no contact with them, only the one asset Winters believes to be employed at the Natanz nuclear facility."

"How trustworthy is this asset?"

"His parents, a brother, and sister live in the US; Winters says he's solid."

"Yeah, I'll bet … the solid ones I distrust the most. Okay, boss, what's this got to do with me?"

"I'm asking if you'd be willing to help."

"Help. What in the hell do you mean, help? Sounds like a job for the marines, not an old, tired wind bag like me."

"We've thought of that and ruled it out, takes too long. And there's no guarantee it'd work."

"And you think sending me in would work? What have you been smoking, Mr. Webster?"

Webster regretted what he was about to say, he knew a friendship, even one as solid as his and Ellison's, could only take so much exploitation, but at that very moment in time their relationship was irrelevant.

Ellison checked the towel, the bleeding had stopped. He opened the hotel room desk drawer and found some stationery and a cheap pen with camel logo on the plastic cap. "Well, director?"

"You're right, Frank; you're out of shape, overweight, underpaid, and counting the days until retirement. You are too damned old for any kind of mission requiring physical, or for that matter mental skill, but in this one case you will be motivated."

"Explain."

"One of the operatives is Crystal Stanton." Webster didn't know what to expect from Ellison after this revelation; he knew, however, he was fortunate the Atlantic Ocean separated them. If the phone conversation had taken place anywhere within driving distance, Webster was confident he'd have a very disturbed visitor on his doorstep.

"I'm sorry, Director, I may have misunderstood, please repeat."

Webster cringed under the heavy tone in Ellison's voice. "Frank, you heard me, and we don't have time to discuss why or how right now. I've got to know if you're willing to put your life on the line, and I've got to know now. After this is over, if you're still alive, you have my permission to kick my butt up Pennsylvania Avenue and torture my dog in front of my children, but right now I have to have a yes or no.

A flash of anger swirled through Ellison like an Oklahoma twister in May. He realized demanding answers at this point would only delay an already critical situation. As he adjusted the fierce rage to a controllable level, Ellison felt the emptiness he'd been experiencing evaporate, he now had a purpose. Crys Stanton was the only woman he'd ever truly loved; there'd been others, but none like Crys. He'd thought about her every day since the official breakup years earlier, and that one single event, of all the bad ones in his life, seemed to be the beginning of what he called his dark years. During Dr. Bethel's vetting process, he'd learned Crys was dating a rancher, but at this stage of his life that didn't matter, she was in trouble. To give his life for someone as special as Crys was far better than sitting in his bass boat the rest of his life.

"Jerry, of course I'll do anything for Crys. Who, by the way, brought her in?"

"A computer."

"Computer?"

"The CIA pulled her agency profile because she matched criteria outlined in the search process."

"Yeah, yeah … I know all that bullshit, but a real person had to ask her, who in the hell was that."

"Me." Webster didn't elaborate; he knew Ellison wouldn't buy the fact he'd tried to talk Crys out of saying yes, and at this stage of the mission, he wasn't so sure he'd buy it either.

"You sonofabitch—"

"I know, Frank, you'd stuff me in a meat grinder and make my family watch. That's for later, right now, put simply, you're all we got."

"But you know I have no skills relevant for extracting operatives out of a hostile country."

"I know that, but in your case, Frank, I think motivation will trump skill."

"I hope … now, what's the plan?"

"There is none."

"No, Jerry, that's not possible. There's always a plan—"

"It's up to you," Webster knew valuable time was being wasted on a matter that under the best of conditions couldn't be explained to Ellison's satisfaction; he had to cut him off. "I can tell you where she is right now, and I can tell you who the asset is, but beyond that, no, there is no plan."

CHAPTER 35

After a short meeting with the vice president, Secretary of State James Parker boarded his plane for Athens, the neutral site agreed upon for the classified diplomatic gathering before flying on to Israel for his speech at the Knesset. The assembly, arranged in secret and to be held in a secure location, was set for six p.m. local time. Parker was chosen as moderator via phone conferencing with the selected parties involved. In addition to the secretary of state, two men representing the Muslim community, and two representing the Jewish antiquities community were present. Each man was acquainted thoroughly with the historical perspective and prophetic nuances concerning the ark of the covenant in both the Qur'an and Old Testament. The first and so far the only rule set forth for the meeting was that discussion would focus entirely on solving the immediate problem and not on opening dialogue concerning the book of Revelation in the New Testament.

At midnight the group proposed their final plan, a ten-

page document stating firmly that the tablets allegedly stolen from the Iraq Museum International in Baghdad were not authentic. Several press releases would be made public in hopes of reigning in some of the more dangerous rhetoric, and the experts on both sides of the issue would formally discount original claims leaked to the media about the ark's location. Parker knew their efforts were a long shot; the opposing factions were already using the ark as an indication of the imminent fulfillment of prophecy.

Winters clicked through every late-night news channel devouring international news as it related to disharmony in the Middle East. Time was passing far too quickly, nearly an hour now since she'd talked with Webster, and with every passing minute, the chances of saving the two operatives grew slimmer. The idea of catching the next commercial flight to Tehran becoming, perhaps, her only choice. Her job was no longer a worry, facing a senate inquest and the loss of her reputation wasn't a consideration; Winters was ready to do something—right or wrong.

The phone in her damp, shaking hand rang. "Winters," she answered.

"Margaret, it's me. Here's what I've got," Webster said.

"I'm listening."

"As part of the plan to further the ark charade I sent two of my agents to Damascus to assist local police with the investigation of Ramirez's death in an effort to delay the forensic results."

"And?"

"The senior agent is a former fiancée of Crys Stanton; they'd planned to marry several years ago when Stanton was given what turned out to be a protracted undercover assignment."

"The agent you had on the Ramirez case from the start?"

"Yes, the same agent."

"So how can he help us?"

"He's motivated."

"As in give his life for a former fiancée?"

"Yeah … there's much more to it, and if you'd like me to spend the next hour explaining it—"

"No, no, of course not," she interrupted. "What's the plan?"

"Like I told him, we're adlibbing all the way. We can get him a car from the embassy, phony press credentials. Can you use your people to get him through the boarder checkpoints?"

"There is no problem getting him out of Syria and through Iraq; the hard part is Iran. He'll be a sitting duck."

"That may work to his advantage."

"I'm not following you?"

"What idiot would drive into Iran in broad daylight headed for Tehran hoping to interview the president but a reporter looking for career-making story? Certainly not CIA or FBI."

"Can he play the part?"

"Like I said, Margaret, he'll do whatever it takes. I know him; it'll be an award-winning performance."

"Okay, I'll send you coded logistical information via an attachment to an e-mail. Call me the instant you receive it. I'll make arrangements for clear sailing through the boarder into Iran. Send me a current photo, some ID, name, height, weight, so I can get it to my station chief," Winters said, her heart pounding at the prospect of a plan. No matter how thin the chances, it was still something she could put her energy into.

"I'm doing that as we speak; you should have it now."

"It's coming through."

"I'll make arrangements for him to get whatever there is in the way of a standard rent car in Syria. Of course we'll have him leave his weapon and FBI credentials at the embassy," Webster said.

"Have you received the e-mail and attachment?"

"Yeah, Margaret, I'm opening it now, I'll print and then delete it."

"You should have the coordinates where our operatives are, there should also be a sat photo of the nuclear plant. All the buildings are numbered; one of the attachments should be an index corresponding to those buildings. I'm also sending an old photo of our Iranian asset and his brief bio."

"Got it."

"Good, make sure your man destroys all of this before he leaves Damascus."

"I will. What are you going to do, Margaret?"

Webster's question reminded the CI chief of her insecurity and how tenuous circumstances were. "I don't know, maybe visit Baghdad; I hear it's beautiful this time of year," her subdued laugh full of absurdity. "Might even get on my knees and pray. In the meantime let's keep each other informed."

CHAPTER 36
0125, SEPTEMBER 16

Jerry Webster closed his cell phone feeling regret deeper than any he could remember. Sending another close friend into unimaginable danger was more than he'd ever bargained for as acting director of the FBI. Knowing the likely outcome of such a spontaneous and unrehearsed mission only added to his growing guilt.

It was nearly noon Damascus time when Erik Booker arrived at the hotel for lunch with his partner. Ellison was halfway through his meal when Booker sat down.

"What happened to you?" Booker said, staring at the conglomeration of gauze and adhesive tap over Ellison's eye.

"I fell."

"Looks like somebody clobbered you with a dull machete."

Ellison repeated his answer. "I fell and hit my head on the metal leg of the bed. Okay?"

"Okay, if you say so."

"Now, listen up, Booker, I don't have time to say this twice."

The young agent recognized the conversation had taken a serious turn. "Okay, Frank, what's going on?"

"Change in plans, your going back to the states today."

"That's sweet, but why, I don't understand. What are you going to do?"

"Our part of the mission has been aborted … don't ask, because I don't know. I'm taking some time off. I have friends here in the Middle East I haven't seen in years, I plan on spending some time with them."

"Yeah, okay, I can buy the mission has been aborted, but I can tell you're not visiting friends in the Middle East."

"Bullshit, what makes you think you know what I'm going to do?"

"You're acting strange, nervous. If I didn't know better, I'd say you were scared about something."

"Booker, you don't know your ass from a hole in the ground. Now, get your bags packed, check out at the embassy, take what forensic material we've collected, and catch the first flight out. Go see your family." Ellison dropped the tip on the table and left without saying anything more. Two hours later, Ellison drove out of Damascus on a twenty-hour journey into a world he knew nothing about, a country he didn't like, a culture that was so very different, and a belief system that put him at odds with everything their government did. He couldn't speak the language, but he did have a letter written in Farsi and a duplicate written in Arabic, along with his new passport, that explained he was a reporter for a major news outlet. His assignment was to gather information about Iran and its president to be published as a series appearing in the Sunday newspapers in many metropolitan US cities. Government analysts stationed at the US embassy in Damascus were aware of the Iranian president's propensity toward ego-mania. Having the world population focused on him regardless of story slant fed his narcissism, and in exchange, the president usually granted safe passage to whoever might immortalize him in print. The letter, signed by the Iranian ambassador to the United Nations, Ellison hoped, would keep him alive. The forgery, according to Ellison's embassy contacts, was nearly perfect.

Ellison—whose new passport identified him as Eli Franks— made Baghdad at midnight. Fortunately Iraqi boarder police assigned him to a small US Army supply convoy, and although they never topped sixty miles per hour, the convoy didn't stop until it reached the green zone. The agent refueled the ten-year-old Mercedes Benz, parked it directly in front of the officers' quarters, and left instructions with the OIC he must be awakened at 0400. Military personnel had been informed a civilian reporter would pass through sometime that night, and he was to be accorded every courtesy and convenience without question. At 0500 Franks joined another supply convoy headed east toward the boarder with Iran. The G-man turned deep cover operative didn't know what to expect at the first Iranian checkpoint, all he could do was play out the role of a reporter and let nature take its course. An hour and a half later, the remaining US Army supply vehicles reached their destinations and Franks was on his own. According to the map, he was only minutes away from the boarder and his first test.

As Franks approached the first checkpoint, he forced a smile and inhaled deeply hoping the extra oxygen would somehow lessen his apprehension. A young man in a tattered khaki uniform stepped from the small shelter pointing an automatic weapon directly at him shouting something in a tongue Franks didn't recognize. He stopped the car and held his hands up so the guard could see he was unarmed, and at the same time motioned at an envelop laying conspicuously on the dash. The guard nodded, and Franks, hoping the gesture meant the same in Iran, picked the envelope up and handed it out the window. Franks could see the guard making a phone call from inside the shelter; he looked at his watch, the second hand moving slowly. Ten minutes passed, then twenty, Franks couldn't tell whether the perspiration soaking his shirt was weather related, nervousness, or the adrenaline rush that hadn't subsided since Web-

ster said the name Crys Stanton. Eventually the guard returned with the letters and motioned for him to proceed. There was no traffic on the two-lane highway, and, except for an occasional pothole, Franks tried to make up time. For the next hour he was able to maintain a high rate of speed, and by noon he was nearing Kangavar. The trek east to Natanz would be slower because of the mountainous terrain. His official destination, according to the letters he carried, was the capital, Tehran. If stopped and questioned why he was on this route, Franks planned to plead ignorance and confess he was lost. To even utter the word Natanz would be a mistake.

CHAPTER 37

NATANZ, IRAN
SEPTEMBER 17

At about the time Eli Franks crossed from Iraq into Iran, Yasmeen Binte Mahir was awakened by her ever-present adversary. Talavi unlocked her door and stepped back allowing Yasmeen room to exit, but only by inches. Without speaking, she headed to the lavatory anxious to discuss a plan of escape with Zayna and find refuge from the sickening smell that clung heavily to Talavi. She noticed, sliding by his huge chest that he was in the same uniform as he was the day before, food stains from yesterday's meal still clearly visible. Yasmeen carefully pulled her hijab down further on her forehead to cover the blond roots, and as she walked through the door into the lavatory, Talavi followed—his leering eyes watching every move she made. Trying to appear calm and uninhibited by his intrusion she washed her face and then checked the dryer for underwear she'd left the day before. He followed, staying not more than a few feet away. Talavi's stench was no longer noticeable; Yasmeen's senses shifted from mere repulsion to an unpleasant odor to fright in a matter of seconds. She thought about the knife but knew she'd be no match in face-to-face combat with him. The knife would only be useful in a surprise attack, and it would have to be lethal, a stab or two to his massive chest would only inflame his rage. The only sure attack would be to cut his throat, and to do that she'd have to approach him from the rear, but that would resolve the problem only temporarily. Yasmeen knew whoever was monitoring the security cameras would dispatch help. The only weapon left—and one she'd used successfully all her life—was talk. Crys Stanton had talked herself out of trouble all her life, a skill she refined as an FBI special agent, and maybe it would work to her advantage today. While folding a few clothes, waiting for Zayna to arrive, Yasmeen, in the most respectful voice she could muster under the circumstances, said, "Mr. Talavi, do you have family near by?" She knew to try and humanize their relationship was her only alternative.

There was a moment of hesitation, Yasmeen kept folding clothes, not making eye contact with her escort.

"Yes, a wife and son."

"Oh … and how old is your son?"

"Nearly twenty-five."

"Does he still live with you?"

"No."

Yasmeen sensed sadness in his reply; she could see peripherally that Talavi's body language was different, less defensive. "What does your son do?"

Another hesitation, Yasmeen could hear him sigh then take a deep breath.

"His mother and I are very proud of our son; he is in Iraq fighting for Allah against the Americans."

"I'm sure you are proud, how wonderful that he's taken up the sword against the infidels."

"Yes, he is a hero to our family name and to the cause."

Yasmeen could tell two things: Talavi's physical presence was less threatening, and he didn't want to talk further about his son. She needed to change the subject, and she needed to keep Talavi talking. "I thought Dr. Sayyid would be with us by now?"

"Dr. Sayyid joined her team earlier this morning. She may be out several days."

Yasmeen tried not to show her alarm; first Faxhir goes missing, then Zayna. She was next, and without her partner, there was no one to talk over options. That is if any options were left. For the first time since the mission began, Yasmeen knew she was alone; she'd felt isolated in her room away from the other team members, but not alone. She now, assuming the worst for Zayna, was the only one that could accomplish the mission, and at the same time, save her own life, a thought no one in their right mind would assume possible. The dismal circumstance ignited a burn in her stomach, causing Yasmeen to retch violently. Talavi stepped back; he said nothing and made no effort to help. Yasmeen splashed cold water on her face while trying to apologize, "I'm sorry ... something I ate."

Dr. Ansari met Yasmeen at the bottom of the stairway, the worried look on his face she read as genuine was comforting. He took her hand as she stepped onto the lab floor. "How are you?"

"Fine, just my aging body refusing to cooperate."

"I'm so sorry we didn't provide sufficient nourishment for you yesterday." Ansari pulled his lap drawer out to reveal various food items, all in violation of plant rules. "If you feel weak, something here might help." He closed the drawer as cautiously as he opened it, hoping not to attract attention from the guards or any nosy scientists looking for a promotion. "I am worried that Sherafat has chosen Talavi to be your escort, as I told you ... he has a reputation."

"You mentioned he is called the eliminator, is that because people who have been in his care tend to disappear?"

"Yes ... that has happened a few times."

"Who is he?"

"He was the only gold medal winner in the 1998 Olympics for Iran. Talavi was the Greco-Roman-style wrestling world champion, and from what I gather, he was held in the highest esteem, almost godlike."

"But how did he end up here?"

"During the Olympics Talavi and his entire family planned to defect to America. His Australian coach had arranged it. At least that's what I've been told.

"What happened?"

"Talavi was with the team in Seoul, and his parents were in route. I understand his son became ill, and his wife had to stay in Tehran to look after him."

"So even though his parents ended up in America, Talavi had to return to Iran," she said.

"Yes. The government tried him, and he was sent to prison. They stripped him of his medal and all his championship honors."

Just then three scientists approached Dr. Ansari, and Yasmeen stepped away to let them talk. Their conversation was short, and the substance of what she could hear was about a problem concerning manufacturing. Ansari motioned for her to join them, and explained that there was an issue at the manufacturing entity of the plant. "The problem has to do with blending elements, and as a physicist you may have some advice for us. Would you like to go?"

There was no way she could object. "Yes, of course, I'd be happy to join you." Her heart pounded as she agreed to a consultation with experts that would most assuredly expose her.

The five left the lab on level ten followed by Talavi, and when they reached the elevator shaft, the four men in white coats got into one elevator leaving Yasmeen to ride alone with Talavi in the next. Her claustrophobia and fear worked in tandem, prompting another major panic attack; she tried to talk, hoping a dialogue with Talavi would keep her mind occupied with survival and not on her shrinking consciousness. But it was no use; her knees buckled, and the last thing she remembered before crashing to the floor was the hope she was dying.

She felt the cool moist washcloth as it moved over her face and neck, a refreshing breeze from an overhead fan stirred the air. Yasmeen opened her eyes to see the men tending to her, Talavi was in the background clutching the Kalashnikov and watching. Someone was talking to her.

"You must have had another episode with your hypoglycemia," Ansari was saying.

"Oh my...I'm so sorry, please forgive me for my weakness."

"Nonsense, we all have weaknesses. How are you feeling?"

"Better."

"Would you like to go back to your room and rest?" Ansari asked.

"No, I'll be all right in a minute." The thought of getting back into the elevator with Talavi was more frightening than being discovered an operative of the US government. She sat up. "I'm okay...help me to my feet." As Yasmeen stood, she paused allowing the remaining dizziness to subside; Ansari and another scientist held her arms for support. She felt someone shove something into her hand, and when she realized what it was, a wave of apprehension hit her like a tsunami. During the mayhem Yasmeen's hijab came off. No one said anything, but she could feel the stares. She quickly replaced the covering acting as normal as was possible under the circumstances and forcing a smile thanked the four men for their assistance.

"I'm all right."

"Are you sure?" Ansari asked.

Yasmeen nodded. "Yes...please, let's proceed."

Working under the assumption her identity was irreparably damaged Yasmeen focused all her attention on escape, and within the confines of the nuclear facility, surrounded by desert and arid mountains, that prospect seemed impossible. As the group entered a sprawling one-story building, Zayna identified as a manufacturing facility of some kind, Yasmeen thought of Xerxes Sattar. She suspected it was Sattar who planted the knife. He was an educated man that spoke perfect English and behaved in a manner obviously influenced by European or American culture. It seemed to her Sattar might be her only hope.

"This, Dr. Mahir, is the manufacturing arm of the plant." Dr. Ansari swept his hand from left to right pointing to the vast expanse of computer-driven machinery.

"I'm confused; I thought Natanz was strictly a nuclear power plant and enrichment facility?"

"It was, correction … it is, but we've had problems recently with the enrichment process. Now we have a centrifuge array sufficient to enrich uranium to weapons grade."

"And you're manufacturing weapons here?" Yasmeen asked insipidly.

"No, what you see here is the manufacturing of engine parts for heavy equipment."

The three other scientists hurried over to an isolation lab. They clothed themselves in bulky protective gear and disappeared through a door marked *decontamination*.

Talavi stood ten feet away, just out of hearing range, scrutinizing every move Yasmeen and Ansari made.

"Why are you making engine parts?"

"As you know, our president is obsessed with the annihilation of Israel. Our military has the rocket power and now we have the expertise to build a nuclear warhead. He suspects, and rightly so, that Israel will bomb the weapons plant soon. What Israel, and the rest of the world, doesn't know is that he has another plan."

"Involving engine parts?" Yasmeen was surprised by Ansari's candor, particularly after the earlier incident with the hijab. Maybe he didn't notice the blonde roots, or maybe it was just that he knew she'd be dead soon. In either case she was anxious to find out more.

"They are not just engine parts; they are highly enriched uranium engine parts."

"I am not following you, Dr. Ansari."

"The parts are sold and shipped to China, they in turn ship them to assembly plants around the world, Israel and the US included."

"But the parts would never get through the radiation monitors. The US, I understand, employs a layered defense system of portal monitors."

"And, Dr. Mahir, they are vulnerable."

"How?"

"Simple, a set of parts is shipped in a box covered by two-millimeter-thick lead, and those boxes are centered in the cargo container. As they pass through a monitor, the ray weakens at two meters."

"So the ray is too weak to detect enriched uranium beyond two meters?"

"Precisely, I'm surprised a physicist of your distinction wouldn't know that."

"Pakistan devotes its human resources to weaponry. Frankly speaking, I don't think we've ever thought this creatively." Yasmeen pressed on with more questions, knowing her efforts were most likely in vain, but in the event of a miracle, she wanted every detail possible. "I'm guessing that the parts are trucked to their various assembly plants, but what happens then?"

"Active loyalist cells in those countries, in some cases assembly plant employees, trade out parts containing uranium for standard parts they machine themselves."

"I would say that this process is taking time?"

"Calculations tell us the cells will have enough to build a one kiloton device within a year."

Yasmeen searched her memory for information involving the power of such a device. "One kiloton, placed in the right location could kill thousands, not to mention the financial crises that would follow," she said while committing the layout to memory, the constant whirring of manufacturing dulling her capacity to hear.

"Dr. Ansari, could we step outside?" He nodded, and Talavi followed them out to the shade of one of the few trees on the plant grounds.

"Is this better?" Ansari asked.

"Yes, thank you. The noise made it difficult to understand what you were saying."

"What I was saying isn't important, Dr. Mahir, I need your expertise to verify my calculations regarding adjustments in the lead shipping boxes from two to three millimeters."

"I thought two was enough. Why risk the additional weight?"

"The new generation of spectroscopic machines will employ both gamma-ray and neutron detectors, we just want to be prepared."

Yasmeen realized additional questions would lead her further down the road to complete exposure. She had exhausted her ability to redirect conversation based on clues and language used by Ansari. His next query might be to review an equation, and that would be the end of what secrecy remained for her to hide behind. The only alternative she could think of was to force a private conversation with Xerxes Sattar and hope he was the one who planted the knife; it was a long shot, but one she had to take. "Dr. Ansari, there are, I hope, some issues I can help you with, but in the meantime…" She dabbed at perspiration that wasn't there with a handkerchief "…I'm sorry for causing you delays; I must eat something. I'm feeling lightheaded again. My condition seems to be worsening."

"We will get you to the nurse." Ansari looked at Talavi. "Get us a vehicle," he shouted, praying his command didn't insult the escort. In a short time Talavi was back with something akin to a golf cart, and the three rushed back to the main building.

So far the plan was working; she successfully avoided further technical dialogue with Ansari and maneuvered herself closer to Sattar's office.

"You are in good hands now, I hope you are feeling better soon, we can resume our talks then." Ansari left the infirmary, and Talavi remained just outside the door. The nurse provided nourishment for Yasmeen and drew a blood sample for analysis.

"I want you to rest, Dr. Mahir. Later the doctor will be by, and he'll look at the test results and tell us what we need to do."

Although the nurse did not smile, she seemed truly concerned about Yasmeen's welfare. She patted her patient's hand. "Now, try to get some rest. I'll be back to check on you later."

"Nurse," Yasmeen said as the woman was leaving the room.

"Yes, Dr. Mahir."

"I feel so badly about my condition interfering with my mission here. I must apologize to Dr. Sherafat. Is there a way for you to arrange a meeting?"

"Dr. Sherafat is not a friendly person. I say that now in case you hadn't noticed." A wisp of a smile and the sidelong glance told Yasmeen that Sherafat must have a poor reputation among staff. "Yes, I know, but I must see him regardless."

"I'll see what I can do. No promises though … understand?"

"Of course." If the nurse could arrange a meeting that would put her within a few feet of Sattar's door, how to get through it without Talavi was an aspect yet unclear.

CHAPTER 38

"Eli Franks, Eli Franks," Ellison repeated aloud over and over. Getting used to his cover name was more complicated than he expected. He looked quickly at his watch. *Taking your eyes off the mountainous road even for a second could be a deadly miscalculation,* he thought, especially at the speed he was traveling. It was nearly noon, and he wasn't far from the city of Arak. According to Webster's information he'd be in Natanz around four p.m. The adrenaline rush Ellison felt after his conversation with Webster was beginning to subside. Fatigue and hunger were factors he tried not to think about, but they were gaining in importance to the point of physical coercion. Ellison pulled next to what appeared to be a roadside cafe and reluctantly entered; knowing his ignorance of the language and the menu would stand out like a clown at a Pavarotti concert, but he could still point. After eating something consisting mainly of vegetables, he returned to the Mercedes, turned off his cell phone to conserve the battery, and leaned back, hoping a power nap would sustain him until he reached the nuclear plant.

The first road sign he saw showed that Natanz was another forty kilometers, Ellison made an attempt at conversion, but gave up knowing his focus wasn't on the metric system. The food and short nap had restored his energy and trying to figure out how far away he was from his one time fiancée wasn't worth wasting one calorie on. Ellison needed to think how to get Stanton and the other operative out of Iran and solutions to that problem weren't readily lining up for consideration. Ignorance and the phony letters of introduction were his only resources, he'd have to let the chips fall were they may.

Eli Franks handed the letters to the first security checkpoint guard and held his breath. The man, obviously a simple fellow, read the letter and said something in Farsi. Franks shook his head. "I don't speak your language."

The guard stared at Franks then back at the letter. Allowing the foreigner to enter was far above the guard's authority to do. He made a phone call, and within a few minutes a white Toyota pickup arrived with four-armed security personnel who surrounded the Mercedes. The senior man opened Franks' door and motioned for him to get out of the car, and while the others searched the vehicle, he read and reread the letters. After thirty minutes spent trashing the Mercedes, the security team ordered him to follow. Xerxes Sattar met the reporter in the lobby. "Mr. Franks, welcome to the Natanz Nuclear Facility." The men shook hands. "This way to my office; we can talk there."

Franks was relieved someone spoke English. "You have quite a facility here."

"Yes, we are very proud of its capabilities. May I offer you some refreshment?"

"Just water, thanks," Franks said as he followed Sattar. His eyes were quickly drawn to the photos covering one wall. Most were taken of Sattar and dignitaries from England and the US in familiar locations. "I see you've been to America … isn't that Congress-man James from Texas you're shaking hands with?"

"Yes, I received my master's degree in public relations at the University of Texas. We actually became close friends."

"Do you remain in contact?"

"A few times a year I'll receive an e-mail, but nothing more. Now, tell me, Mr. Franks, what we can do for you."

"As you can tell from the letters, I'm a reporter doing a series of articles on your president that will appear in newspapers around the US. Our ambassador met with your ambassador, and they worked out the details—"

"Yes, Mr. Franks, I can read, but why are you here at this facil-ity?" The friendly, public relations smile had disappeared.

"The article will include information about Iran's nuclear potential, both from a domestic-use perspective as well as military." Franks knew Sattar was smart enough to smell deceit, there was no use pretending.

"Mr. Franks, when will you people learn that this plant is exclu-sively for the purpose of generating power? We've been above board on this with the IAEA."

"Then you won't mind me taking a look around before I meet with your president?"

"I'm afraid that is impossible; you have no authorization to do that."

Franks pointed at the letters. "What about that?"

Sattar reread the letter from the ambassador adding a toothy smirk as he handed the letters back to Franks, "This may authorize you to visit with our president, but that's all. If the president wishes to let you see the plant, he will let us know. For now, Mr. Franks, you'll have to be satisfied with seeing my office and talking with me." Sattar's sarcasm was obvious; he stood, an indication that the conversation was over.

Franks ignored the hint and remained seated. "Mr. Sattar, maybe we should start the conversation over."

"No. It is over, I have nothing left to say or show you, so if you'll be so kind," he said, gesturing toward the door.

"Since the article will be written, regardless of your cooperation, I suggest a little more teamwork—"

"Mr. Franks, as you Americans say, you are on thin ice. This is typical US imperialism, thinking you can bully people. Take a look around, Mr. Franks." Sattar was seething; his dark eyes wide with anger, even the sarcasm had disappeared. "All I have to do is say the word, and you'll find yourself in more trouble than you've bargained for."

As Franks stood, he opened a small notebook and took a pen from his breast pocket. "I want to make sure I get the correct spelling of your name for the article, Mr. Sattar. Is that with one or two *t*'s?" His intent on turning up the heat worked, Sattar was furious. He picked up the phone and announced some kind of crises code over the intercom, and within seconds security filled the hallway outside Sattar's office and Franks found himself face down on the concrete floor, his arms wrenched back, and someone's knees planted strategically in vulnerable spots over his body. Mechanical restraints were placed around his waist and his arms locked tightly in back. Two men raised him from the floor, and he was ushered out of Sattar's office at the same time Talavi was escorting Yasmeen next door to meet with Sherafat.

Talavi held her back as the small security force dragged Franks down the hall toward them. As the two former lovers passed, their eyes fixed on each other, and in the turmoil of the moment he managed a wink without anyone noticing. He shot a disgusted look at Talavi as he was being dragged by him in the narrow hall. "You're an ugly bastard," Franks uttered. Talavi reached out and grabbed his insulter and, with one blow, sent teeth bouncing across the floor and blood flowing from the mouth of a now unconscious man.

"Take him to level three and put him in room seven. I will take care of him later." The sound of Talavi's angry bellowing echoed off the concrete walls.

Sherafat heard the disturbance and stepped into the hall. "What is going on?" he shouted, aggravated by the commotion.

"A very rude American reporter, sir," Sattar said, watching the incapacitated man being carried away.

Yasmeen struggled to make sense of what was happening. Conflict raged within her, instinct spurring her to act, while reason cautioned against such a flagrant mistake. Obviously a rescue attempt was unfolding and to react even in the slightest way might thwart what efforts were in play. She watched as Sherafat and Sattar whispered. Finally Sherafat turned to Yasmeen gesturing toward his office.

"I understand you wish to speak with me?" he said closing the door.

"Yes, please, I want to apologize."

"And what do you want to apologize for, Dr. Mahir?"

"I have not been helpful to Dr. Ansari; my disease has overtaken me at the most inopportune time."

"What disease is that, Dr. Mahir?"

Yasmeen felt a shudder that left her cold. Sherafat was intentionally belittling her, toying with her, a cat and mouse game was in progress. "Hypoglycemia, Dr. Sherafat," she said as convincingly as possible.

The chief of science and technology didn't respond, remaining aloof, uninterested in her reason. Sherafat lit a cigarette and studied a document he pulled from his lap drawer. Several minutes dragged by as the scowl deepened on his leathery face. "Dr. Mahir, I am a very busy man, and I don't have time to play silly games with imposters." Sherafat's voice was calm but intense. His stare now cold and fuming. "According to this," he held a sheet of paper up shaking it menacingly in her direction. "There is no one by the name of Dr. Mahir or Dr. Sayyid in Pakistan. You and your friends are spies. We will find out who sent you, then you will serve our country as buzzard food." Sherafat's words came fast, spittle flying and spotting her uncovered hands and face. Yasmeen reached for the knife, but something told her it wasn't time. How would she explain a bloody mess to Talavi, who was standing just outside the closed door?

"Talavi," Sherafat screamed. "Lock this imposter up."

Talavi grabbed Yasmeen by the neck, lifting her off her chair, shoving her toward the door. As Talavi escorted her past Sattar's open door, she looked in hoping to make eye contact, but it was no use, Talavi shoved her hard, face first into a wall, and she crumpled to the floor. Excruciating pain radiating from her bloodied and broken nose, Yasmeen braced for another blow as consciousness faded.

CHAPTER 39

FBI Agent Erik Booker arrived at Dulles International where he was met by an agent-in-training ordered to return him to headquarters for a short meeting with the director.

"Relax, Booker, I just wanted to visit about Damascus," Webster said, hoping to put the young agent at ease.

"Yes, sir."

"I'm assuming Ellison explained the mission was being aborted?"

"He did, but no explanation as to why."

"Well, I'm not surprised; he's always been a man of few words." Webster opened a desk drawer and rifled around, trying to hide the desperate feeling that had welled up unexpectedly. It was difficult to maintain the illusion that everything was okay because it wasn't. In reality, Webster thought to himself, the situation was without a doubt the worst he'd ever faced. He took a long slow drink of very hot coffee, the burn, purposely intended to shut down the emotional calamity he was experiencing, worked. Webster cleared the sting from his throat. "I want you to arrange a reunion between Dr. Ramirez and Dr. Bethel. Although part of the mission has been altered, I want the meeting to remain confidential, use whatever stealth measures are necessary. Understand?"

"Yes, sir."

"One more thing, Agent Booker... I want you to smooth the way for Bethel, his wife, and mother-in-law to get back home. They've suffered enough; we need to let them get back to some semblance of normalcy."

"Yes, sir."

"Any questions?"

"Only one, sir."

"Well?"

"I've been away from my family for several days. May I go home first?"

"Take the rest of today and tonight; spend it with your family." Webster stood and extended his hand. "Thanks for your hard work and your dedication. Ellison tells me you've got what it takes to be a great agent."

"He did?" Booker looked surprised.

"Yes, he did."

The young agent tried to cover his smile. A compliment coming from someone he thought had only contempt for him was a shock, and to think the compliment was passed to Jerry Webster was nothing short of a miracle.

Webster's assistant knocked and stepped through the door. "Winters on line one." The woman stepped back and held the door open for Booker. She knew her boss would want to take the call, and he'd want to do so in private. Webster returned to his desk and as his assistant closed the door he reached for the phone.

"Margaret, what's going on... have you heard something?"

"A text message over my non-secure personal phone, about ten minutes ago, I'm assuming from our asset in Natanz."

"What, what was the message?"

"Eli Franks and Dr. Mahir locked up at nuclear plant."

"That's all?"

"I'm afraid so. If I return the text message and someone is tracking, they'll know right away who I am."

"You mean your people, NSA ... who?"

"No, of course not. I don't give a damn about the US, but if Iran has intercept capability, it could expose our asset. He took an enormous risk sending the message in the first place, and I don't want to risk his life, especially if there is a chance in hell he can help our people."

"Agreed. Do we just wait for another text message?" Webster asked.

"That's all we can do—just wait. And it's driving me nuts."

Webster could hear what sounded like the unfolding of paper. "Margaret, you still there?"

"Yeah ... did you read the morning paper?"

"Not yet."

"Front page, and it's all over the cable networks and Internet."

"What is?"

"Authorities claiming the tablets found by marines in Baghdad are bogus. Al Jazeera is saying the US planted the tablets and made up an elaborate hoax about the ark in a veiled attempt to initiate conflict between opposing religious factions."

"Isn't that what you wanted in the first place, Margaret?"

"No, Jerry, it isn't. I wanted a distraction so we could find out about Iran's nuke capabilities, but, Jerry, to be perfectly frank, I don't give a damn what the extremists do to each other, it's what they're trying to do to the rest of us I'm concerned about."

Webster knew the CIA chief was right, and it was easy to see it was a burden of monumental proportion. "I understand, Margaret, it's the rest of us that concerns me too."

"Jerry, I've got to go. If I get another text message, I'll call."

Zayna Binte Sayyid watched the sunlight crest the rugged Zagros Mountains. Hours earlier she faced a one-man firing squad. Her hands and feet bound tightly and blindfolded, she lay helplessly in a crevasse high on an abandoned mountain pass far from civilization. The hour had come, as she always knew it would, when death was imminent. Slow-motion images of her family slaughtered by Somali gunmen when she was young flooded her mind. The years of abuse at the hands of her abductors and finally her rescue that led eventually to adoption and life in America. Sayyid's penchant for danger, driven by anger she'd harbored for so many years, had come full circle; she was about to die at the hands of a murderer too. Her accomplishments would be recorded in a closed file in the archives of the Secret Service; words would be spoken on her behalf at the memorial eventually. No one knowing exactly what happened to her, the mission would remain secret, concealing from friends and family her true dedication to the people and country that saved her life. She closed her eyes and waited for the mechanical click preceding by milliseconds the bullet that would end her life. Instead she felt the cold blade of a knife slipping between her wrists, and in one sawing motion, cut the bindings. Her captor ordered her to stand. She got to her feet, rubbing the circulation back into her hands. She reached for the blindfold and was ordered to not touch it.

"Here," the man said. Sayyid felt a piece of paper forced into her hand. "A map, some instructions."

Zayna listened as the truck started and drove away. The shear terror she'd experienced since being bound, gagged, and hauled away from the nuclear plant along with the frigid night caused her to shake uncontrollably. She squatted down and leaned against the rock wall that just minutes before was destined to be her tombstone.

Sayyid welcomed the sun and the warmth it would bring. She opened the note still held firmly in her hand. A map showing a road that led to the nearby town of Shushtar. According to the crudely written note, Shushtar was a known staging area for radical Islamic revolutionist awaiting opportunities to smuggle rocket-propelled grenade launchers and bomb-making paraphernalia into Iraq. The note went on to say she should find the staging area and "tell the leader *you* wish to seek martyrdom."

"Of course," she said aloud. Sayyid realized her ticket into Iraq would be as a suicide bomber. She tore the note in pieces and buried it and then followed the memorized instructions to the road south into Shushtar.

Yasmeen awoke realizing she was back on level three in her room, the fullness of coagulated blood in her nose blocking airflow she desperately needed. She grabbed a washcloth and blew her nose; pain streaking out in all directions reminded her of the collision with the concrete wall at the hands of Talavi. In the dim light, Yasmeen could barely see her reflection in the stainless mirror, but it was enough to distinguish a crooked nose and the flesh discoloration beginning to appear around her eyes and cheeks. As consciousness returned, her recollection of what happened before the wall encounter began to clear, and the most vivid memory was that of Frank Ellison. She cringed at the image of him being pummeled by Talavi, but puzzled why a perfectly intelligent human being—she knew Ellison to be—would intentionally insult a monster like Talavi. She sat down and leaned back against the wall, holding the bridge of her sore nose hoping to stop the bleeding. Her ears stopped ringing, another effect of being knocked unconscious, and the quiet gave way to tapping. Yasmeen paid no attention at first, she'd grown used to various sounds emanating from within the huge underground structure she was presently a captive of, but the sound persisted, it had a rhythm unlike any of the other sounds and that drew her attention.

"Morse code," she whispered. It was Ellison trying to communicate from the next room. Almost everything Yasmeen learned at the academy about the Morse code she'd forgotten. There had never been an opportunity for her to use it, and to now recall the dot-dash system of communication was a struggle. She turned to where she thought the tapping was coming from and said, "Frank, can you hear me?" The tapping continued, evidently the sound of her voice couldn't pervade the thick wall.

Time and ideas were slipping away, pushed to one side by frustration and anger over the fact another person had been added to the list of mission casualties—this time a person Yasmeen had deep feelings for. Overcome by her thoughts, all she could do was sob. Pulling her knees as tightly as she could to her chest, Yasmeen buried her face in the blood-stained hem of her tunic.

Zayna walked into Shushtar just before noon. She had avoided the main road, advice she'd taken from the note, staying on pedestrian routes not routinely traveled by Iranian military. Near the center of town Zayna found an open-air market. Butchered goat hung from rafters, a woman fanning the flies from the carcasses eyed her suspiciously as she walked by. A stranger in the midst of routine customers drew attention, a fact Zayna hoped she could take advantage of. She examined an orange and returned it to the pile; grapes and pears were plentiful. The smell of fresh-baked bread filled the air around kiosks of clothing, jewelry, and pottery. A bearded man wearing a white turban tending a tobacco stand beckoned to her. "You are a visitor to Shushtar, yes?" His smile revealed years of smoking stains so embedded in what was left of tooth enamel they couldn't be eliminated with a wire brush.

"Yes."

"I've been watching you eye the fruit stands, maybe you are hungry, yes?"

"You are a perceptive man."

"And you have no money to purchase."

"You are not only perceptive but clairvoyant as well."

The man handed Zayna some coins caressing her fingers as he slowly dispensed each Rial. "It is my lunchtime. If you'll be so kind and purchase bread and fruit, I would share my feast with you."

Zayna's beauty beguiled the old man, and his misguided perception of her vulnerability was what she'd hoped for. Just to the man's right was an automatic weapon telling her there was more to the tobacco vender than stained teeth and lust. She returned quickly, he pointed to a rug for her to sit on, and as the man sliced the pear and divided the grapes, Zayna broke the bread, laying the largest pieces in front of the vender.

"Where are you from?" he said.

"Originally from Pakistan."

"And what is a beautiful woman, without money, doing roaming the country unescorted?"

"My husband, Nadim, was murdered by the Americans in Iraq ... and I'm ..." She dropped her head and hesitated, hoping her affect would be convincing.

"Yes ... you are what?"

"I'm on a mission of retaliation."

The man laughed. "And how will you, a woman, retaliate against such a formidable army?"

She looked away as if to realize the folly of her intent. "I don't know, I was told to come to Shushtar and someone would help me find a way. It is unlikely I'll be able to do anything, but I must try. Nadim was an honorable man, a hero in his hometown. I'm willing to do anything."

"Anything?"

"Yes, my life is useless without my husband, I'm ready to ..." Zayna intentionally allowed her voice to take on an air of melancholia. She had to sound sad, but even more importantly she must convey desperation.

"Ready to what?"

"To give my life."

"Hmmm ... that is quite a sacrifice. Your family must be very proud of you, yes?"

"My family is gone, died many years ago. I have no one now that Nadim is dead." She thought about her real family in Somalia, and unintentionally, tears welled, streaking her dust-covered cheeks.

"I'm sorry for your grief. You deserve to rejoin them if that is Allah's will."

The man's sentiment was insincere, but Zayna could see he was contemplating a move she hoped would put her closer to the insurgents. "Thank you, I pray for Allah's will, I hope to see my family soon." She stopped eating, true sadness curbed anyone's appetite, and she had to appear genuine. A customer came, distracting the vender for some time. Zayna studied the kiosk for more clues to the man's true occupation, but the weapon was the only irregularity.

The customer left and Zayna stood. "I must go. I've bothered you enough and thank you for the food—"

He interrupted. "Go where? I thought you had no family, and you have no money. What will you do?"

"I don't know."

"I may be able to help. If you will wait until my shop closes, we can talk without interruption."

CHAPTER 40

Yasmeen's thoughts bounced from praying death would come quick to escape. Sleep was not an option, her mind in a tumult searching for illusive answers. The only glimmer of hope was the unexpected appearance of Frank Ellison. Something was in play. *An all-out military rescue attempt*, she thought, *hardly*. Winters said the risk was too high. That left only one plausible explanation—Ellison was the only person on the face of the earth dumb enough to try a rescue. As Yasmeen thought through the possibilities, it became clear that he must have talked with Webster. She knew Ellison better than anyone else, and if he had an inkling she was in trouble, he'd make the stupid mistake of trying to rescue her, now they'd both be used as symbols of Western aggression and in the end—slaughtered.

Yasmeen's attention shifted to the thin stream of light drifting quietly from under her door. It remained fixed, meaning the elevator had stopped on level three. She got to her feet and tried in vain to see who it was, but all she could make out were shadows illuminated by the open elevator door, then the scraping sound of the heavy bolt being slid back on the room Ellison was in. Yasmeen strained to listen; at first she thought she could hear a muffled conversation, but even that faded to silence. In a few minutes darkness blotted the light that once passed through the small window; someone was standing at her door, an unmistakable stench of garlic and sweat wafting in the air. Yasmeen drew the knife from the scabbard and held it hidden in the folds of her tunic. The metallic sound of the latch being lifted and sliding sideways was terrifying. She moved close to the door, her one and only chance was to act offensively, Yasmeen had to take Talavi by surprise. The door opened, and she lurched forward, driving the knife toward his mid-section with as much force as she could mount, but with a reflex action any Kung Fu master would be proud of, he deflected the blade. The next thing she knew her right shoulder dislodged from the socket, sending debilitating pain from one extremity to another; she fell hard to the concrete floor. Before passing out from the throbbing injury, she heard the familiar tearing of duct tape. Shock and the resulting unconsciousness were a blessing, at least for a while.

Sometime later Yasmeen opened her eyes to the night sky, and along with her awakening, the pain returned. Her mouth was covered by tape and her arms and legs were wrapped painfully tight. She turned her head and saw Ellison's bloody, distorted face staring at her. His bloodshot eyes searching hers for a sign, she blinked and he returned the signal. The vehicle they were in hit a deep rut in the road tossing them into the air, they bounced in the truck bed for what seemed like an eternity, each impact sending wave after wave of pain through her. The ride to wherever they were going was torture enough; she could only pray that death would be immediate. The truck came to a skidding stop near a ridge running north and south high in the mountain range hours from Natanz. Talavi got out and opened the Toyota tailgate. Yasmeen could only watch as he lifted Ellison out of the bed and set him on a flat outcropping of rock protruding from the embankment. She felt her entire body tense when Talavi pulled a knife from his boot. It was still dark, but from what she could make out, it appeared he was cutting Ellison's bonds. Once his hands and feet were liberated, he pulled the blood-soaked tape from his mangled mouth. Forgetting temporarily about her own pain, her eyes filled with empathy, but alert to the fact something she hadn't expected was taking place.

Talavi approached and ordered her to turn over; she did and soon was free. Ellison helped her from the truck bed; their spontaneous embrace was intense, rekindling old feelings for each other that hadn't faded with time. Talavi stood in the darkness watching; feeling gratified he'd accomplished something far more rewarding in his life than carrying out Sherafat's horrendous dictates. He cleared his throat and in English said, "I'm sorry...but you must move quickly while it's still dark." He handed Ellison a map and explained how to get to the boarder of Iraq. "I can't tell you what you will encounter at the border, all I can say is that as you approach a US checkpoint, be very careful not to appear excited, the soldiers might interpret your delight as aggression. They shoot first and ask questions later—as you Americans like to say." He motioned for Yasmeen to step closer. She did, and he took her dislocated arm in one massive hand, and in a single motion, reset the joint. She dropped to her knees; both men knelt beside her, but they could only watch her writhe in pain. A few minutes later, Yasmeen stood holding her shoulder.

"I'm okay. Mr. Talavi, I have to know what happened to Nadim Faxhir and Zayna."

"Yes, of course." His once formidable manner tempered now by sorrow. "The news is tragic for Mr. Faxhir."

"Is he ... dead?" Her voice tentative, trembling.

"He is ... I am sorry."

"How?"

"It's complicated, and you don't have much time."

"I must know, please."

"Mr. Sattar and Dr. Sherafat knew almost immediately you were not scientists."

"How?"

"Please, Crys, we don't have time, let him finish."

"Sattar ordered Mr. Faxhir interrogated, but he wouldn't talk. After several hours of torture Sattar ordered me to kill him, bury his body in the desert, and bring him Mr. Faxhir's head as proof he was dead." Talavi explained he took Faxhir to the desert and was planning to let him go, but Faxhir insisted Talavi follow orders.

"He said that if I returned without his head Sattar would know for certain you and Dr. Sayyid were imposters. Not only would that be your death sentence, but it would be mine also. He said I was the only one at the plant capable of helping you, so I had to follow Sattar's orders."

"Oh my God...you killed Nadim."

"No, I did not." Talavi looked away searching for the right words to describe what had happened. "We sat for a while discussing ways of getting the two of you out safely. He was calm, the pain he had endured while being tortured seemed not to affect him. He'd lost a lot of blood during the interrogation...the bastards cut his toes off, and before they ordered me to kill him, they castrated—"

"Oh my God...oh my God," Yasmeen doubled over, choking back the horrific image.

"Yasmeen." Talavi touched her hand.

"What happened then?" She asked gasping for air.

"He prayed for sometime, and when he was finished his face was full of peace and in spiritual union with Allah. He looked at me and smiled, and before I could do anything, he grabbed my weapon and shot himself."

There were no more tears for her to cry, sorrow was now repressed, the anger Yasmeen felt just minutes before securely compartmentalized, a numbing sensation engulfed her. With words she hesitated to utter, Yasmeen asked, "And what about Zayna?"

"She is alive and in the town of Shushtar. Dr. Sayyid has a plan, a dangerous one, but one I think will work. Now, no more talk, you must be on your way." Talavi handed Ellison the truck keys and his previously confiscated cell phone and the Kalashnikov to Yasmeen. "There are two fully loaded pistols under the seat; you have enough fuel to get you into Iraq. Now go."

"What about you? What will you do?" Ellison asked.

"Don't worry about me; I have a plan."

Yasmeen embraced him, ignoring his smell. "I have to ask … are you the one that left the knife tucked in the towel?"

"Yes, I only had one, and you looked more vulnerable than Dr. Sayyid."

"So you gave it to me, and I tried to kill you with it."

"And you were nearly successful; I am sorry about your shoulder."

"The shoulder will heal, don't worry. But thank you for the knife, it gave me a sense of security I wouldn't have had otherwise."

"The knife was never intended to provide you a sense of security; I'm glad it did though."

"If not for protection, what was its intent?" she said. His eyes, observable in the breaking daylight, answered the question.

"Sometimes, death by our own hand is better than the alternative." Talavi shut the truck door and waved. "You must go; it will be day soon." He watched as the truck disappeared over a ridge carrying passengers he prayed were destined for safety. Talavi dropped to his knees, praying forgiveness on his soul. He petitioned Allah for strength, then slowly got to his feet and walked the short distance to an embankment standing far above a rocky canyon. The one-time Olympic champion took his cell phone out of his pocket and sent what was to be his last message to the director of the CIA, then reached toward heaven and jumped.

"There's no way he can survive, is there?" Ellison said.

"No … if he shows up at the nuke plant without our heads, Sattar will have him killed," Stanton said checking the weapons to make sure they were loaded. "And, of course, he couldn't go with us because his wife is still in Tehran."

"What do you think he'll do?"

"I think he answered that question earlier, don't you?" she said, her feelings well concealed behind fresh motivation to survive. Her instincts to stay alive had returned as sharp as ever, and it was not the time to allow anything, not even sentiment, to interfere with that objective. She knew there would be ample opportunity during many future sleepless nights to rehash the mission and particularly the loss of human life. Those memories had to be carefully moved somewhere they wouldn't interfere.

"By the way, Ellison, what in the hell are you doing here?"

"Just vacationing, then I ran into you, and you looked like you needed assistance."

"My ass ... you dumb sonofabitch, you could've been killed. Did Webster send you?"

"Well, we did have a casual conversation about Middle East politics, and yes, your name came up sort of in passing."

"You lying sack of shit—"

"Whoa ... what's with all this foul language?"

"Shut up and let me finish. I'm trying to get all this hostility out, and the cuss words just seem to emphasize the meaning of what I'm trying to say."

"Let it out."

"When my shoulder heals, I'm kicking both your butts. I can't believe two of my best friends are the stupidest people on earth. I have absolutely no talent for picking friends." A heavy interlude followed her tirade. Ellison picked up on the double meaning and reached over, giving her hand a soft squeeze.

"You didn't know Talavi was a CIA asset?" he asked, changing the subject.

"The crack I made about having no talent picking friends ... the same goes for allies."

"Explain."

"I was relying on Sattar to be helpful, certainly not Talavi. Hmm, just thought of something."

"What?"

"If my mother said you can't judge a book by its cover once, she said it a million times. Obviously I ignored that bit of homespun wisdom." Stanton tried to chamber a round in one of the hand-guns Talavi left under the seat but the shoulder pain was too much. "Damn it, a lot of good I'll be in firefight. I hope you've honed your diplomatic skills since the last time we were together."

"Meaning?"

"If I remember, Frank, you had none."

"Age must be affecting your memory... I was always a mild-mannered agent."

Stanton smiled, the first in nearly a month. "Mild mannered my ass. You were a bull, on speed, in a china closet." They both laughed. "By the way, did anyone ever cite you for saving the president's daughter?"

"Oh yeah... big event in the director's office. Webster and the director were the only attendees."

"What?"

"It was a hoot. The director said some kind words and handed me a framed citation signed by the president, we shook hands, and he took the citation back."

"Come again?"

"He took it back and said I could have it to hang wherever I chose five years after the president was out of office. By my calculations that should be in about six years."

"What did Webster say?"

"He gave it the bureaucratic spin, said words like 'for the greater good,' the daughter's drug history and near kidnapping had to remain confidential during and for a short period after his presidency."

"What a crock. If I recall, everyone knew his daughter was into drugs."

"Yup, you recall correctly."

The washed-out road they were traveling suddenly got worse, forcing Ellison to slow to a crawl. "I don't like this."

"Yeah, driving this slowly just makes us sitting ducks."

"I figure, by Talavi's map, we're about a hundred miles from the boarder, at this rate we won't make it anytime soon."

"Just as soon as Sattar realizes Talavi hasn't returned with our heads, he'll notify the military, and boarder crossings will be closed."

Stanton took the map from Ellison's hand so he could tend to driving. It was nearly eight a.m. and the cold high altitude air was losing its grip, giving way to a September sun promising a hot day. Wind picked up from the south, and dust off the arid landscape pelted the truck. "Roll your window up," she said. Stanton spread the rudimentary map on the seat and studied the handwritten details. "Looks like Talavi has us moving off road to a dry river bed at the base of the ridge we're on. The road goes northwest and the river goes southwest."

"Then where?" Ellison asked.

"That's where the map ends. I guess the river goes on into Iraq."

"And the road?"

"It winds around to a settlement, and he's written *don't go there,* so we probably shouldn't."

Ellison nodded. "And we won't."

The road began to smooth, allowing Ellison to speed up. "If we can maintain this speed, we should be near the boarder in four or five hours."

Stanton held her shoulder and turned to view the ridge they'd just come down from. No one was following, it was clear, Talavi plotted their escape through a remote and isolated area of southwest Iran, but they were a long way from safety with few places to hide in the event they were pursued. Somehow, Stanton thought, the danger didn't have the same intensity as long as Ellison was near. "So you knew Talavi was an asset."

"Winters shared that with Webster along with logistical information. I guess Winters was planning some kind of military rescue."

"What?"

"Yeah, a C-130, couple of helos, and Delta Force, but then our friend came to her rescue."

"I'm not following."

"Webster called me and asked if I'd like to go instead. I said what the hell, didn't have anything better to do. So they took my badge and gun, gave me a fake passport and a ten-year-old Mercedes, and sent me in."

"I'm so glad I didn't marry you," Stanton said.

"Why?"

"'Cause you are a fool, a Neanderthal, and…"

"And what?"

Stanton didn't answer, she was afraid it would complicate an already very complicated life she was trying hard to simplify.

"Come on, Crys… and what?"

"You're a throwback, Frank. Look at yourself… thinning hair, overweight, several teeth missing; you should've taken better care of yourself." Her criticism belying her true feelings.

Ellison's consciousness was inundated with escape strategies, a never-ending composition of scenarios playing over and over like an unfinished symphony in his mind, but still attuned to Crys' humor. "Have you taken a close look in the mirror lately? You ain't no prom queen. And speaking of fools, what in the world enticed you into this mission?"

"Aw shucks, Frank, I just wanted to save the world. You know, write a book, be on Oprah's show." Stanton laughed, but the pain once localized to her face and shoulder now radiating everywhere turned the chuckle to a groan.

"Crys." Ellison's urgent tone grabbed her attention. "Look behind us, I think someone is following, and they're moving in fast."

CHAPTER 41

SHUSHTAR, IRAN
1800 HOURS, SEPTEMBER 17

The tobacco vender led Zayna through the backstreets of Shushtar to a warehouse district and knocked on a door of a well-hidden Quonset attachment. The narrow street dead-ended near a walled courtyard. Zayna noticed security cameras positioned in various secluded areas around the entrance and assumed the delay in answering was due to whoever was inside trying to identify her. Finally a dark, bearded man opened the door and allowed the vender in, but ordered Zayna to remain where she was. The late afternoon sun was still hot, her tunic and hijab absorbing every degree, concentrating the heat full force next to her skin. There was no shade and no breeze, just the stifling warmth. The man finally opened the door and gestured for her to enter, his face showing no signs of hospitality, only suspicion. He led Zayna into a small windowless room where the vender was waiting and disappeared down a short hall. The vender pointed to a chair. "Our leader will be with us in a moment."

Zayna sat down. "Who is he, this leader?"

"I don't know, only those that serve closest to him know, and I've never heard them say."

"He must be very important?"

"Of course he is important. He is personally blessed by Allah and talks with him often."

"Then he shares those talks with you and the others?" she asked, hoping to coax more information from the vender.

"Of course…he is a rising prophet; the one that will bring worldwide peace."

"Ahh…then Allah has truly blessed me by guiding me here, I will be so thankful to be in your leader's presence." Just then the door opened wide, and a young man in a tailored business suit walked in. His demeanor was the opposite of what she expected; he greeted her in European fashion, a kiss on both cheeks, then invited her to sit down. "I've been told you wish to aid in our cause against the infidels. Is that true?"

"Yes…for my husband's sake and that of my family."

The man's expression grew serious. "You are Pakistani?"

"I am."

"And you are prepared for martyrdom?"

"I am."

"You will attain the highest rank in paradise, rewards will be plentiful, and you will be nearest the throne of God."

Zayna lowered her head, an endeavor to dramatize humility before the self-proclaimed leader of terrorists. "Allah Akbar…Allah Akbar," she said reverently.

"Allah Akbar," he repeated. A brief pause followed the dual proclamation. The vender watched closely as his leader and the woman communed in the presence of God himself, hoping his recruitment efforts would win him praise.

"Please excuse my forwardness, Mrs. Sayyid, but with your unmistakable beauty and depth of spirit, I firmly believe you will be able to penetrate the infidel's most fortified compound and do the most harm…or should I have said *good* on Allah's behalf."

"This would be my most fulfilling moment, sir."

"Then indeed you shall be a martyr of the highest distinction.

You are but days away from reuniting with your family and sharing with them blessings beyond your imagination, Allah Akbar."

"Allah Akbar," Zayna and the vender repeated.

The leader stood and issued orders to an aide standing just outside the room. "Show Mrs. Sayyid to our guest quarters, provide her with all she asks for, and tell Kalid to prepare her respectfully for her mission."

The vender left the room first and turned left toward the exit door. He'd been dismissed to return to his duties at the tobacco stand. Her escort remained in the hall, leaving the leader and Zayna alone in the room. She stood to follow the escort then hesitated.

"Is there something else?" the leader asked. "You appear apprehensive?"

"Yes, your name. I want to be able to speak of your dedication when I meet Allah."

"If you won't share it with anyone; you understand it is better for me to remain anonymous."

"Of course."

"I am a banker here in Shushtar; my name is Akil Ibn Bilal. That is all you can know. Now you should be on your way into Iraq in two days; we will not see each other again."

"I will prostrate myself before Allah and petition on your behalf, Akil Ibn Bilal."

Bilal bowed slightly, an appreciative smile barely distinguishable. He gestured toward the door, and Sayyid followed the escort to the right.

Kalid followed Bilal's orders; although aloof, obviously a proponent of a male-dominated world, he did what he was told. His reluctance noticeable and his courtesy stiff, Kalid introduced Sayyid to others, and then opened the door to the warehouse. The sight made her gasp. Stacked along each wall were anti-tank weapons, missiles, manufactured in Russian and China, some US- and British-made surface to air missiles. In the center were crates of grenades, launchers, AK-47 assault rifles, and handguns. More firepower than she'd ever seen. Sayyid looked carefully around the room. "This is very impressive."

"Yes ... and, useless."

"I don't understand?"

"We can't get it to our forces inside Iraq. The Americans and the Brits have successfully shut down our smuggling efforts."

"There is no way of getting any of this into Iraq?" She faked her disappointment well.

"Only bits and pieces by mule over rough terrain, but much of that is intercepted. Our most successful strikes are the martyrs that give their lives. The explosives they carry strapped to their bodies and blessed by Allah are our most devastating weapons."

"How do we carry the explosives over the border without being detected?"

"You won't carry anything. It is all prepared for you in your target city. You show up, and our freedom fighters fit you with the device and drive you to the location. It is simple."

Sayyid kept the conversation going while making an accurate survey of the gymnasium-sized room. Stacks of ammunition sat randomly and several crates marked *explosives* rimmed the far wall. At the opposite end of the building, boxes of detonators, cell phones, and handheld remote control devices were kept separate from the explosives. Hundreds of double-A batteries were still in their original packaging strewn around on tabletops ready for quick assembly into a tool of death and destruction.

Kalid closed the door, locked it, and motioned for her to follow him to the guest quarters. She was surprised; the room was large, a bed, chair and lamp table on one side and a full kitchen on the other. The only other door led, she hoped, to a bathroom. Although the room was austere, it was clean. Kalid pointed. "You will find clothing in the closet, and of course, there are bathing facilities in that room. I will leave you undisturbed the remainder of the day and night."

"What happens tomorrow?" she asked.

"Instruction, map study, target identification."

"And then?"

"You will be escorted to the border."

"How do I cross? I thought the border was sealed."

"To weapons, men with no familial ties to Iraq, yes, but not to attractive females."

"I don't understand; why are females allowed to cross?"

Kalid looked at her for the first time, his stare hollow as if he were peering into darkness. He inhaled. "Mrs. Sayyid, they are allowed to cross for the same reason they have always been allowed to cross."

Sayyid knew why, but thought it wiser to appear naive. "I am sorry, I just don't understand."

"The Americans turned border control over to the new Iraqi army; they are poorly trained and undisciplined. Most are very young, some teenagers, and they have their cravings that go beyond nourishment." Kalid's strict Muslim upbringing permitted him to go no further discussing the world's oldest profession satiating the appetites of lonely and isolated soldiers. The thought of being forced to act out the part of a prostitute repulsed her, although, she thought, a relatively small price to pay for her freedom. A fact of life she'd endured at the hands of her captors so many years earlier.

A west window provided a view of the small courtyard and of the setting sun. Birds hopped from branch to branch on an ancient olive tree standing in the middle of a beautifully landscaped garden, a stark difference to the entrance she'd passed through just hours before. The sight from her window was serene, stirring her first peaceful thoughts in a very long time. Sayyid closed her eyes, allowing the rare moment to bathe her. She'd never been a religious person, but the cleansing feeling somehow felt spiritual as if lifted from the dark where everything was obscured into daylight. Sayyid held fast to the experience as long as she could, drifting in and out of conscious euphoria until daylight was gone. Her mind, just an hour earlier full of strategic maneuvering drenched heavily with fear, was now free of clutter, ready to scheme without the doubt driven *what ifs.*

Sayyid fixed a light meal of goat cheese and bread while surreptitiously searching for surveillance equipment, but found none. She stepped into the hall and looked toward the door leading to the armory, amazed that there were no cameras; she walked toward the door she knew was locked. Her story, if intercepted, would simply be that she was looking for Kalid to explain that her toilet wasn't working. To back her story she'd disconnected the flushing mechanism. Wandering the hall for what seemed like a long time brought no one to check on her. She gently opened the door leading to the outer offices. Sitting not far away was the night security, head pitched to one side snoring, his chair pulled close to a table where he'd propped his feet. Sayyid stepped in and touched his shoulder; he didn't stir. A set of keys lay on the table next to a flashlight; she picked them up quickly and turned toward the hall door. She hurried to the armory and after trying several keys found the right one. All her Secret Service bomb-defusing training came flooding back.

Constructing a bomb would be complicated not to mention dangerous, a matter of reversing the defusing process, she hoped. Sorting through the box of phones, she found a powerful older model bag phone that still worked; on one side someone had written the number on adhesive tape. Sayyid sorted through the cell phones until she found one that indicated residual power and dialed the bag phone number, it rang. After wiring the phone to a detonator, she embedded one end into a package of explosives with Chinese lettering on the container. The only two English words distinguishable were *Danger: Explosives* printed in red along with the same warning written in five other languages. She placed the improvised device behind a stack of ammunition and the cell phone in her pocket then headed for the door. As she reached for the handle, the door swung open. There crouching, poised and ready to take action was the man she'd lifted the keys from.

"What are you doing in here?" he shouted.

Sayyid assumed the submissive posture she knew the guard would expect; speaking softly and with contrived respect, she whispered, "I am so very sorry, sir. I'm embarrassed, humiliated."

"What are you doing in this room?" he demanded.

"The stool in my room is not working properly; I was looking for a tool—"

The guard interrupted, furious with her. "Looking for a tool? What kind of tool? Why did you not ask me to help?"

"I humbly beg your forgiveness, sir, but I came and tried to wake you, and when you didn't respond, I made the very serious mistake and borrowed your keys. I should never have done that. Please forgive my foolishness." She took a chance and, looking into his eyes, forced a shy, obedient smile.

The guard, disarmed by her charm and beauty, fell quickly to her feminine wiles. He motioned her out of the armory, realizing if Kalid discovered he'd been asleep, his reputation would be lost and his family disgraced. "I will fix your toilet."

"You are too kind, sir, and please keep my ignorant and foolish behavior to yourself. I am to be martyred soon, and I don't want even the smallest detail to distract from that glorious occasion."

The guard didn't answer, but it was clear to her he knew the predicament he'd created, and the only solution to his dilemma was to remain silent about the incident. The only witness to his transgression, after all, would be dead soon.

He followed her into the guest quarters and quickly repaired the stool, then left without saying anything.

Sayyid shut off the cell phone she'd smuggled out of the armory to conserve what battery power was left, wrapped it in a wash cloth and slipped it into her underwear just below her belly-button. She drifted off thinking of her team, doubts about their chances of survival preventing the deep sleep she so badly needed.

CHAPTER 42
ZAGROS MOUNTAIN FOOTHILLS
0800 HOURS, SEPTEMBER 18

Stanton forced her pain-racked body around to see what, if anything was in pursuit. "All I see is our dust."

"Look again, back about a mile."

"Yeah … I see the sun reflecting off a windshield, and more dust."

"They're coming fast, Crys."

"Speed up."

"I can't … the damn road; some of these pot-holes are a foot deep." Ellison turned hard to the left, narrowly missing a washed-out area of the road and sending Stanton crashing into the door. She held her shoulder, screaming in agony.

"Sorry, Crys."

"No, no, Frank, its okay. Just get us out of here." She bent forward searching frantically for a more comfortable position, but the effort was futile. Stanton straightened her body, tears turning the grit and dried blood around her eyes into a blinding concoction, making the yellow and black bruising appear all the more horrid. She turned slowly to look back, every degree of twist brought searing pain, pain she could no longer allow. Stanton pulled herself around and braced her hand against the dash. "They're still gaining, going too fast for casual traffic. How far to the border?"

"At least thirty, maybe as much as fifty; hell, I don't know."

"Make it thirty... at this rate whoever that is will be in rifle fire range soon."

Ellison handed Stanton his cell phone. "They gave me this phone at the embassy along with the Mercedes."

She moved back to her original position and stared at the phone. "And who do you suggest I call, Superman?"

"Hang on we're taking evasive action." Ellison shouted. He guided the truck from one side of the road to the other, zigzagging fiercely.

"What are you doing?" She shrieked bouncing like a pinball inside the truck.

"We're taking fire... see that hole in the tailgate?"

"No, I can't turn around again."

"Trust me; it wasn't there five minutes ago. Looks like a fifty caliber to me." He no sooner spoke when another round shattered the rear window.

"The phone, Frank, what about the phone?"

"Nine-one-one."

"What?"

"Nine-one-one. Do it now."

Stanton pushed 9–1-1. "Now what?"

"Give it back." Ellison stuck it in his shirt pocket.

"What happens next?" she yelled, forcing her words through the din of noise from the screaming engine. The broken rear window allowed hot dust filled air to circulate fiercely through the cab making any communication almost impossible.

"I don't have a clue. Boys at the embassy just handed it to me... said dial nine-one-one if I got into trouble near the border."

"What?"

Another round obliterated the driver-side review mirror, showering glass inside the truck cab. "You okay?" Stanton said.

"I'm okay. You?"

"Yeah." Stanton shouted picking small shards of glass from her tunic as another round missed her sore shoulder by inches.

"Hang on, I'm gonna try and put some distance between us." Ellison gunned the engine. "Crys, if you can, take a few shots, make 'em back off."

Stanton pinned the barrel against the truck dash with her sore shoulder, and with her right hand chambered a round. She lifted her left knee onto the seat and swiveled her body facing Ellison and stuck the business end of the Kalashnikov through the broken window and fired a burst. "They're still coming."

"Yeah, we're outta range for the AK, but in range for their fifty. They probably don't know we're shooting at 'em—aim higher."

Stanton lowered the butt end of the Russian-made assault rifle slightly and fired another burst. "They swerved, Frank...they swerved."

"Are they still coming?"

"Yes, but they've dropped back a ways."

Another round from the high-powered weapon grazed Ellison's shoulder and tore through the truck dash sending an explosion of plastic inside the truck.

"Frank, you've been hit."

"Just a flesh wound, but got something in my eye that's stinging like hell. Take another shot, Crys."

"We've only got twenty, maybe twenty-five rounds."

"We've got to put another two hundred meters between us, Crys. You shoot; I'll speed up."

Stanton took aim, hoping the bullet velocity and the speed of the oncoming vehicle would work mathematically in their favor. She fired another burst. "They swerved again, Frank."

"Are they dropping back?"

"Can't tell for sure, too much dust."

CHAPTER 43

SEPTEMBER 18

Margaret Winters' jet landed in Baghdad just before noon. She had authorized an unauthorized visit to Iraq to meet personally with her CIA chief of station and the commanding general in charge of Middle East operations. Winters didn't have a plan, but sitting in her office pretending the world was flat wasn't working. She hadn't slept in a week, and to make matters worse, the bottle of Chivas was becoming close company, too close. The desire to do something, even if it was wrong was overwhelming, and now she was in the thick of things with no option for turning back.

General G. L. Dobbs stood as his aide announced her arrival. "Director, it's been a while." His greeting was friendly but the general's curiosity was apparent.

"About a year, General, I believe it was at a White House briefing."

"That's right; we sat next to each other." He motioned for her to take a seat, tipping his shaved head to one side, staring, wondering why an unannounced visit.

"I know this is unusual, no notice and all."

"Yes, highly unusual … what's going on?" he said.

Winters explained the mission in brief. "As some operations do, this one took a turn for the worse."

"And you're trying to cut your losses?"

"I prefer to think of it as trying to save a couple of lives."

"What do you want from the military?"

"I'm not sure, let me discuss a possible scenario, we'll work around that."

"Should I summon logistics?"

"Not yet, hear me out before we brief others."

Dobbs nodded, his slow response implied skepticism, not necessarily skepticism of Winters, but of her reference to Iran. Border events, particularly military action of any kind were always provocative to the Iranians. Any action near the boarder was just grist for the propaganda mill, and the opportunistic Iranian president was a master at generating worldwide misinformation. Saving CIA operatives on or near the border was a troublesome prospect, not to mention against his better judgment. "I'm listening."

"What we know for sure is one of the original team is dead, a man. The two other members, both women, were being held at the Iranian nuke plant at Natanz—"

"Women," he said, his eyes widened. "You sent women into Iran to snoop around for nukes?"

"I did, no time to explain my reasons now. We have information I have confidence in: the two women and an FBI agent were ushered safely out of the nuke plant to locations near the Iraq boarder."

"Hold on a minute, Director Winters…you say an FBI agent…how'd he get in the mix?"

"It's a long story; I'll explain later."

"I can't wait…go on." Dobbs was intrigued.

"We believe one operative is in Shushtar, and the other two are driving a truck in a remote area near the border south of Shushtar."

"And you know this how?" Dobbs asked.

"Text message from an asset at the facility."

"You trust the asset?"

The director grimaced at the realization that at this stage of the operation it was all guesswork and praying for good luck—trust was no longer a realistic variable she had the luxury of considering. "General, it's all I have."

"Okay, but I still don't see how that involves the military."

"I hope it doesn't, but just to make sure, I'd like to prepare an extraction plan."

Dobbs picked up a telescopic pointer. "Here's Shushtar and you say the other two are headed our way and are somewhere in this vicinity." He drew an imaginary circle around an area roughly the size of New Jersey. "How do you propose we narrow the area down in order to pin-point their location?"

"Good question. When the agent left Damascus, he was given a cell phone with a tracking device embedded. He was instructed that if he was near the border, near rescue assets, he could punch in nine-one-one."

"And the local police show up and rescue them?"

"I wish … but no, the nine-one-one signal alerts our tracking team that danger is inevitable. We locate them and do our best to rescue without jeopardizing rules of engagement."

"Director Winters, you're dreaming. If we get within a mile of that border on anything more than bicycle and we're spotted, that goat-herding fanatic in Tehran will turn it into an international crisis."

"I know, General … that's why the operation is my doing, not yours."

"Explain."

"I would if I could, but I'm flying by the seat of my pants on this one. All I can say is its evolving, and as it does, we—my operatives and me—will take action accordingly."

"That kind of strategy doesn't play well under battlefield conditions. I admit … sometimes we have to make it up as we go, but I'm not committing lives and assets to an ill-contrived covert operation." The general stood his ground, making the only rational move he could, and Winters understood why. If the rescue attempt failed, he would share in the blame, and if failure resulted in a diplomatic disaster, Dobbs would be retired in disgrace, just what every four-star dreaded most.

Winters realized, for his sake, the conversation should end. To draw him further into a clandestine action would force him to take necessary steps to prevent a rescue operation from happening. The result, a war of wills—the general trying to avoid an incident of extreme proportions and Winters attempting to rescue people that deserved rescuing.

"I see your point, General, and it's right on target." She stood, forcing a smile she hoped conveyed the proper meaning. "Thank you for your time...all this worry may be for nothing. They're resourceful people, hopefully they'll make it." She didn't try to hide her disappointment.

"I hope so. What will you do now?"

"I'll hang around the office here in Baghdad until we know something."

"Why don't you join me for dinner at the officers' mess...come over I'll introduce you around."

"Thanks, I just might do that...time?"

"1800."

On her way out of military headquarters, Director Winters wound through the maze of desks, planning tables surrounded by command officers and armed soldiers to the lobby where her entourage of security and assistants' waited. She looked at her deputy. "Any news?" Winters asked quietly.

"No, nothing new. We're still tracking Ellison."

"Where is he?"

"South of Ahvaz headed west on an old road leading out of the Zagros foothills."

"Terrain?"

"Flat, lots of agriculture, small farm communities."

"How far to the border?"

"Fifty, maybe seventy-five miles."

Winters moved quickly out of the building to her vehicle and slid in behind the driver. "Headquarters," she said loud enough to be heard over the sound of doors slamming and her protection detail yelling cryptic instructions only they could understand.

The director's caravan skidded to a stop in front of the hotel that doubled as CIA headquarters in Baghdad. Dust swirled, mingling with the security detail rushing into position around her Humvee. Her door opened, and three men and a woman carrying assault weapons ushered her and the deputy inside. They made their way to the chief of station's office who had been briefed about the circumstances surrounding Winters' visit.

"Henry, good to see you."

"Likewise, Maggie."

"You remember my deputy, Tom Owens."

"Of course." The men shook hands.

"Sorry, I didn't come here first, but you understand protocol."

"I do, think nothing of it. Now, some refreshment?"

"Please, anything with ice; I'm burning up."

"Maggie, you're getting soft … it's only a hundred and five. The maintenance crew has assured us the air conditioner will be up and running just as soon as the part is flown in from Delaware," he said, laughing cynically at his stab at humor. "Now, while we wait on that, tell me about this operation."

"I'll tell you more about the mission later, right now my one and only goal is to get our team out of Iran." The shrill alarm from Owens's phone halted the briefing.

The deputy answered and listened intently. He glanced at his boss. "When?" He repeated the answer: "Five minutes."

Winters knew this was the news they'd been waiting for. Her heart raced, rushing adrenaline-laced blood coursing in preparation to act.

"Okay, sit tight, we'll be back to you in a few." Owens closed his phone.

"What's going on?" Winters said.

"The nine-one-one code we gave Ellison, he just used it."

"How long ago?"

Owens glanced at his watch. "Six minutes."

"Do we have his exact location?" Winters was already standing. "Yes."

Winters turned to the Baghdad COS. "Agency has two UH-60s, don't they?"

"Ready to fly at a moment's notice," he answered.

"How're they equipped?"

"Six rockets and a door gunner."

She turned to the deputy. "Is he in trouble?"

"We know he's on the move, traveling at a high rate of speed for those road conditions, and we told him the code was to be used only if he was in trouble and close to the border. The answer to your question is *yes*, there's a high probability he's being pursued."

The director paced around the conference table mumbling; the two men watched, knowing Winters worked best under pressure and without interference. She opened her cell phone. "Henry, do you have the general's private number?"

He scrolled to a number, wrote it down, and handed it to Winters. "I'm goin' to call and see if I can get some military help. Is the helo equipped to haul?"

"Yes, with webbing, it'll bear a load of a few tons."

"How long till it's ready to fly?"

"Thirty minutes."

"Tell 'em I want to board in twenty."

"You're going?" Martin's ruddy face twisted to a doubtful frown.

She nodded and turned to Owens. "Get an exact fix on Ellison, and any known Iranian military camps along his escape route, I want that info in ten minutes." She dialed the number Martin had given her. "General … sorry, I won't be able to join you at mess, but I have a request I think you can live with."

CHAPTER 44

Ellison jerked the wheel hard to the right, narrowly avoiding a rock the size of a basketball. Stanton's head collided with the doorframe, reopening the scabbed over cut.

"Sorry." Ellison shouted as he guided the truck back on to the road.

"I'm okay," she uttered between agonizing groans as the surge of pain flowed mercilessly through her body.

"Yeah, right."

"What?"

"Yeah, right, I can hear it in your voice." Ellison's quick response to the road hazard saved the truck from certain irreparable damage. He accelerated, alternately swaying the vehicle from side to side hoping to evade another round from the fifty. Ellison estimated the vehicles' distance at around five hundred meters, certainly within range of the big gun, but he knew a hit on a moving target would be by chance only, maybe.

Stanton wiped the blood out of her eye with the hem

of her tunic and, with all the strength and pain tolerance she could muster, pulled herself upright and pointed the assault rifle out the broken rear window. "Tell me again about this nine-one-one call we made."

"Forget it, Crys. I'm sure it was just CI's way of offering me a security blanket … you know, something to hang on to."

"Right … guess I'd opt for my teddy bear." They laughed.

"Can you see 'em?"

"Looks like they've fallen back, maybe they're running out of gas. Wouldn't that be a hoot?" she said.

"Yeah … but don't count on it."

"Damn it, Frank."

"What."

"You ruined my moment in la-la land."

Ellison was about to apologize for bursting his friends imaginary balloon when a loud pop ended the repartee.

"What was that?" Stanton shouted.

"We blew a rear tire … we're slowing down."

Ignoring her condition, Stanton turned, scouting for something that might give them shelter from attacked. "I don't even see a tree we can hide behind."

"We'll use the truck. I'm gonna skid to the left and stop in the middle of the road. Grab the weapons, and when the truck stops, bail out and take up whatever defensive position you can find." Ellison veered right then left bringing the truck to a standstill. They both tumbled out and crawled behind the wheels. Stanton tossed one of the handguns to Ellison. "These have a full mag and no more than ten or fifteen rounds in the rifle."

Ellison looked around the front of their metal bunker. "Looks like they've stopped."

"How far?"

"Five, maybe six hundred meters." He no sooner got his words out when a round penetrated the rear fender exiting out the wheel well on the opposite side, missing Stanton by inches. "They're shooting at the gas tank, Crys, get over here." Ellison grabbed her uninjured arm and dragged her behind the front wheel. "We've got a better chance here … that fifty won't go through the engine block."

The second round collided with the nearly empty gas tank and the explosion sent shrapnel flying. The remaining fuel ignited the rear tires, and they burned furiously, sending clouds of black smoke swirling in the wind. Ellison picked up the assault rifle and fired a burst; the Iranians returned fire with one single shot striking the engine. Pieces of the valve cover ricocheted through the grill, striking Ellison's neck and chin. Blood was everywhere; he fired another burst and dropped next to Stanton, awaiting the next enemy round. She hadn't moved, laying face down on the dirt road; Ellison realized something was terribly wrong. "Crys … Crys." He screamed lifting her head and rolling her body toward him, the front of her tunic soaked in blood, too much blood, he knew for her to survive long. He located the severed femoral artery and made a tourniquet, her breathing growing weaker by the moment. Ellison pulled her next to him and held her. He leaned his head back against the tire ignoring the fire inching closer, the acrid smoke stealing what breathable air remained. Ellison picked up one of the nine-millimeter handguns; he and Stanton were out of options, save one.

CHAPTER 45

The CH-60 crossed the border at 1700 hours flying fast and low, the eleven on board, including Winters, were armed and ready for a fight. Martin and Owens were ordered to remain in Baghdad against their fervent objections, but Winters knew their active participation in an unofficial operation could cost them their careers. The action was her responsibility and hers alone, she wasn't about to ruin their lives as well.

The pilot picked up the road Ellison was supposed to be on and headed north, the twin GE turboshaft engines screaming as they picked up speed. Winters headphones crackled.

"Director," the pilot said.

"Yes," she yelled into the mic.

"This is the pilot; we've got smoke ahead."

"How far?" She pressed the earphones tight against her head.

"Five kilometers."

"At one kilometer, swing right over the road and hover."

"Yes, ma'am."

Winters adjusted the binoculars and knelt near the door gunner. The helo slowed to a crawl, and the pilot announced, "We're at one K, banking right."

"I see a vehicle on fire and two people on the ground, but I can't tell if they are alive," Winters shouted.

"One is waving. Looks like they are taking fire from a truck up the road another half K," the co-pilot answered.

"Fly over the other vehicle, we need an ID."

"Yes, ma'am. Prepare for altitude climb and evasive action," the pilot announced calmly. Winters refastened her tether just as the Blackhawk soared skyward.

"Ma'am."

"Yes."

"The objective is a truck with five armed occupants. They've fired on us, but we're out of range."

"Can you confirm the occupants are firing on the burning vehicle?"

"Affirmative."

"The next time they fire … return it."

"Ma'am."

"Yes."

"You want the site sanitized, right?"

"Absolutely."

"I suggest we go in low and let the door gunner spray 'em."

"What about a rocket?" Winters asked.

"A rocket would scatter pieces, make clean up difficult."

"Do it."

The pilot flew a wide arch around the objective and came in low, taking the first round through the cabin, destroying communication equipment. He held the Blackhawk steady at five hundred meters from the target, and the gunner squeezed off a hundred rounds in a tight pattern. The pilot cautiously approached the vehicle; there was no sign of life. Two paramilitary carrying light assault weapons jumped to the ground and approached the truck. Seconds later one gave the all clear signal, and the pilot landed a few meters away. Four crewmembers dragged the heavy canvas webbing out of the helo and began spreading it near the truck. Winters checked the time, from target acquisition to present had taken less than five minutes. She gave the go signal, and the pilot lifted off, heading for the burning vehicle.

Ellison shielded Stanton from the wash of dirt stirred violently by the landing Blackhawk. Two medics scrambled out and headed toward the injured pair as the co-pilot and Winters emptied fire extinguishers on the fire.

One of the medics approached Ellison. "Don't worry about me," he yelled. "Take care of her." The confidence and levelheaded resolve Frank Ellison was known for vanished as he watched the medics trying desperately to save Stanton's life. He dropped to his knees, the mix of terror and utter exhaustion, but mostly his fear of failing the one person he'd gladly give his life to save overcame him. "Oh God…oh God…save her," he pled, the noise of the Blackhawk and the shouting silenced by his passionate begging.

Winters tossed the empty extinguisher in the truck cab and gave the pilot a signal. The Blackhawk lifted a few feet and headed back to pick up the others. The pilot skillfully hovered over the net filled with the remains of the truck and five Iranian soldiers while the crew secured it to the helicopter. The pilot moved the contents a few feet away to allow the men on the ground room to rake the area for any remaining telltale signs of the truck. The nearby spinning rotors landscaped the kill site giving the dirt road a natural wind-blown appearance, seconds later the Blackhawk, and the ground crew clinging to the net, was on its way back to where the others were. The pilot made a distant pass to avoid sending debris over the medics and their patient, descending just enough to allow the netted cargo contact with the ground. After the crew had cleared the net, he released the hook, securing it to the helicopter, and set the Black-hawk down ready for passengers. Winters approached the cabin.

"Can we load this truck too?" she shouted.

The pilot shook his head vigorously. "No ... too heavy."

Medics were loading Stanton, and one of the crew was seated on top of the cargo net ready to reattach it. Winters ran back to the burned Toyota and retrieved the fire extinguisher, the Kalashnikov, and both nine-millimeter handguns. Once aloft the pilot hovered over the cargo and the crewmember reattached it. Another of the crew lying on his stomach peered under the helicopter. "Go, go, go!" he shouted over the cabin noise, and the Blackhawk climbed.

"What about that guy?" Winters pointed down, fumbling to get her communication headset on.

"No room in here; he'll ride the net," the co-pilot said reassuringly. The guy was probably as safe as anyone else, and wind chill on a hundred-degree day wasn't much of a factor, she thought.

"What's her condition?" Winters asked one of the medics who was working to insert another needle in a vein; he didn't answer. She wasn't used to being ignored and asked again.

"Wait," he said with enough authority to remind the director of Central Intelligence who was in charge at that very moment. She sat back and watched the two men working anxiously to save Stanton's life. Even Ellison knew better than to interfere by asking unanswerable questions. Winters closed her eyes, her thoughts on Limber Crisp.

"Ma'am," the pilot said, louder than was necessary to communicate over the head set.

"Yes."

"We're in Iraq, approaching the drop zone. ETA five minutes."

"I hope the general followed through." Winters crossed her fingers.

"Affirmative. We'll know in three and a half minutes."

Winters looked at her watch. "How long will the drop take?"

"To be conservative, ma'am, I'd say thirty seconds."

"Nothing to it…huh."

"Nothing to it, ma'am."

"What happens to the guy riding the net?"

"He can ride back with the combat engineers." The pilot spotted the zone. "Ma'am," he shouted.

"I'm here," Winters said readjusting the headphones.

"I have engineers at a thousand meters."

General Dobbs agreed to pull a hemmit loaded with a Cat D9 off a nearby road construction crew and dig a hole deep enough to bury five thousand pounds of truck. Winters hadn't mentioned the truck would be loaded with human accessories. He didn't ask, and she didn't tell, a workable arrangement for both.

The pilot's approach was skillful. Once over the target, he edged the cargo close to the embankment and waited until the crewman had cleared the netting; he nodded and the co-pilot disengaged the hook. The D9 operator gave the thumbs-up, and Winters watched as black smoke bellowed out of the bulldozer's exhaust stack signaling burial was in progress, the Blackhawk, free of its cargo headed toward Baghdad.

CHAPTER 46
SHUSHTAR, IRAN
SEPTEMBER 18

A loud knock startled Zayna Binte Sayyid out of her shallow sleep. "Yes, what is it?"

It was the security guard. "Mrs. Sayyid, Kalid wants to see you right away, please ... come now."

"In five minutes," she said eyeing the clock. She couldn't imagine what was occurring at that hour that would require her presence other than the possibility Kalid had heard about her nighttime prowling, regardless Zayna was prepared to stick with her story.

The guard escorted her down the hall past the armory. Kalid met them and, after dismissing the guard, opened the door to a large conference room and ushered her in. The leader Akil Ibn Bilal sat at the head of the long rectangular folding table surrounded by ten men Sayyid assumed were Bilal's lieutenants. There wasn't a friendly face among the group, and her growing anxiety was getting difficult to conceal.

Bilal pointed to an empty chair at the opposite end of

the table, and Sayyid sat down. "I trust you rested well," he said, his tone and body language exposing nothing about what he was thinking.

"Yes ... thank you."

"There has been a change in plans."

"Oh."

"Yes, we have reliable information that America's war-mongering vice president will arrive in Baghdad tomorrow morning, and you'll be there."

"But how?"

"When the vice president arrives, he will be escorted under heavy security into a fortified hangar. He will present combat ribbons to a few soldiers and hold a brief news conference. One reporter from several news outlets will be allowed to attend and ask questions. We have arranged for the reporter representing Al-Jazeera to be delayed and for you to take her place."

"As you said, there will be heavy security ... won't they use detection devices?" Sayyid was cautious about the use of language that might suggest she was more than the wife of dead Muslim patriot.

"Of course, we've had such a plan in place for over a year, and we believe it has been perfected. Unless something goes terribly wrong, our plan is foolproof."

"I am truly blessed to be a part of your plan, sir."

"Ah ... not my plan. My plan would doom it to failure; this is Allah's will and his plan. You, Zayna Binte Sayyid, have been delivered to us by Allah's own hand, a positive sign the plan will work." Bilal dismissed the men and left the room after whispering instructions to Kalid.

"We have a lot of work to do and very little time to do it ... if you'll come with me."

Sayyid followed Kalid back to her quarters; he pulled a chair away from the table but didn't sit down until she had taken a seat. "I will explain," he said as courteously as a man from such a fundamentalist culture was willing to be, his eyes showing traces of compassion. "We will prepare you a passport and media credentials; people are working on those things now. You are correct; security at the airport will be very tight, and you'll be required to pass through several precaution levels before you'll be admitted into the hangar." He paused, watching her eyes for signs of regret, regret that could later turn to reluctance.

Sayyid sensed his search for burgeoning weakness and held her determined stare. "How do I get the explosive vest?"

"Iraqis are now sharing some of the police and battlefield responsibilities, and one of our own is a trusted high-ranking officer." Kalid pulled a photo of the officer out of a folder and slid it across the table. "Take a close look so you'll be able to recognize him."

"Does he know I'm coming?"

"He knows the Al-Jazeera reporter is his contact."

"I'm still puzzled about the bomb … with security so tight."

"The only items you'll be allowed to carry into the hangar is your notepad and a pencil. Once inside all the reporters will be required to stand in one designated location about ten meters away from where he'll make his presentations. You will be required to stand in the designated location until the vice president has exited the hangar. The reporters will also be required to be in their places thirty minutes prior to his arrival." Kalid moved his chair closer to Sayyid, suggesting the plan was to take on an even higher level of secrecy. His dark eyes contrasting against the white turban conveyed an intensity she'd not seen before. "Listen carefully," he said. "The reporters won't be told this, but I understand it to be true. If one of the reporters needs to go—"

"You mean to the toilet?" She interrupted.

Kalid nodded. "Yes … to the toilet. They must be escorted by one of the armed security, and they may only go one at a time. You must enter the designated area, wait ten minutes, then make eye contact with the man in this photo. That won't be hard, because he'll be watching you. Once your eyes meet, hold the look several seconds, and then raise your hand. He will come to you and ask what you need. He will be abrupt; he'll act impatient when you tell him you must go to the toilet." Sayyid listened carefully, she had no idea her mission would include assassinating the vice president of the United States and invited soldiers. The plan was in place and operating at full speed, all in a matter of a few hours, and following through was the only way to thwart it.

Kalid pointed at the photo. "After you have made your request of this man, he will lift the warning tape and escort you to the toilet. Inside he will quickly disassemble his assault rifle from the stock and bind the barrel and trigger housing to your body under the tunic. The barrel will lie here." Kalid pointed to Sayyid's torso, being careful not to make an indecent gesture toward her breasts. "The trigger housing and magazine will be here." Indicating her belly. "Your tunic should hide it as long as you remain standing."

"My ignorance is getting the better of me, sir. I've never shot a weapon before, I wouldn't know the first thing, and wouldn't I draw attention trying to get it out from underneath my clothing?"

"No, no … you will not be asked to shoot him."

Sayyid had already begun to put two and two together, but she couldn't let on, her role required an air of innocent ignorance to be played out until the final act. "I am so sorry, please forgive my constant questioning."

"You have nothing to be sorry for … you are about to be martyred, and I …" He hesitated and looked away. Sayyid sat silently knowing her place was not to ask.

Kalid slowly faced her allowing his usual stern appearance to mellow. "I admire you. I'm nothing but a middleman, an organizer of sorts … never fighting, never giving my life for what I believe in, but you are perfection embodied within Allah's will." His confession spawned an awkward moment. Kalid waited for an approving word from her, but knowing their traditional fundamentalism wouldn't permit such an expression. He quickly gathered his stoic pretense and continued with the instructions. "Zayna. Do you mind if I call you by your first name?"

"No."

"Zayna…you won't be required to shoot the weapon, the parts bound to your body are full of explosives, and you will be given a detonator. When the time comes, you will just press the button, and your magnificent afterlife will commence." His eyes returned to their former intensity. "Allah Akbar, Allah Akbar."

"Allah Akbar," she repeated.

Akil Ibn Bilal rushed into the warehouse conference room ten minutes late for a meeting with his most-trusted revolutionaries. Kalid ordered the men to be seated.

"Is Sayyid on her way yet?" Bilal asked.

Kalid looked at his watch. "Yes, thirty minutes ago."

Bilal smiled, energized that a plan was in place that would rival even the worst assault against the infidels. "Allah will be pleased." He raised his fist, shouting, "Allah Akbar." The noise died momentarily, and Bilal began an emotion-filled tirade against the West, condemning democracies for the spread of lawlessness and sin around the world.

Sayyid's driver reached the outskirts of Shushtar and turned southwest toward Iraq. "I am sorry for the inconvenience," she said quietly from the backseat, "but I must use the facilities. Could you stop there?" Sayyid pointed to a fashionable hotel. The driver pulled under the stone canopy and stopped in the shade. "This will only take a minute…I am so sorry." Her contrite behavior and imminent martyrdom afforded her concessions she would not normally be privileged to. She hurried into the lobby and down the short hall to the public restrooms. Sayyid punched each number—she had memorized off the adhesive tape—cautiously into the cell phone taken from the armory. Sayyid heard a click then a ring, then another, she waited, but there were no further sounds. She wiped the phone clean with a wet paper towel and threw it in a waste container and returned to her waiting driver.

The meeting concluded, and as his lieutenants filed out of the room, Bilal embraced each man, offering victorious words of encouragement. Kalid was standing next to Bilal as the last man received his blessing, a phone rang in the armory, and he reached for his key to unlock the door.

By the time Sayyid returned to the car, the driver was outside the car looking back toward the city. "I am sorry I took so long," she said as she opened the car door.

"Did you hear it?" the driver said.

"No ... hear what?"

"The explosion." He no sooner got the word out when several more explosions scattered debris skyward. Employees and hotel guests rushed out to see a large plume of gray smoke rising from somewhere in the city.

Knowing she shouldn't appear too eager to leave, Sayyid said, "Do you think we should return? People might need our assistance."

"No," he said firmly. "I have my orders; we must be on our way to the border."

She sat down and closed the door.

CHAPTER 47

The CH-60 landed north of the building housing surgical units managed by joint operations medical staff from the army, air force, and navy. A medical team rushed to the helicopter, pushing a gurney arrayed with life-saving equipment. A flurry of organized chaos surrounded Crys Stanton as she was moved efficiently into surgery.

Frank Ellison sat motionless on a narrow bench inside what used to be one of Saddam Hussein's military academies. The building was now being used by coalition forces as a hospital. Margaret Winters paced from the surgery room door to a window and back, the pit of her stomach raw and burning from an acid overload. She walked back to where Ellison sat waiting on word about Stanton. "We've never formally met, Agent Ellison; I'm Margaret Winters." She didn't extend her hand; it was obvious he was in no mood to be social. The blood from the gunshot wound to his shoulder had dried; small pieces of metal fragments embedded in his chin and neck, his right eye swollen shut.

Without looking up, Ellison nodded. Then with some effort, he rolled his left eye up and focused it on Winters, studying the face of the women that most likely saved his and Stanton's life. "Call me Frank."

Winters smiled. "And you can call me Maggie."

A brief pause followed; Ellison forced his eye up again to meet hers. "The hell I can."

"What?"

"My dumb-ass boss would demote me."

"Dumb-ass boss, let's see … would that be Jerry Webster?"

"It would."

"I thought you two were friends?"

"The best, but that doesn't mean he isn't a dumb-ass."

"I guess your feelings arise from the belief he got Crys involved in this mess?"

"Yes, my feelings arise from that belief." His sarcasm overt, emphasized with a roll of his eye.

"You should know Webster was against asking Crys to participate, but when the vice president orders you to do something, it's wise to follow through."

"Oh."

"And if you want to be angry with someone, be angry with me. This whole mess is my concoction."

One of the surgical team members stepped into the hall. "She's fine. Wounds were ugly but superficial, except for the metal frag that nicked her femoral artery. We gave her blood and cleaned her up; she'll be in post-op for an hour or so then to a bed for a few days. Oh yeah …" The woman looked at Ellison. "You Frank?"

He nodded, tears flowing and afraid to open his mouth, afraid he'd bawl like a baby at the news Crys was okay.

"Before we sedated her, she demanded to know where you were and how you were doing. We told her you were fine just to shut her up. Glad to see you're alive; I hate lying to a patient."

"When can we see her?" Winters asked.

"Tomorrow," the woman said. She opened the door to the surgical unit and then stepped back out looking interested in Ellison's appearance as if she'd just noticed his condition. "See door number five down the hall?" the woman said, pointing.

"Yeah."

"Go there now; we'll be with you in fifteen minutes."

"But—"

"But nothing. Now do it," she ordered.

After the woman returned to the surgical room, Winters sat down next to Ellison. "I don't think you've taken a look at yourself. You are a mess, and you need attention. Do what she said. I'll go back to headquarters and see how things are going, then I'll be back."

Ellison stumbled down the hall to room five, and Winters left the building through a heavily guarded side door. The CI chief of station and his security detail pulled into the parking lot just as Winters stepped into the late afternoon sun. She got in next to Martin, and he handed her a bottle of water. "Just debriefed the pilot. He said everything went well, but he didn't know Stanton's condition."

"Doc says she'll be fine, said they'd likely downgrade her from serious to stable condition tomorrow."

The small caravan of armored SUVs sped the short distance to CIA headquarters where Winters and Martin were joined by Owens. "How's Stanton?"

"She'll be okay, so is Frank Ellison."

"Good." The deputy was relieved, as much for his boss as for Stanton and Ellison. He knew better than anyone what a toll it had taken on Winters. "I have some news to pass on," he said.

"Hope it's good news." The CI Director set her empty water bottle down and pointed at Martin's desk. "Anything in there stronger than water?"

"That would be a clear violation of agency policy and the pact we made with the Muslim clerics. Absolutely no alcohol. Don't you remember? You signed the document."

"Oh … of course, sure I remember. Now, do you have anything stronger than water?"

Martin punched an intercom button on his desk phone and ordered three Cokes with ice and lime wedges. After the refreshments were delivered, he dug to the back of the bottom desk drawer and lifted a bottle of Bacardi out and poured some in each glass.

As they slowly nursed their drinks, the deputy explained what he'd just learned. "According to CENTCOM in a message issued this afternoon, the vice president will make a surprise visit to Iraq—"

Before he could finish Winters interrupted, "When?"

"Tomorrow."

"Why?"

Owens smiled. "Ours is not to wonder why, ours is—"

"Blah, blah, blah; okay, what time is he coming?"

"ETA 1030 hours Bag time."

"Itinerary?"

"He will de-plane inside hangar four at BIAP and present combat ribbons to about twenty soldiers and marines. From there he'll tour some former Baghdad insurgent hot spots then return to the green zone. By the way, Director, he knows you are here."

"Yes, I know he knows I'm here, I told him." Winters swirled her drink around the melting ice trying to cool what remained of her Cuba Libre. "I suppose he wants a briefing?" she said more to herself than the others.

"Yes, he does."

"What's the other bit of news?"

"Today at 1400 hours Bag time, signals intelligence reported communication emanating from Tehran that an explosion occurred in Shushtar. We tasked a satellite for photos and confirmed it."

"Details?"

"Iran issued a release to their news outlets claiming the explosion resulted from a natural gas leak."

"What's the real story?" she asked.

"The signature was not that of natural gas, probably gun powder, C-4, something of that nature."

Winters' mind was churning up possible scenarios that would fit with knowledge she already had. She set her empty glass on Martin's desk. "Got a map of that area?"

Martin rolled a four-foot-long map out on the conference table and pointed. "We've always suspected Shushtar was a staging area for insurgents. A prominent citizen there by the name of Bilal, we believe, is the organizer."

Winters looked at her deputy. "Our Natanz asset said Shushtar was where Crisp was headed."

"Crisp is one of the team members?" Martin asked.

"She is." Winters studied the map. "Henry, where is she most likely to emerge on this side of the border?"

"That's impossible to say; there're so many places. Lots of tunnels; just as the military plugs a tunnel, another opens up." Martin hesitated, sliding his bifocals higher on his nose. "She might just wiggle across right there." He pointed to a well-guarded border crossing.

"Wiggle?" Owens asked.

"Wiggle, which means a person wanting to enter Iraq from Iran, will negotiate his or her passage. The Iraqi military began playing an active role in border security about six months ago. Most of these so-called soldiers are nothing more than twenty-year-old, inexperienced, undisciplined, untrained, testosterone-driven knuckleheads. They work hard at trying to enforce border security against men carrying grenade launchers and assault weapons, but that's about it."

"In other words, if an insurgent approached them unarmed and offered money, they'd be allowed to pass through."

"Precisely, unless, of course, US troops happen to be in the area."

"What happens then?" Winters asked.

"The Iraqis tell 'em to come back later."

"Shit."

"My sentiments exactly," said Martin.

Winters paced around the conference table, muttering options. "I don't see any way to identify her route, assuming she is in fact mobile, but from what I know about her, she will be maneuvering in some way toward and through the border. I have confidence in her. Gentlemen, I absolutely hate this."

"What?" Martin said.

"Helplessness, we can't do a damn thing to help Crisp." Winters checked her watch. "I'm going to check on Stanton and then try to get some sleep."

Martin picked up his phone and ordered the director's security detail to stand ready. "What can I do?" Martin asked.

"You two stay on top of the intelligence … anything coming in about Crisp I want to know immediately."

CHAPTER 48

SOUTHWEST OF SHUSHTAR
NEAR THE IRAN, IRAQ BORDER
1615 HOURS, SEPTEMBER 18

The driver stopped. "This is as far as I go."

"How far to the border?" Sayyid asked.

"Over that rise about one kilometer. Tell the border security your car broke down, show them your Al-Jazeera press credentials, and tell them you must get to Baghdad to cover a story."

Two Quonset huts sat side by side along with an array of military vehicles, some with heavy armament protruding from behind fortified shields. A bunker between the huts gave the area an unwelcome appearance, just as it was designed to do. As Sayyid approached, a sentry using a bullhorn ordered her to stop. She knew this to be standard procedure. The man ordered her to raise her tunic neck high and to turn slowly while another studied her shape with binoculars. "Identify yourself."

"I am Sayyid of Oman; I am a journalist with Al-

"Yes, the group is made up of scientists, none of whom have animosity toward the other. They're only interested in the knowledge from a scientific point of view."

"And you trust that?"

"I've no choice. However, I do respect these men, they are not fanatics, and they don't believe the discovery, should there be one, is a sign from God to start killing one another."

"Are you one of the five?"

"No, but I've been asked to be a part of the expedition, and—"

Lee interrupted. "If you're going to ask me to be a part, please don't."

Carlos stood and walked to the window and leaned on the chair railing watching two marshals secure the boat used for patrolling the shoreline. Without turning to face his friend, he said, "Don't ask now or don't ask ever?"

CHAPTER 50

CIA Director Winters spotted Ellison sitting on the floor next to Stanton's room, his bandaged head against the wall. "You look a bit better than you did yesterday."

"Yeah, the docs patched me up, brought me these clothes, and I've had a steak dinner. All that, plus Crys is better. As they say, it doesn't get any better than that." He forced a weak smile.

"How long's it been since you've slept?"

"Hell, Director, I don't even know what day it is."

"Go somewhere and sleep. I'll call my deputy at head-quarters, and he'll arrange for you to get inside. By the way, I called Webster and told him you and Stanton were okay."

"What'd he say?"

"That he wasn't worried."

"That shit." Ellison smiled. "That's his way of admitting he was in a panic. When we partnered, he'd make some stupid remark like that followed quickly with 'paradoxically speaking.'"

"That was apparent," Winters added.

"Meaning?"

"I could hear his voice quiver." Winters looked at her watch. "Can I see her?"

"They kicked me out, said it was time to change dressings. The nurse said it'd be another thirty minutes."

Winters looked at her watch again. She wanted to see Stanton, but Crisp was on her mind. Stanton was safe, Crisp wasn't, and that was all she could think about. She looked through the window to Stanton's room but a temporary curtain blocked her view, just then her phone rang. "Winters, here." Her caller ID indicated the chief of station was on the other end.

"Just got a call from General Dobbs thought you'd be interested."

"And?"

"MPs and Iraqi security discovered a homicide bomber amongst the press entourage at the airport."

"Oh my God. The VP hasn't arrived yet has he?"

"They've re-routed him to another hangar. He's been informed, says he'll conduct the presentation there."

"What about the bomber?"

"They're getting ready to question her now."

"Her? It's a woman?"

"Apparently. Had Al-Jazeera press pass and passport was from Oman."

"Where is she?" Winters asked.

"Here at headquarters, Dobbs thought it best that our interrogators do the questioning … you know."

"Know what?"

"In case we wanted to send her to Egypt." Martin didn't use the word rendition; he knew his boss would pick up on the intimation.

"No, we're not doing anything until I lay eyes on her. I mean it, Henry; no one is to get close to her."

"Sorry, Director, the MPs already are questioning her."

"Stop them. I'll be there in fifteen minutes."

Winters closed her phone and turned to Ellison. "I'll be back as soon as I can, and if anything changes about her condition, call me." She didn't wait for a response. Winters ran out of the hospital and climbed into her armored vehicle. "Back to headquarters, fast." A frenzied exchange of radio chatter followed her order. The first vehicle headed straight for a short flight of steps leading from the former military academy, passed a decorative courtyard fountain to the street. The remaining two vehicles followed, jarring Winters brutally. She grabbed the seat in front of her attempting to steady herself, "Shortcut?" she uttered.

"Yes, ma'am. Cuts two minutes off driving time, plus we're not as likely to get ambushed," the driver shouted.

"Oh. That's good. I suppose an ambush would slow us down," Winters said humorously, but the security detail paid little attention. They had a job to do, and it was routine to choose an alternate route just in case someone had them in his crosshair.

COS Martin met Winters in the lobby and pointed to elevator doors held open by Owens. Martin punched LL2, and the elevator descended. The lowest level of the hotel had originally been parking and building maintenance, but when the CIA took charge, it was converted to offices for interrogators, interrogation rooms, and secure holding cells. Two women watched observation monitors, and a young man listened to mostly silence coming from the isolation rooms. Martin pointed to the man. "He's CIA Mid-East translation expert. Once in a blue-moon, these guys will start talking to themselves just to hear sound, and every so often they'll say something worthwhile."

Martin walked over to the control panel and asked the red-haired thirty-something observation tech to pull camera six up with sound. She complied by pressing two buttons, never taking her eyes off the monitors. Neither woman knew they were in the presence of Director Winters. They had been trained well. Watching monitors for hours at a time could be hypnotic, if not down right boring, leading to little details being missed. Those held in

"Humor me, young man; I really want to know why you'd jeopardize your career."

Sweat trickled down the sides of Skinner's face, but he remained straight as an arrow holding onto what was left of the prestige he worked so hard to attain, "Sir," he said in a command voice. "I thought she was a very attractive woman ... I entertained the idea of asking her out. I was shocked when I saw her lying on the restroom floor with a bomb tied to her chest."

Martin laughed.

"Sir, what do you find humorous?" Skinner asked.

"Hormones ... I find hormones humorous. Sometimes I wish I had 'em back, then there's times I'm glad they're fading." He shook his head still smiling. Martin gave the major a pat on the arm. "Did you learn something in all this?"

"Yes, sir."

"Good. Now then, Major Skinner, here is what my report of this incident will say." Martin went on to explain an order had come down not to interview the suspect, but by the time the order was delivered, its origin was confusing. Being the ranking officer and an interrogation expert, Major Skinner directed everyone but himself to exit the room awaiting clarification of the proper procedure for follow through. Martin could tell Skinner was having difficulty accepting a perspective that would in fact benefit him but wasn't true. "Major Skinner, that is what I'm going to say; you say whatever you think is appropriate. Now go."

"Yes, sir."

Martin went back to control and ordered the video and audio to be shut off in room six; he then joined Winters and the deputy who were with Crisp.

CHAPTER 51

The physical and mental well-being of Limber Crisp and Crys Stanton was Winter's primary concern. Secondly, she wanted to put distance between the women and curious journalists that were quickly gathering clues to the event surrounding Unger's arrival. Winters wasn't worried about what Crisp and Stanton would say if confronted by a scoop-driven reporter, but what those sources who asked for anonymity would tell just to make points with the media. She posted CIA paramilitary at the hospital and blocked visitation from anyone other than one attending physician and one primary nurse on each shift. The need for medical care lessened dramatically for Stanton, but the physician wanted her to have twenty-four hours of undisturbed rest before discharge. COS Martin saw to it personally that Crisp got the same security at CIA headquarters. Before Winters left interrogation room six to attend dinner with the vice president, she informed Martin, Owens, and Crisp she'd be leaving Baghdad with the two women and Frank Ellison at 1800 hours the next evening.

Winters got out of her chair to leave the interrogation room. When she got to the door, she turned and faced Crisp. "I'm truly thankful you're okay. You, Stanton, and Faxhir, God rest his soul, should have a ticker tape parade down Broadway for what you've accomplished." Winters paused, unconsciously shaking her head. "Unfortunately only a few will ever know your sacrifice." She stepped into the hall. "Anyway, you are true heroes...God bless." As Winters passed the control console, she asked the technician to play the last fifteen minutes of video and audio from room six. The tech now knew who Winters was but still didn't take her eyes off the monitors or stand out of respect. "You ordered no video or audio, ma'am."

"Exactly, now run the last fifteen minutes of audio and video in room six."

The tech flipped two switches underneath the number six stenciled on the console. Winters watched five minutes of dead air then instructed the tech to shut it off, "Thank you."

"No problem, ma'am."

At five thirty, Winters joined Owens in the waiting Humvee. She was wearing the required flak jacket; he handed her a helmet. Winters turned to Owens. "I bet you're getting a real kick out of seeing me smash delicately coiffed hair a few minutes before dinner with the VP, aren't you?"

"No comment."

Martin and a team of armed men and two women escorted Limber Crisp to her room where she would be residing for the next full day. The windows had been fortified; it would require a direct hit from a very powerful projectile to penetrate the metal reinforcement. The interior, however, was homey. Lamps, end tables, two large couches and several chairs all covered in a fabric of Asian design arranged tastefully around a large coffee table bearing a hand-carved palm tree. The bedroom was through a door on the right and a small

kitchen through a door on the opposite side of the room. The chief
of station handed Crisp several color photos of clothes and introduced her to a woman that had just joined them. "Ms. Crisp, this
is Angela Morgan." The women shook hands. "Mrs. Morgan has
been with the CIA a long time, and for the past ten years she's been
in charge of wardrobe." Martin noticed Crisp's double take. "Yes,
even the CIA has a wardrobe department." He pointed at the photos. "Look through 'em, pick a few things out, and Mrs. Morgan
will have them ready to go in the morning. In the meantime, you
have time to freshen up before dinner is brought in."

"Thank you, Mr. Martin. I'm looking forward to a good meal
and a soft bed." Crisp's smile was nearly free of the vestiges of
tension.

Martin's next stop was on the same floor four doors down from
Crisp. He knocked softly. He could tell from a flickering shadow
that the occupant was checking him out through the peephole. The
door opened quickly, and Ellison, dressed in athletic shorts and a t-
shirt boasting the official emblem of the CIA invited the COS in.

"I see you've decided to come over to the dark side," Martin
said.

"Meaning?"

"The t-shirt, I assume you're making the transition from G-
man to spook." He didn't know Ellison or his present state of mind;
Martin added a wink, hoping the crack hadn't offended the agent.

"Oh. Yeah, a woman stopped by earlier and brought me some
stuff to wear."

"That would have been Mrs. Morgan, great lady, been with the
agency a long time."

"Yeah, now that you mention it, Morgan was her name. She
seemed nice, helpful."

"Have you had a chance to rest?"

"Couple of hours. Right now I'm starved, waiting on room
service."

"This isn't the Waldorf, but it's better than HoJo. I think you'll
be pleasantly surprised."

"Doesn't matter. Hell, I'd eat the north end of a southbound skunk right now."

"Well, anyway, Agent Ellison, I just wanted to stop by and see how you were doing. I'm sure your meal will arrive soon; I'll let you eat in peace." Martin turned toward the door. "I understand you'll be flying back to the states with Winters and the two team members. Guess she wants some time to debrief. Her plane leaves at—"

"Nope, I've made other arrangements."

Martin turned back quickly. "I don't think you have that option. As I said, she wants some quality time to debrief all of you."

Ellison wasn't about to tell anyone, no matter how important they were, that he'd decided the best thing for him and Stanton was to make a clean split. He wasn't sure about her, but he was dead certain about his own feelings, and it wouldn't take much for him to try and disrupt the relationship she had going with the cowboy back in Oklahoma. No one understood what was going on in his heart; Ellison didn't expect understanding, but he did expect to handle the dilemma his own way and spending sixteen hours on board a plane with Stanton would only complicate matters. "Sorry, Mr. Martin, I've made my decision."

"She is the director of Central Intelligence, you know."

Ellison opened the door for Martin to leave, both men looking for something in the other's eyes that would bridge the gap. "And, Mr. Martin, I'm just an old fart on my way out."

Martin smiled. "I'll pass that along."

Special Agent Frank Ellison left the Baghdad CIA headquarters at eleven p.m. for BIAP and was on board a C-130 headed for Germany at midnight. He hadn't mentioned his departure time to Martin on purpose. Ellison didn't always trust the FBI, his own agency, but he trusted the CIA even less. He imagined a scenario where CI operations people would swoop in and put him bodily on Winters' plane. He knew he'd have to talk to her soon but not in the presence of Crys Stanton.

CHAPTER 52

Carlos Ramirez stood on the second-floor deck, his armed
security detail on either side watching Lee Bethel and
Agent Booker disappear down the narrow road.

"To the airport?" Booker asked.

"To the airport. I'm ready to go home." Bethel couldn't
help thinking about Ramirez's not-so-veiled offer. Another
once-in-a-lifetime chance staring him in the face, but logic
prevailed, at least for the moment.

———

Vice President William Unger completed the presentation
of combat medals to the soldiers and marines, concluding
the event with a short patriotic speech about the high cost
of freedom. He shook hands with all the recipients and
chatted informally with them. A *Stars and Stripes* photog-
rapher by the name of Erin Butler took individual photographs, and her assistant typed names and addresses into
a laptop so they could be sent to hometown newspapers.

Reporters, still unaware of the homicide bomber, shouted questions to Unger which he ignored. The vice president motioned for an aide and whispered, "Change the itinerary. I want to talk to Margaret Winters next." His tone left no room for uncertainty.

In less than an hour, Unger's motorcade jammed the entrance to CIA headquarters. MPs working with the Secret Service established a perimeter of military vehicles around the building. The vice president made his way through the arched main door and straight to the elevator and down to the lowest level. He and his group of assistants and Secret Service agents were granted entry into the interrogation and isolation unit. A brigadier general met them as they passed through the bulletproof glass door. Another officer called all military personnel to attention, and the general saluted. The only people that did not respond were those watching the monitors. Their orders were clear: eyes on the monitors at all times.

"General Walker, it's been three or four years," Unger said extending his hand toward Walker.

"It has, Mr. Vice President."

The two old friends exchanged pleasantries. Unger moved a step closer. "Are you having dinner with us tonight?"

"If you're inviting me, then yes."

"Consider yourself invited. It'll be a small gathering: you, me, Gen Dobbs, Margaret Winters, her deputy, maybe a few others."

"Yes, sir, I'll be there."

"Okay, now I need to find Winters. She's here, right?"

"Yes, sir, room six interrogating the bomber." Just then Major Skinner came from the hall into the control center. Walker saw the major and motioned. "Major Skinner, I want you to meet the Vice President of the United States." Skinner saluted and then shook Unger's outstretched hand. Walker slapped Skinner on the shoulder. "Major Skinner and his men are the ones who prevented the bomber attack."

Skinner felt his throat swelling, a crimson flush, noticeable even under his dark skin, inciting sweat glands into action. General Walker took control of his command post at the interrogation and isolation unit just minutes before Unger arrived, and there was no way for him to know circumstances had changed considerably. Skinner was embarrassed. He couldn't pull the general away and give him the new information, which would only add the appearance of incompetence. The major swallowed hard and, after a congratulatory handshake from Unger, said, "Mr. Vice President, General Walker." Skinner made eye contact with each of his superiors. "There has been a change to the information given earlier."

Both men turned toward Skinner, Walker spoke first, "And when did this new information come about?" The general's proud expression because of the quick and decisive action of his men quickly faded.

"Just this minute."

"Explain, Major."

"Preliminary information from the suspect would appear to clear her—"

"Her? This homicide bomber is a woman?" Unger's eyes flitting back and forth at the men.

"She is a woman, but—"

"But what?" Walker said louder than he intended. Most of the eyes in the control center looked at the small huddle of men surrounding Skinner.

"It appears that she actually saved Mr. Unger...I mean, the vice president." Skinner's awkwardness was barely perceptible to those around him, but to the major it seemed extreme. He didn't know whether to proceed with what he'd just learned or wait for questions. Skinner was now the center of attention, and rather than try to explain a complicated situation, Skinner tossed the ball to Winters' side of the court.

"The director of the CIA has taken over the interrogation; she asked me to leave."

The vice president looked at Walker. "Meet us at Dobbs's pri-

the fifteenth up to an including the meeting with the vice president on the evening of the twenty-third. "By early in the morning of the twenty-fourth, the vice president and the other attendees had unofficially sanctioned the operation Director Winters proposed." Owens noticed that Sylvia was typing everything he said. "Sylvia, uh, delete the part about the operation being unofficially sanctioned, please."

She nodded without looking up.

Crisp finished jotting a note and said, "Would you be clearer on what you mean by that?"

"Unofficial sanction?"

"Yes," Crisp pressed.

"Federal agencies, all of them, but especially the CIA, have to give the president wiggle room—" Owens stopped in mid-sentence. "You're shaking your head?"

"Sorry, I understand. We moved so quickly from the real world to the political one I just got lost."

Owens knew Crisp wasn't lost, she'd made the remark facetiously and felt obliged to call her on it, yet he agreed. "Sylvia—"

"I've already deleted her comment."

"Thank you."

By midnight the timeline matrix was completed. Dates and times of events covered the board. Owens laid the marker down for the first time that evening. "Okay, let's get some sleep. We'll do breakfast at 0700 and get back to work. I'd like to have the outline completed by this time tomorrow." He turned toward the matrix again. "Check that, we *will* have the outline completed tomorrow."

They left the room exhausted, the adrenaline rush driven hard by the intensity of the past few days had dwindled to a trickle, and sleep was demanding its due. The only other thought Stanton entertained was of Robert Gray; she hadn't talked to him in over a month. The exhaustion she felt served only to emphasize her loneliness for him. She reached for her cell phone and punched in his number, but when she got to the last digit, she shut the phone and cried; her sequester had not yet been lifted.

CHAPTER 54

Newly appointed FBI Director Jerry Webster unpacked the last box of books and was arranging them on shelves when his assistant, Ms. Ferguson, opened the door. "Director Webster, Special Agent Frank Ellison is here."

"Show him in."

The good friends wasted little time complimenting each other on recent actions. Webster finally achieved his goal as director, and Ellison found purpose in helping Stanton out when she needed it the most.

Webster ordered coffee, circled the desk, and sat down in a leather wingback opposite Ellison. "I've heard all about your motor tour through the Middle East countryside."

"Yeah, not my favorite vacation, but, you know, Jerry, maybe the best thing I ever did."

"'Cause you were able to get Crys out, right?"

Ellison nodded. "The most significant accomplishment in my life. You may not believe this, but I'm glad you gave me the opportunity."

"Frankly, I thought you'd be angry—"

"Angry," Ellison interrupted. "Oh yeah, I was angry at first, but Winters told me she was the one who wanted Crys contacted. That you tried to discourage her."

"I tried, but you know Crys better than me; she wouldn't listen. As soon as she heard the words 'of national importance,' she was in."

"Yeah, that's Crys. I hope for the rancher's sake she never hears 'em again." Ellison's voice was quiet, as if talking only to himself. Webster understood why.

"Well, aside from your head looking a lot like ground hamburger, how are you feeling?"

"Good, never better, and on top of that, I'm only six months away from mandatory retirement."

"But, Frank, you surely don't want to retire?" Webster leaned forward to make his point. "As director, I can waive the age requirement and keep you on payroll another five years."

"You're joking. Why in the world would I want to hang around?"

"'Cause the agency needs you. Hell, Frank, I need you. You know the field better than anyone. I need someone with your knowledge to help me stay in touch with the folks doing the job."

"Sorry, Jerry, I'm gonna fish. As a matter of fact, I'm headed to HR now to start the paperwork."

"Six months gives me time to talk you into staying; I'll throw a wrench into the works one way or another." Webster smiled and extended his hand. "You're the best, Frank."

Ellison stood after shaking his boss's hand. "You too, Jerry. The agency couldn't have picked a better man for the job. Now, where in the hell is HR?"

Webster shrugged. "Beats me. Remember, I'm new around here."

Agent Ellison finished the ream of retirement papers required to start the process and grabbed a sandwich in the cafeteria before heading to the parking garage. His orders were to meet Winters at Quantico and review the portion of the report involving his participation from the time he left Damascus until he boarded the C-130 in Baghdad for Ramstein. He was intentionally dragging his feet, not wanting to show up while Crys was still there. Frank just couldn't trust himself, fearing in a weak moment—and there were many—he'd try to convince Crys to come back to him.

It was nearly one p.m. when Ellison cleared the heavy DC.traffic on I-95 crossing south into Virginia. He drove as slow as the traffic would allow that time of day, and as he passed the sign indicating Quantico was just five miles ahead; he felt his heart race. Ellison made his way through the marine base to the secure unit where Owens and the women were converting raw data into finished intelligence. He pulled into a spot in the empty parking lot and got out. He'd made up his mind about what to do when he saw Crys. His decision might be the wrong one, but regardless, it was made.

CHAPTER 55

Margaret Winters stretched her arms above her head, trying to get feeling back in her hands. She rolled to her stomach, forcing her body closer to the edge of the bed, and
stared in murky disbelief at the red numerals—it was six
a.m. Her mind raced to clear the sleep-induced stupor and
put events of the past few days in perspective. She pressed
a button on her secure phone, and a male voice answered,
"Yes, ma'am."

"I'll be ready in forty-five minutes. Confirm."

"Forty-five. Yes, ma'am."

The director's security detail was on notice. The ten-
person unit checked their weapons and helped each other
tighten gear belts and fasten Velcro straps on flak jackets.
The drivers re-checked fuel gages, coolant, and oil levels
and struck each of the heavy reinforced tires for bounce. A
routine the security detail practiced religiously ten minutes
before each trip. In the beginning, Winters thought the
three-vehicle transportation team a bit extreme, but it was

policy, and after only a few months as director of the most secretive agency in the world, she realized why. Not only did the director attract the standard gathering of political paparazzi but also a range of kooks, some with genuine mental illnesses and some harboring a need to play spook—the wannabes. The heavily armed and well-trained detail dealt mostly with the kook category but were prepared—twenty-four hours a day—for an all-out attack on the director.

Winters slid in next to Stimmon who was on the phone and pecking on the laptop keyboard at the same time. She buckled in, and the driver gave the go order to the lead vehicle. Stimmon closed her phone. "Good morning, Director." Before Winters could return the greeting, Stimmon interjected, "Change in plans."

"What now?"

"Breakfast with the VP in thirty minutes, his office."

"Reason?"

"None given."

"Okay, Jonni, call Owens, tell him I'll be there sometime today, just not this morning." She gazed out the shaded window at the Washington Monument half-hidden by the morning fog. The window tint and heavy mist cast a colorless pall over the shrine-covered landscape. The usual emerging vibrant fall tapestry of red and gold somehow consumed by gray, a depressing sight for Winters. A fitting metaphor, she thought, for the way her life seemed to be going.

Stimmon called Owens and relayed the message. While continuing to talk, she typed out two sentences and swiveled the screen so Winters could see.

> From Owens: Sylvia's a miracle wkr. Draft will be
> ready by 1600.

Winters gave Stimmon thumbs-up, and her assistant relayed the message.

The director's detail weaved through early morning traffic, periodically the lead driver would turn the SUV's grill-mounted strobe array on to encourage slow drivers to move right. Within twenty minutes, they drove into the vice president's private parking area next to an elevator door. Stimmon pressed the button and entered the elevator ahead of Winters.

"Good morning, Maggie." Unger was standing in the doorway as the two women entered the suite of offices. He pointed to an uninhabited cubicle. "Jonni, you can set up in there for the time being. This shouldn't take long. Oh, help yourself to coffee." He motioned for Winters to follow.

"Door shut?" she asked.

"Yes, please." Without looking at the conference table, he waved his hand in that direction. "Fill a plate and join me." Unger sat down behind his desk and bit into a burned piece of bacon. "Sorry. Got a busy day; had to start without you."

Winters surveyed the fare, which was abundant, and chose toast and coffee.

Unger leaned forward looking at her plate. "That's all?"

"Yes, thanks. In my state of mind, greasy bacon and scrambled eggs wouldn't stay down. Toast is fine."

"So, Maggie, as we say back on the ranch, wired tight and wrapped loose," he said breaking well-done bacon in half and stuffing it between biscuit halves.

"I'd say so."

"Then what I'm going to tell you might even make you hurl toast."

Winters leaned back in the chair and closed her eyes. "What's going on now?"

"Just as we predicted, it was inevitable in an election year, House Committee on Intel wants to see you Wednesday bright and early."

"How early?"

"Nine, you'll be first up, but if I were you, I'd plan on all-day."

"No doubt, no doubt." Winters took a bite of toast, contemplating her next move. Finally she looked at Unger. "You know we have enough trouble with our enemies; why in the world do we have to put up with bastards like Paul and Murphy?"

Her question was rhetorical, Unger knew that, and frankly he'd wondered the same thing. "Maggie, you're the director of Central Intelligence, can't you just make them disappear?"

Winters smiled. "I wish."

"One other thing, Maggie."

"Oh?"

"Murphy is energized by the prospect of his man becoming president, and in keeping with his party's philosophy, he is advocating more transparency regarding national security issues."

"You mean allowing journalists to listen in?"

"Yes."

"That can be a two-edged sword," Winters mumbled finishing her toast. "Bill, remember our conversation the other evening in Bag?"

"Verbatim."

"I think I have a plan."

"You think? What do you mean you think?"

"No, I do have a plan. That's if I've anticipated Murphy's next move accurately."

Unger refilled his plate and freshened his coffee. He held the pot up, and Winters nodded. "I'm listening," he said, trying not to spill the hot liquid as he poured.

"Let's let him sink his own ship; maybe Mr. Paul will go down too." Winters went on to explain her plan. The mission, according to what she'd heard aboard the plane, revealed precisely the kind of intelligence lacking when the US and coalition forces decided to remove Hussein. Winters planned, organized, and oversaw the mission out of her office because the original intelligence—concerning WMD—gathered by Doug Paul had been inaccurate. She'd taken responsibility for the inaccuracies once, but swore it wouldn't happen again. Although Paul knew some things about Operation Moriah Ruse, neither he nor his following were aware of the team's insertion and reconnaissance efforts in Iran. The ruse had worked in more ways than one, and if the committee pushed too far, Murphy's reputation would be damaged.

Unger listened thoughtfully, rubbing his chin and rocking in his cowhide-covered executive chair. "Maggie, are you sure your team has accurate intelligence?"

"I haven't seen the official report yet, but from what they told me, I'd give it a 99.9 percent on my confidence scale."

"I guess your answer, then, is yes."

"Yes, it is."

Twenty minutes later, Winters headed south to Quantico. As her detail pulled into the parking lot, she spotted Ellison on the sidewalk near the building where Owens and the team were preparing the report. "Honk," she ordered. Ellison heard the short blast from the SUV horn and stopped. He watched the three vehicles park one behind the other parallel to the curb and facing the street. Two armed security escorted Winters to where Ellison was standing and then took up observation positions on either side of the director and the agent. Winters presented a friendly appearance, even a warm smile, which Ellison found oddly attractive. He'd been so preoccupied with Stanton and his part of the mission, he hadn't taken a close look at her. She was younger, maybe ten years, was his guess. Winters acted happy to see him, which he thought strange given the fact he'd refused to fly back to the U.S. with her. Ellison figured Winters would be upset, but her smile said otherwise. "You look a lot better than you did a few days ago. How are you feeling?" she said.

Ellison managed a nod. "Okay."

"You joining the group?"

"That's it," he said, puzzled over what appeared to be real concern for his welfare.

"Let's go in before we draw attention."

Ellison followed, thinking what he'd say when face to face with Stanton. He was dreading every step that brought him closer to a moment and a conversation that would change his life forever. Winters knocked on the door to the debriefing room, and Owens opened it. "Come in," the deputy said with an assurance in his voice Winters took as a good sign.

"Tom, did you and Frank meet when we were in Bag?"

"No, but I've certainly heard a lot about him."

The two shook hands, but Ellison's mind wasn't on the introduction. He glanced quickly around the room. "Stanton, where is she?"

"She finished dictating her contribution, and I cut her loose."

"Cut her loose?"

"She'd been through enough, Agent Ellison, as you well know. We arranged a flight for her back home, and she left about fifteen minutes ago." Owens could tell that wasn't what Ellison wanted to hear. The agent stood with a blank look, staring at an empty chair next to Crisp.

Winters touched his elbow. "Are you all right? You've lost your color, Frank."

"Yes, yes, I'm fine. I just wanted to see how she was." Ellison inhaled deeply, forcing a smile Winters recognized as artificial.

Two hours later, with Ellison's part of the story nicely blended into the document, Sylvia pressed print times four. The copier printed out a document for each person in the room. Every page embossed with a heavy notation signifying its classified nature. Each person read the twenty-eight page mission draft in awe of Sylvia's talent for conceptualizing the drama. It was a government report all right, free of embellishments that read like a *New York Times* best seller. After some minor tweaks, Winters looked first at Crisp. "Accurate?" she asked.

"My part, according to my recollection, is accurate."

Winters turned to Ellison, who had recovered somewhat from his earlier slump, "Accurate?"

"Yup."

Sylvia took Winters' copy and placed it into a metal case along with a CD, locked it, and handed it to the director. She gathered the other three copies and dropped each one in a shredder and bagged the contents in a thick plastic container marked with the word *destroy*. She signed an electronic device attached to the container and handed it to Owens. The chain-of-destruction document was activated and would be traced electronically all the way to the incinerator. She then placed the hard drive from her laptop in another plastic container marked the same way. It would also be incinerated.

Winters leaned forward in her chair resting her elbows on her knees, both hands massaging her scalp. Ellison watched her run her fingers through her short dark hair, marveling that every strand fell back into place. The bright overhead light exposed freckles stretching from cheek to cheek across the bridge of her nose.

"Operation Moriah Ruse is officially over." Winters crossed her legs and sighed. "But, as you all know, this document, even after I've prepared it for committee consumption, will set events in motion, both good and bad, and no one will be able to predict the outcome. Whatever happens post OMR is anyone's guess." She paused, gathering her thoughts. Winters pointed at Crisp. "You, Stanton, and Ellison deserve an award and the thanks of a grateful nation, but sadly, you'll get neither. All you will receive for your bravery and incredibly hard work is prison time if you ever mention anything about OMR. I hate to look you two in the eye and say that—I hate it—but you know it has to be said."

Ellison and Crisp nodded; they'd heard the spiel before.

Winters stood, and in a gesture characteristic of the female gender took Ellison's hand and Crisp's and added, "However, you have my everlasting gratitude. And now, you're free to go."

Ellison left the building feeling somehow revitalized, and as he cut across the well-manicured lawn toward his car, he heard Winters call his name. "You forget something, Director?"

"What are you going to do?"

Ellison thought about her question as she approached. "Nurse-maid a wet-behind-the-ears rookie for a few months and then fish." He emphasized fishing with a voice nuance she knew sealed the deal.

"No, I meant now."

"Right now?"

"Right now."

"Eat, I guess. Why?" An awkward tingle originating from somewhere in his chest and lodging firmly in his throat made him blush.

"Frank, I make the best, heart-clogging nachos you've ever tasted. You want to share a plate?"

"At your house?"

"At my house."

"Tonight?"

"Yes."

"Ah, hmm, I don't—"

"You're blushing, Agent Ellison; you're red as a beet."

"I am?"

"Yes, now stop it. Here's my address. It's about an hour from here. Pick up some beer. If we get moving, we can catch the second half of the Redskin and Dallas game." She handed him her card with home address and private phone number scrawled across the back. Winters didn't wait for an answer, by the time he'd read the address, she was climbing into the backseat of her SUV.

CHAPTER 56

MARGARET WINTERS' HOME
CLASSIFIED LOCATION
2015 HOURS, SEPTEMBER 22

Sometime later, Ellison located Winters' home and encountered her first level of security. A young man dressed in a dark suit minus a tie exited a vehicle sitting just on the other side of the small barricade blocking entrance to a well-concealed home. Ellison badged the guard, and he pulled the reflective white and bright orange barricade away just far enough for him to pass through. Although he was expected, it took Ellison another ten minutes to reach the front door of Winters' modest ranch-style house. He rang the bell and within seconds the door opened wide. Winters, still dressed in her pantsuit, smiled and invited him in, and as he walked by her into the foyer, she remarked, "My, my, Frank, you are still blushing."

He didn't have to be told, he could feel it, especially the wetness soaking through his undershirt and likely staining the under arms of his white dress shirt.

"I'll take your jacket." She reached for the lapel of the tan blazer, but he pulled away. "I'll just keep it on for a while." He didn't dare take it off until he had a chance to inspect the damage privately. Ellison handed her a six-pack of Bud Light but could tell right away Winters disapproved of his selection. "What?" he said, following her into a large combination kitchen and TV room.

"Men and their Bud. I'm curious." She opened the refrigerator and set the beer on the lowest shelf.

"About?"

"Does Bud really taste that good, or is it the buxom blonde in short shorts that sells the beer?"

Ellison didn't say anything; he knew the answer had very little to do with taste. His face flushed, and he continued to perspire. He looked over toward the large screen obviously trying to change the subject. "Whose winning?"

"Washington's ahead by a field goal. Want a beer?"

He turned away from the game and watched her layer shredded cheese and jalapeños over a concoction of Tostitos and cooked hamburger meat. "I can get it." Ellison retrieved two bottles while Winters slid the tray into the oven to warm. The mental picture left him doubting his own eyes. Watching the most powerful woman in federal government fixing nachos she was going to share privately with him was an image that required, as he'd heard in training sessions, the suspension of reality.

Neither said much during the game. It was easy to see Winters was a football fan. She was ecstatic when Washington scored and criticized the coach when a play faltered. Winters put aside the refined and assertive dignity she was known for that evening in favor of just being herself. She'd dropped the persona of her office and the arcane nature of her profession easily. Ellison admired that in her, wishing he knew her secret. The transformation from a well-trained government investigator to a regular citizen had always been difficult for him and probably the crux of his failed relationships. He watched Crayton catch a pass in the midst of three Redskin defenders and score to win the game. Winters was livid. "I know Joe Gibbs." She pointed in a northerly direction. "He just lives about a mile from here. He's a great coach, but if you want my opinion, he's a has-been. We need new blood, new enthusiasm, a new game plan."

"Sounds like you're really serious about this stuff."

Winters laughed. "Yeah, guess I am. With the world on the brink of disaster twenty-four-seven, this is my sanctuary. I get wrapped up in it, and for a few hours I don't think about genocide in Darfur or the craziness on Capitol Hill. It's fun, Frank—it's an escape."

"Yeah, I hear that."

The late news came on, and Winters shut the TV off. The nervousness Ellison was finally able to overcome began to edge its way back bringing images of possibilities with it. He didn't know whether she wanted to just talk or if she was about to make a pass. Ellison quickly discounted the latter after a quick inventory of why that thought was silly. He'd hidden his balding scalp with a burr cut; his once thirty-four-inch waist and forty-four-inch chest were working hard at trading places. He excused himself to relieve the fluid buildup and check his underarms. The wetness was returning. When Ellison got back to the TV room, he started picking up plates and empty beer bottles. "I'll help you clean up."

"Put that down, Frank. You won't believe it, but the agency provides a housekeeper, probably the only housekeeper in the world with a top-secret security clearance."

Ellison sat the dishes back down but remained standing. "It's late; I'd better be going."

"Yeah, it's past my bedtime too, but tell me, please, before you leave, about your relationship with Crys Stanton."

Ellison was relieved in a way, but at the same time didn't feel it was anyone's business. "Why?"

"I know you were engaged at one time, and obviously, by your actions the last few days, you'd give your life to save her." She paused and downed the last of her beer. Ellison didn't say anything during the lull. He knew she was still crafting a question; what he did not know was why.

"When I told you earlier that she'd gone home, you looked devastated, not just disappointed you'd missed her, but down and dirty devastated." They stared at each other a long moment, he made no attempt to respond. "I'm just curious; why?"

Ellison realized an explanation needed to be made, not because it was a part of a clandestine mission but because it was personally important to him, and Winters had obviously sensed his dilemma. "I suppose what you saw was a complex collection of feelings that were at war. I wanted to be with her. I still love her, I think. Letting her get away was the dumbest thing I ever did." Ellison walked to the refrigerator and opened the door. "Two left. Want one?"

"Sure."

He twisted the cap off and handed one to Winters as he returned to his seat. He placed his bottle carefully on a coaster and sat back. "In Iran, during the heat of escape, I was prepared to rekindle the relationship—"

Winters gently interrupted. "Even knowing she was engaged?"

"Oh hell yeah. I even imagined going to Oklahoma and kicking his butt just to prove I was the better man."

Winters laughed quietly. "I'm sure that would've impressed Crys."

"Big time." He shook his head and smiled at the absurdity. "During her stay in the hospital, I came to my senses and realized what a mistake that would have been. That's why I flew home alone. I didn't want to spend hours aboard your plane with Crys. I wanted a clean break. And then." He took a deep breath and looked at Winters.

"And then you changed your mind again, right?"

He turned his eyes from her to the blank TV screen and took a long drink and nodded. "Webster said you wanted me to join the team for a final debriefing at Quantico. That's when I decided to ask her to stay here, with me, and not go home to the cowboy."

"And when I told you she was gone all the emotion came crashing in."

"Exactly." He finished the beer, staring at the TV.

"So, Frank, how are you feeling now?"

"You know, Maggie, I was agency ordered into therapy once for killing a man, a righteous kill, mind you." He tried sucking what was left out of the empty bottle. "And this is sounding a lot like that therapy."

"Well, how are you feeling?"

"Actually I feel pretty good. Guess I can chalk one up to fate. No telling how badly I would have screwed up her life if she'd been there when I arrived." He still wasn't convinced the bottle was empty and took one more pull. He turned to Winters. "Hey, it's empty and time I should be going."

"So it's back to the agency for a short and then on to the lake."

"That's it, Maggie."

They both stood, and she walked him to the door.

"Thanks for the nachos and *therapy*." He turned and took the two shallow steps to the curved stone walkway.

"Hey, Frank."

He turned back.

"Thanks for the beer and … the best evening I've had in a very long time."

Ellison waved and followed the walk to his car.

CHAPTER 57

EARLIER THAT SAME DAY, SEPTEMBER 22

Jonni Stimmon finally found a routine air force flight from Andrews to Vance. The crew chief said the supply flight would leave at 1700 hours, and there were two available seats. She knew her boss would be tied up at the debriefing until early evening and wouldn't need her transportation. With Winters' approval, she directed a driver to take Stanton to Hangar Ten at Andrews.

Stanton, dressed in the loose-fitting clothes she'd worn the day she arrived at Quantico a month earlier, tossed her two bags in the SUV and waved to Owens. She was grateful to be released, at least temporarily, from the mission. All she could think about was getting back to Robert and repairing damage the separation may have caused. Winters had cautioned her about OMR. She had to stick with the original story, and to do that she'd have to work in an explanation of her injuries and rather severe weight loss.

As the SUV exited the FBI training center, Stanton saw Frank Ellison drive in. "Stop," she shouted.

"Ma'am, if we get caught in traffic, we won't catch your plane," the driver said, pulling the vehicle to the curb.

Stanton watched Ellison's car heading to where Owens was waiting to debrief him, where she'd been just minutes before. She was sorry they'd missed each other; it was her plan to say a proper good-bye to the man who'd saved her life. A familiar tug rose somewhere in her chest, a feeling she hadn't had since they'd met twenty years ago, a feeling she hadn't experienced again, not even with Robert.

"Ma'am?"

His car turned onto a tree-lined side street and disappeared. Stanton dug a bandana out of one of her bags and dabbed at her tearing eyes. "Ma'am, what do you—"

"Andrews." The word came slowly.

───────────────

"You Stanton?" the crew chief yelled over the noise as she stepped out of the SUV. She nodded.

"Follow me." The sergeant led her through a maze of supplies being loaded on a C-130 to an office. "You can stay here until we're ready."

"How long?"

"Forty-five minutes."

"Flight time?"

"We'll be fighting head winds, count on four hours." Before she could ask another question he put his ear protection on and was out the door yelling instructions to several young airmen. Stanton put her bags on the floor and looked around the office. The only other inhabitant was a senior airman monitoring radar displayed on a large LCD monitor and talking with air traffic control. He took his headset off, swiveled around in his chair, and faced her. She smiled; he smiled. "I gotta go," he said breaking for the door marked "men/women." Stanton could see there was no lock on the door; the absence of privacy reminded her of the open lavatory on level three.

The airman came out a minute later obviously relieved. He smiled again and returned to his chair.

"May I use a phone to make a long distance call?"

He pointed to a multifunction phone. "Press five-five and wait for the beep, then nine, wait for the tone, then your number."

"Thanks."

The airman didn't hear her; he was already involved in a crucial conversation with the C-130 pilot and the controller.

Stanton hesitated a long while, rehearsing the first greeting since her abrupt departure. She thought about not calling, but that wouldn't be fair to Robert, for her to just show up without giving him an opportunity to sort through his feelings and prepare for her return. Stanton dialed his number, when she heard the answering machine she hung up. He was probably having dinner with his folks, she thought, but she didn't want to call there and take a chance Fred or Helen would answer. They too would have questions and she wasn't ready for that. Time alone with Robert first was the most important thing. Everything else would fall into place, one way or the other, depending entirely on the outcome of their reunion.

Stanton thought about calling his cell phone, but his number was on speed dial and her phone battery was dead. She couldn't remember his number, the only time she'd ever seen it was the day she entered it into her cell phone log. The crew chief hurried through the door just then headed for the restroom, and as he passed Stanton he gave thumbs-up and said, "We're leaving." She picked up the desk phone again and called Robert's home number and waited for the machine to pick up. "Honey, I'm leaving now, should be at your place between midnight and two, but don't hold me to that, we have strong headwinds. Don't try my cell; the battery is dead and no way to charge it. I-I-I've missed you." She stumbled over the right words, her plan was to say she loved him, but something held her back.

Six hours later, Stanton picked up state highway thirty-four out of Woodward headed north; another twenty minutes and she would be there, her mind considering the possible conflicts facing her. She turned off the state highway onto the dirt road, and as she crested a hill, Stanton saw Robert's house, always dark at that hour except for the security light, but not tonight. The front porch light was on, so was the back porch light. She could see lights in the kitchen and front room, even the garage light was on. Stanton slowed her truck so she could take in the sight. She hadn't seen Robert yet, but she knew this was his way of showing his excitement. The welcome was obvious.

By dawn the two were exhausted, six hours had evaporated like a summer shower in the Sahara. Stanton had explained away her bruised nose and the visible cuts and abrasions as the result of a fender bender where she had forgotten to buckle her seatbelt. She hated lying, but knew it was necessary, and thankfully, Robert didn't probe. Trying to keep the dialogue focused on the fact she was back safe and sound without getting into details was difficult only in the sense that every word out of her mouth was untrue and would remain so for the rest of their lives. Robert was like a giddy adolescent after his first kiss. He talked about all that had happened during her absence, including ideas about a honeymoon. After breakfast they went into the living room and the comfort of a new couch to continue the conversation. Robert called his dad and reported in with a story about needing to buy tractor parts. He said not to expect him around until late afternoon. Robert hung the phone up and turned to Crys, and they embraced. He kissed her, being careful not to aggravate her injuries. "You're even beautiful with yellow and purple eyes." They leaned back against the cool softness of the leather couch, and with their arms wrapped tightly around each other fell asleep.

Buffalo, Oklahoma, was a small town in a sparsely populated county made up of wheat farms and cattle ranches. The inhabitants said there were two kinds of weather in Harper County—hot and windy, then there was cold and windy. Both weather patterns were for the most part dry. Being a small town had its advantages, far more, as a matter of fact, than disadvantages, but the speed in which information got around was one of the big negatives. Stanton knew that in the month of her absence everyone would have heard that she was in New York, hidden by US Marshals, testifying against terrorist, just enough information to start the gossip mill churning. She also knew word of her return would spread quickly, and there were four people she wanted face time with before the rest of the town found out. Stanton felt she owed Robert's parents the first visit then her chief deputy and Maude Bingham.

Robert called his mother. "What's for dinner?"

"You coming over?"

"Thought I would; that's if you're fix'n something good." He laughed.

"I suppose I could pull something together. What time you coming over?"

"Six. Is that okay?" Robert wanted to give Crys time to rest.

"Sure, we'll eat at six-thirty."

"Oh, Mom, another thing."

"I suppose you want banana cream pie."

"That would be great, but what I was going to say is would you set an extra plate?"

"Robert. Is she home?" her voice excited.

"Yep, late last night." He thought about how his mother might take his answer so he quickly added, "We talked all night, she's asleep now, but she's anxious to see you and Dad."

"Oh my, that's such good news. I've been so worried."

"Yeah, me to. She said the marshals took good care of her, except for the fender bender."

"She okay?"

"Fine, she's fine, a few bruises around her eyes and a few cuts. She'll never live this one down."

"I don't understand."

"She's a cop, and she wasn't wearing her safety belt."

"Oh my, I should say so. She needs a good stern talking to."

"Well, Mom, you can let her have it tonight." They both laughed.

Robert hung up the phone and peered into the living room. Crys was still asleep on the couch. She hadn't moved, never had he seen her so exhausted. *The flight from New York, long drive home, and the all-night emotion packed reunion had to have been draining,* he thought. She'd done all that just for him, and he had allowed it. Now he felt guilty. The first thing he should have done when she walked through his door was insist she sleep, but he wanted to talk, get reacquainted, and she obliged. Crys was finally home, and he was happy, maybe the happiest he'd ever been. *Never again,* Robert quietly promised, *would he think of himself first when it came to the future Mrs. Gray.*

Winters slept in that morning; instead of the usual five a.m., her alarm didn't disturb her until six thirty. She felt rested, wondering if the relaxing evening with Ellison was perhaps the reason. Winters hadn't had a nice time in so long she couldn't remember what the previous occasion was. Nothing spectacular happened during the evening, but then she hadn't set any expectations.

After thirty minutes on her Stairmaster and a shower, she was ready to tackle the report. The twenty-eight-page document would be no more than ten when she finished editing. After culling out the team selection method, training, the insertion process, the complicated trek to Natanz, the interaction between the team and Dr. Sherafat, Xerxes Sattar, Karush Talavi, Dr. Ansari, and Nadim Bin Faxhir's horrible death, as well as the escape, the remaining draft would merely report that the plant in Iran is enriching uranium and shipping equipment parts infused with it to the US, among other places. The document summary would be made available to HPSCI committee members and only then to the media after the minority and majority co-chairmen were convinced the information would not be a threat to national security. The entire twenty-eight-page report would be made available to the committee upon their request, but customarily the members only wanted the condensed version. Most legislators thought they had too much to read as it was—an abstract was typically sufficient.

Winters kept this in mind while she rewrote the report; it had to be crafted for consumption by everyone, including the Iranian president. It had to be written in such a way that put Iran's leadership on notice without revealing how the US got the information. Of course the Iranians would deny the contents of the report and act out their indignation, at such a grievous accusation, with contemptuous anti-American rhetoric. That much Winters understood as standard rules-of-the-game, but what she didn't understand was the fact many Americans and some legislators bought into the propaganda spread by fanatical regimes. A mystery that in all likelihood was unsolvable.

It was nearly noon on Saturday when she put the final touches to the sanitized version of Operation Moriah Ruse. Winters got the vice president and the secretary of defense together on a conference call. "Gentlemen, I've completed the report and will dispatch one of my drivers to deliver the full report plus the abstract; all I need to know is which golf course."

The men laughed, a few seconds of garbled words followed when they both tried simultaneously to muster a clever comeback, but the conference line would only transmit one voice at a time. Winters was finally able to coordinate their amusing responses and bring the conversation back to reality. "Okay, where?" she asked.

"The Pentagon, where else?" August Jefferson said.

"And you, Mr. Vice President, where are you?"

"The office, where else?"

"Okay, gentlemen, it's on its way, happy reading. Oh, by the way, how soon can I get a response?" She listened, smiling, as the two men bashed her for being such an aggressive broad.

"How's 1600?" Jefferson said.

"The same," Unger added.

"I guess that'll have to do if you two can't read any faster." Winters gave an exaggerated sigh. A conglomeration of laughter and female insults followed. The repartee tapered off, and Winters picked up the conversation again. "Seriously, gentlemen, don't let anyone see either of these docs yet; as a matter of fact, when you've finished reading them, I'll send the driver back to pick 'em up, if that's okay."

"Sounds good to me. I'd prefer being able to say that I don't have a copy, should the question come up," Unger said.

"Me too."

"Okay, I'll send the driver over about 1600."

Dinner that evening with Robert's parents was a relief for Stanton. Talk about her accident and resulting injuries was brief; there was no probing, Helen and Fred weren't like that. They didn't pry into anyone's business, and they appreciated people not prying into theirs. The entire conversation centered on how glad they were to have her back home. By the time Stanton said goodnight, she was finally beginning to feel like both feet were firmly planted on solid ground. The previous month she'd felt like a climber on a mountain ledge, un-tethered during a windstorm, a prevailing sense of disaster every minute of every day.

Stanton's alertness was returning as the pain medication and sedatives flushed from her body, but physically she was a wreck, exhausted from the emotional highs and lows. Her only objective right then and there was sleep.

They stepped off the curb onto the gravel drive holding hands.

Fred shut the door but left the porch light on so they could see their way to the trucks.

"You want to stay with me tonight?" Robert asked carefully, not wanting to crowd Crys into doing something other than what she wanted.

"Yes, I want to, but I need to see my place, sleep in my own bed. If we go to your place, I'm not sure we'd get much sleep." Her demure smile brought a blush to Robert's face hardly noticeable in the dim light of the porch lamp. "Besides that, I've got the meeting with the deputies, and I have to have my sheriff's hat firmly in place when I see them."

"I see your point, but, honey, I promise to keep my hands off you and let you sleep."

"Sorry, cowboy, I'm not sure I could keep mine off you."

He stammered, his complexion getting redder. "Okay, okay, I'll cut you some slack, but not for long. I want to spend every minute of the rest of my life with you, dear."

She nodded vigorously as she opened the door of her truck. Crys started to step up on the running board, but Robert pulled her back and kissed her, a long passionate kiss that intensified quickly. She felt him slide his hand down her back to the top of her jeans, minutes later they were in his bedroom, the room Robert hoped to call *theirs* very soon.

CHAPTER 58
SEPTEMBER 23

Margaret Winters looked through the sunroom window at the clock above her stove. She finished reading the OMR report for the tenth time. It was practically memorized, and that's the way Winters wanted it when the questions were asked. She leaned back in the padded lounge chair next to the pool under the shade of a newly constructed pergola. It was late September and too cool to swim, but the day was perfect. A few fluffy clouds drifted southwest pushed by the first of autumn winds. She closed her eyes, triggering an image of the night before. A smile led to a soft chuckle thinking of Ellison's obvious apprehension and reoccurring embarrassment. In many ways she found it endearing, even attractive. Ellison's career had tempered him rough and inflexible—a black or white world—a true cynic that saw people divided into two camps, those that knew the US was in a world of hurt and were trying to fix it, and those that didn't have a clue and couldn't care less. All criminals and many politicians fell into the latter category. Cops, nurses, doctors, schoolteachers and all the blue-collar folks were in the first. *To him,* she thought, *it's just that basic.* She envied his simplified version of the way things ought to be, but obviously it wasn't that way, and try as she might, she just couldn't compartmentalize, therefore her world, she knew, would remain gray.

Winters collected her water bottle, the report, and the phone and went inside. The breeze had picked up, and her wind suit wasn't enough to keep her comfortable. Just as she traded the empty water bottle for a full one, her phone rang. It was ten minutes after four p.m. and the caller ID showed a code, not the originating number. The code, she knew, was that of August Jefferson.

"Winters here."

Jefferson was all business—no hello, how are you, no banter, just business. "Just talked to Unger; we were both blown away. This intel is exactly what the president needs to make his decision; you and your team did a great job. I can't imagine what everyone has been through. It's a miracle the women weren't killed too." His conversation pace was rapid, packing in all the verbal high fives he could in a short amount of time before moving on to the core of his call.

"I understand the House Committee on Intel wants to talk with you."

"Right."

"Has either co-chair seen the report?"

"No, just finished it this morning."

"When do you have to turn it over to them?"

"Twenty-four hours prior to when I'm to meet with them."

"Do you submit both reports?"

"They have the right to see both, but usually they only want the condensed version."

"How's that determined, and who makes that decision?"

"The co-chairs. As for how, I suppose they flip a coin. In other words, August, I don't know." A long silence followed her answer. Winters knew Jefferson was doing the math.

"Okay, you've got to turn it over to them by noon on Tuesday, and this is Saturday." His words were audible, he meant for Winters to hear, but not necessarily respond. He wanted her to listen and his tone communicated that clearly.

terrorism division, the agency tried unsuccessfully to mold Stanton into a bureaucrat. She looked good, presented herself professionally, articulated the agencies mission statement perfectly, and was experienced, but she hated Washington and the games. In the midst of learning the political two-step, her mother called to explain her dad's condition had worsened, and she was considering selling the feed store so she could take care of him. She didn't ask Crys for help—she knew how important the FBI was to her daughter—and Crys didn't offer. Although there was no discussion about her helping, she'd made up her mind before saying goodbye, and the next day, much to the director's dismay, she submitted her letter of resignation. Within a month Crystal Stanton was back home, living with her parents and learning to operate the feed and hardware store her father had run since before she was born. Within a year both parents died. It was a sad year, but also a year she was glad to have spent with her mom and dad where memories were made—wonderful memories that professional success could never have provided.

Three weeks after her mother's funeral, a few of the town's citizens paid Stanton a visit. It wasn't an official meeting, according to the high school principal; it was merely for information sharing. The representatives explained how unhappy the people of Buffalo were with the present sheriff and wondered if she would be willing to consider running in the upcoming election against him. Stanton thanked them for the confidence they had in her—it was flattering—but she would have to decline. That decision, of course, like so many others she had made, was not to be.

Deputy sheriff over administration, Maude Bingham, was the last to leave Stanton's house that afternoon. Wiping away tears, Bingham left the sheriff's home joyful for Stanton and her excitement difficult to contain, especially after the sheriff asked her to be maid of honor.

Stanton's realization there was something wonderful between her and Robert came at a snail's pace on purpose. She knew having something wonderful between them and being in love were two separate issues and shouldn't be confused when thinking seriously about marriage. There was something wonderful between her and Frank Ellison—after all he'd risked his life to save hers and that was a very powerful attraction, but at the same time she was afraid the attraction would evolve out of obligation.

The first thing she had to do was write a letter of resignation. Stanton planned to submit the letter to the board of county commissioners the next morning. She would give a month's notice and recommend the chief deputy be promoted to acting sheriff until the voters decided who they wanted permanently. As she added the closing the phone rang, the caller, her friend in DC, and against her better judgment she answered. "Hey, Jerry, what's going on?" she said casually, hoping the conversation would stay that way.

"Great news, Crys," he said.

Stanton could tell from Webster's monotone greeting it wasn't. "Oh no, what?"

"An all-expense-paid trip, including air fare, hotel, and meal accommodations to your nation's capital."

"Oh shit, Jerry. Who wants me, and why?"

"House Permanent Select Committee on Intelligence wants to question Maggie about OMR—"

"To hell with that hipsy-dipsy bunch. I'm planning a wedding and a honeymoon."

"You are?"

"Yes."

"You and the cowboy?"

"Yep, me and the cowboy."

"I'm thrilled for you, Crys, just thrilled. Does the cowboy know how lucky he is?"

"Of course not." They both laughed.

"Big wedding or small?"

"Very small, but you're invited."

"I wouldn't miss it." Jerry Webster knew how to stretch a pause. He was a master at moving the conversation with the use of well-placed silence from one subject back to where he wanted it.

"You gonna finish the thought or just sit on it hoping it'll hatch on its own?" she said.

"Crys, here's the deal. The committee, or at least some of the committee, wants to see her crash and burn."

"Why?"

"It's the political bullshit agency heads deal with during every presidential election year, especially if the other party seems positioned to assume power. It's Washington, its politics, its crap, but the game goes on."

"So the wolves can smell blood, and they're in attack mode."

"Exactly."

"Will I be subpoenaed?"

"No, it isn't a committee hearing, it's only fact-finding, supposedly."

"Supposedly?"

"Yeah, supposedly, but the majority chair and a few committee members have an ulterior motive. They want to accentuate the negative of the president's period in office. James Murphy believes tying the president to what he perceives as a botched CIA operation will engender more public discontent in him—"

Stanton interrupted. "Why, Murphy's not running for president?"

"No, but he is hoping for a cabinet position."

"Such as?"

"Secretary of defense."

"Oh my God. He's just what we need in a time of crises."

"Yeah, right, just like I need another hole in my head. Anyway, Crys, it's Winters that needs you as support for her account of what the OMR accomplished."

"Why didn't Winters call instead of you?"

"She was, but I told her we hadn't talked since you got back, and I wanted to say hi."

"Okay, for how long?"

"Three days, a week at the longest."

"I'll agree under one condition, Jerry."

"And?"

"I'm not going to lie to Robert again. I know I'm under agreement not to divulge anything about OMR, but there must be a way for me to tell Robert."

"Actually, Crys, I anticipated this, I have a plan."

"What would that plan be?"

"Does Robert have a dark suit and black dress shoes?"

CHAPTER 60
SUNDAY, SEPTEMBER 24

Doug Paul, director of intelligence for the CIA, exited his security-chauffeured SUV in the protected underground parking lot and was escorted to the elevator doors that would take him to the office of Congressman James Murphy. It was late afternoon, and Paul wasn't happy about being summoned from his golf game. Ordinarily he would have refused, but under the circumstances he thought better of declining. At this stage of his career any misstep he made would have a domino effect; his ambitions now were tied directly to political maneuvering and no longer a matter of skill or knowledge. To say no to the man most able to help him nudge Winters out of her office and leapfrog Owens for the top Central Intelligence spot wouldn't be wise.

Two attractive legislative interns looked up when Paul walked into Murphy's area. "Yes, sir, may we help you?"

"Doug Paul to see Congressman Murphy."

"May we say what your visit is in regard to?"

"No, we may not." Frustrated with office protocol and determined to demonstrate his authority to the clueless young ladies, he walked past them and into Murphy's office without knocking.

The congressman stood and offered his hand. "Thanks for dropping your game, Doug, sit, please." Murphy returned to his chair and pulled it to his desk. "You want something to drink?"

"No. Now, what's this about, Congressman?"

Murphy thumbed through some papers, as if he'd misplaced something important, then gave up and leaned back in his chair. "I was informed earlier today that Winters will submit the OMR document Tuesday. Two things, Doug."

"Shoot."

"I need a copy of that document before the meeting; can you get one for me?"

"No, I can't. Those docs are closely guarded under the for-your-eyes-only rule. I don't have a legitimate need to see it until after Winters releases it to your committee."

Murphy pulled his glasses off and tossed them across his desk. "You are the director of intel, and you can't get me a report," he barked.

Paul sat quietly, not in the least intimidated by the congressman's outburst. "I'm sorry, Congressman; it's protocol. I assure you the rule has a vital role in the grand scheme of things when it comes to matters of national and global security."

"Of course it does, I'm not a fool, and I take offense to your wiser-than-thou attitude," Murphy said. The men were silent, locked in a stare, wondering how much lower they would stoop in acquiring their personal ambitions. Each man had worked hard to get where he was, but the last rung on the ladder of what they called success was apparently attainable only by scheming, neither man proud of what he was doing, but neither one willing to lose footing.

Paul had put all his eggs in Murphy's basket and knew his only chance was through the congressman. He straightened his lanky slouch and corrected his demeanor to reflect respect even though

the specifics of why, just a gut feeling. To me, it's like she's gone rogue."

"Legitimately. How do you launder money legitimately?"

Paul caught himself in mid-sigh and coughed to cover the slip-up. "Excuse me, Congressman." He coughed again. "Sorry, something in my throat. Anyway, there are a number of ways to do it."

"And that'll make it easier for you to bump her and her buddy Owens."

This time he gave Murphy's comment some thought. Put in those words made what he was doing sound evil; nevertheless, it was reality, cold and harsh.

CHAPTER 61

Stanton thought Webster's question over; she couldn't remember ever seeing Robert in a dark suit. "I don't know, Jerry, why?"

"You can't tell him without running the risk of jail time, Crys, so here's my plan..."

Webster explained that being director of the FBI gave him certain privileges, and one was access to meetings conducted by the House Permanent Select Committee on Intelligence. From time to time, when the previous director attended, he would take someone with him, usually an agent directly involved in a matter being discussed by the committee. "My attendance will not be questioned, and bringing someone with me will not likely be challenged—"

Stanton cut him off. "So, if I'm hearing you correctly, you're saying you'll sneak Robert into a highly classified meeting, and if caught, you two would go to jail instead of me?"

"Yeah, something like that. What do you think?"

"It's beyond me how you made director. Next to Ellison, you take the prize for being smart and stupid at the same time."

"Nevertheless, Crys, it's about as foolproof as any other plan I can think of. The chance of a committee member asking me to introduce a colleague is remote. Hell, Crys, most of those guys still believe the FBI has a dossier on 'em."

"Do they?" Crys asked suspiciously, remembering stories of the Hoover days when that possibility existed.

"No comment. Anyway, it's perfect. You don't tell Robert anything, but he gets the complete story from all the participants firsthand." Webster didn't want to say more, the decision had to be Crys'. To talk her into the plan and for something to go wrong would be unforgivable on his part, something he couldn't live with.

"Okay, Jerry, let's say Robert will go for the plan eyes wide open, and believe me it'll be his choice. What's the next step?"

"I don't know what Robert looks like, how he dresses, what his mannerisms are, you've got a couple of days to make him look and act like an agent. If he's going to sit next to me in the meeting, he has to at least assume the appearance. Oh yeah, Crys, can you e-mail me a recent photo of him, preferably two, one full face and the other profile?"

"What else?"

"Bring him with you. Another thing, tell him to keep his emotion in check and not utter a word to anyone around here beyond a friendly greeting, okay?"

"Yes, of course, that'll be drilled in deep by the time we get there."

Stanton called her fiancée and explained that unfortunately she had to go to Washington, DC, to add some final touches to what she'd been doing the last month. At first, Robert was angry; Crys could tell by the hard tone his voice took on as he began to throw questions at her.

"Robert, hang on. Let me finish, please." She gave him time to catch his breath.

"Sure, sorry, please finish." Some of the edge mellowed away.

"I want you to go with me," Crys said.

"What?"

"Go with me."

"Oh, well... guess there's no reason why I can't. Dad can look out for things around here. How long?"

"Maybe a week."

Robert protested, claiming the cattle couldn't do without him. It was a weak protest, and the reason even weaker, but she knew he had to say it, it was just his way.

"So, you'll go?"

"Yeah, got nothing better to do. Guess I can be a tourist while you're doing your thing."

"Well, dear, we need to talk about that. Can you come here tonight?"

"What's going on, Crys? Your voice it sounds different, like you're trying to hide something."

"I'm sorry, sweetheart. I can only imagine how it sounds, but you've just got to trust me... okay?"

"You know I trust you. It's just that..." Robert hesitated, searching for the right way to express what he was thinking. "I know this sounds silly, Crys, but it all sounds cloak-and-dagger to me."

"Yeah, well, come over about six; we'll have dinner and talk."

That evening, after they'd eaten, Crys and her fiancée filled the dishwasher and tidied the kitchen, neither spoke of their earlier conversation. Crys grabbed the half-empty bottle of Merlot and two fresh glasses, and motioned for Robert to follow her into the den. The room was small, a bank of windows on the east looked out over what used to be a well-tended flower garden. After her father died, the flowers were her mother's comfort, and her death left the garden abandoned. She set the glasses down on a table her father made when she was still in high school and poured each half full.

Most of the north and south walls were oak bookcases from floor to ceiling, another of his projects. A doeskin tan area rug covered the center of the room and four comfortable chairs sat on the polished wood floor rimming the carpet, an arrangement obviously designed to encourage conversation. There wasn't a radio or TV, only antique lamp tables arranged so two people could sit close and read when talk of the day waned.

Crys held her glass up. Toasting was a custom he'd seen only in the movies, an act the cowboy had never put much thought toward; however, he did know it required him to clink her glass with his and repeat whatever she said. It wasn't difficult, just unfamiliar. "To us," she said softly.

"To us," he repeated awkwardly.

The conversation between Crys and Robert was complicated and lengthy. Explaining the unexplainable was like dancing blindfolded on the edge of the Grand Canyon, and skirting classified issues while trying to make a shadowy point clear was impossible. Finally, Robert reached over and caressed Crys' hand and said, "Let me see if I've got this straight."

Stanton looked relieved and nodded. "Okay."

"I'm going to a meeting of some oversight bunch with the director of the FBI. I'm supposed to look FBIish, right?"

She nodded. "So far so good."

"I'm supposed to keep my mouth shut and look stoic, whatever the hell that means."

Crys smiled. "Indifferent."

"What?"

"It means indifferent to passion or pain. So in the meeting, just look like you don't give a crap."

"Oh, that's easy, no problem. Okay, as I was saying; I'm to sit there in a dark suit, white shirt, and tie and look like I don't give a crap. Nothing to it."

"All right, Mr. *Nothing to It,* let's say one of the legislators calls me a liar and threatens me with jail time. What will you think; what will you do?"

"I'll pull the sonofabitch off his chair and make him apologize, for starters."

Stanton's head dropped to her cupped hands, she inhaled deeply. "Look," she said sternly.

Robert patted her hand again and with an impish smile added, "Just kidding, just kidding."

CHAPTER 62

An oak worktable—matching the office furniture in Winters' home—was topped with a white linen cloth and an array of silver trays of nourishing snacks. The chief of the agency's hospitality department arranged a centerpiece of fresh flowers and stepped back to survey her creation. She was in the process of making minor adjustments when Winters said her guests had arrived. That was her signal to leave; she quickly pulled cellophane wrap off two hors d'oeuvres trays and disappeared into the kitchen.

Winters opened the door and motioned everyone into the office. "Please, help yourself to the goodies; sit wherever you wish."

The five visitors milled around the spacious office, looking at framed photos of famous people and a couple of pictures taken by a war photojournalist depicting Margaret Winters, during her early years with the CIA, dressed in combat attire. She appeared to be talking to Afghan military at a base camp surrounded by rugged snow-capped mountains. Another showed an injured Winters being loaded onto a helicopter during a desert dust storm.

The three men filled their hors d'oeuvres plate with cubes of cheese, Swedish meatballs, and sliced fresh fruit. The two women poured themselves tea from a narrow-neck glass pitcher and sat down. When Winters reentered the room, Stanton stood. "I'm sorry, Director Winters, let me introduce my fiancé, Robert Gray."

"Oh yes, I've heard good things about you."

Robert tried not to show the awe enveloping him just then. He was in the presence of not only the director of the FBI but also the chief of Central Intelligence, and to add more wonder to his astonishment, his fiancée was right in the middle of something big, something he didn't understand. Robert smiled and returned the greeting.

Winters closed her office door. "Thank you all very much for being here and supporting me." She nodded at Stanton and Crisp. "You'd think you hadn't already done enough, and, of course, you have. I wouldn't have blamed either of you if you'd rejected my request, but you didn't, and that means more to me than I can adequately say." Winters paused and poured some tea. "Tomorrow is a big day for me." She sat down next to Robert and took a sip of her drink. "My plan, all along, has been to retire this year, but I'm not going out with a cloud over my performance."

"And what would cause you to have a cloud over you?" Crisp, who usually refrained from getting involved in people's personal matters, asked, her dark eyes wide with genuine disquiet.

"It's a long and complicated back-story, Limber, and I don't want to bore you with intricate details that would have to be explained. What I want you to know is that political conniving and manipulation has begun. Both parties do it. This is simply a time, and era, if you will, where conservatism must make room for liberalism. Now, for that to happen, self-centered and ambitious people pull out the big guns and try to shoot down their opposition."

Everyone sat silent; even the men put their half-eaten finger food down and were listening intently. Tom Owens was nodding as though he'd listened in on Winters' rehearsal of the evening's talk.

"Try not to think of me as paranoid." Winters smirked and went on. "At least I don't think I am." She took another sip of tea. "Here is the way it's playing out…"

Winters explained the House Permanent Select Committee on Intelligence and how the majority co-chairman was, she thought, going to use that forum to discredit the president, the vice president, her management of the CIA, and ultimately the party. "Unfortunately I have a senior level staff member that is sympathetic to the co-chair's philosophy and is trying to ride into my position on his coattails, and that, ladies and gentlemen, would be a mistake." She pointed to Owens and finished her thought. "He should be the new director."

Winters looked around the room, then at Webster. "Where's Ellison? I thought you were going to have him here?"

Webster sighed; he was embarrassed. He'd ordered a subordinate to attend, and Ellison didn't show. "I'm sorry, Maggie; but you know how he is, especially now that he's a short-timer."

Winters smiled; she knew the reason he didn't come, and the reason was sitting right across from her. "Is he coming tomorrow?"

"Said he wouldn't miss it."

"Okay then, I want to discuss what I think the committee will ask, and I want you to hear my response. Fair enough?"

Winters pointed over her shoulder and reminded everyone about the hors d'oeuvres, "Please eat. Martha went to a lot of trouble; she'll be disappointed if the trays aren't emptied." She turned to Robert. "Sorry, but I have to kick you out."

Robert nodded; he'd been told earlier there would be a limit to how much he could hear. Curiosity about his soon-to-be wife's past life and recent activities prickled inside him like a Fourth of July sparkler that wouldn't go out. His concern for her welfare was indefinable, largely because there was nothing yet he could wrap his understanding around. Robert looked at Crys, her eyes told him she understood his quandary, she smiled, and that made it okay for the time being.

"Fill your plate. I'll show you to the TV." Winters returned shortly and closed the door. The guests had eagerly taken Winters up on her invitation to finish off the food, two meatballs and three apple slices were all that remained. "It's late, I know. Hopefully the food will energize you, and you won't fall asleep."

A quiet laugh floated around the room. Regardless of the hour, no one was sleepy; they all wanted to hear what Winters had to say.

Winters crossed her legs and leaned her elbow on the chair arm. The body language was clear—her words to follow were important. "Again, I can't tell you how much this means to me. All of you have sacrificed so much already." Winters paused to let her thanks settle in. "Now, let me tell you what I think will happen tomorrow. Late yesterday afternoon I submitted the condensed version of the mission. Unlike the twenty-eight-page report, the shorter version excludes the complexities of acquiring the intelligence. The committee is interested in the information, not how we got it. In most cases they wouldn't understand the nature of counterintelligence." Winters hesitated, and for a short moment gazed at the wall of awards, citations, and photos commemorating accomplishments over the more than twenty years she'd been with the CIA. "On their behalf, I'm not so sure I understand it all myself." She laughed. "But don't tell them I said that. Anyway, Mr. Murphy will make introductions, then, as always, he'll pontificate. He likes to politicize morality and associate his position with what's good for the world."

Two hours later, Winters and her group knew what had to be done. The agreed-upon tactic was simple; let Murphy say his piece and offer, for his own personal political notoriety, his rant on what's wrong with America. His practice was to follow with specific questions related to whatever was on the minds of committee members at that time, and tomorrow's subject was OMR. Winters would answer questions and when called upon for intelligence gathering verification Stanton and Crisp would elaborate only as far as the committee questions probed.

The CIA chief stood, making eye contact with each person in the room. "I'm not calling for a group hug here, but you have to know how important this is to me." She didn't say anything more as she went from person to person offering a firm handshake and confident smile. No one doubted her sincerity.

Stanton patted Robert's shoulder until he opened his eyes. "Wake up, sleeping beauty. We're going back to the hotel."

He pushed the chair to its upright position and looked at his watch. "It's two. Have I been asleep since midnight?" The question he mumbled was more to orient himself than to initiate conversation. Winters shut the TV off and disappeared into the kitchen. Crisp and Owens had already gone. Crys, Robert, and Jerry Webster were walking toward the front door. "Hold on, Robert. Before you leave, I have something for you." The FBI Director set his briefcase on an entry table and opened it. "Crys, could I have a couple of minutes with Robert?"

"Sure," she said, puzzled, but nevertheless trusting, she continued on to their waiting car.

Jerry Webster fished a black leather wallet slightly larger than a man's billfold out of a side pocket and handed it to Robert. "This is yours to keep, but don't say anything about it to Crys just yet. It's for her sake, understand?"

CHAPTER 63
WASHINGTON DC
0850 HOURS, SEPTEMBER 26

Robert Gray grew up on a large ranch in northwest Oklahoma. His only exposure to the world was as a young man
in the U.S. Army. Like the other soldiers he served with in
Germany and Korea, he was too immature to appreciate
the countries' history or culture. The opportunity to learn
about other people was, for the most part, wasted. Two
years of college satisfied his quest for education; he already
knew how to raise cattle, grow wheat, and fix machinery.
The ranch was where he felt comfortable, and the ranch is
where he settled.

Robert followed his fiancée into the US Capitol and
down a hall populated by tourists and their cameras, men
and women in business suits talking fast and motioning
faster with their hands. Everyone with briefcases; some even
carried on face-to-face conversations while pressing a cell
phone to their ear. "This is a madhouse," he said quietly.

"What?" Stanton said without looking at him. The

crowd was heavy, and she had to keep her attention on openings to cut through in order to get to their destination on time.

"Nothing."

The crowd began to thin, and Robert could see Winters just ahead talking with several people. He recognized Crisp and Owens but no one else. Winters spotted them and motioned. "Good, you're here," she said to Stanton. Robert held back a few feet. His orders were to be inconspicuous and stay with Jerry Webster at all times. Webster hadn't arrived yet, and Stanton was pulled quickly into the midst of the huddle. Robert watched and listened, the people, crowds, everyone talking, cell phones chirping, and the noise—a dull, constant roar of unintelligible babble. He shook his head bewildered by it all just as Webster approached. They shook hands.

"I noticed you shaking your head," the FBI director said.

"I'm puzzled. How does anything get done around here?"

Webster laughed. "That's an age old question. No one I know of has ever come up with an answer." He took Gray by the elbow and pointed. "They're going in; come on."

The room was small compared to other hearing rooms. Typically a HPSCI meeting was attended only by members and government officials carrying high security clearances, but today was different. A few journalists were allowed to attend under strict guidelines. There would be no photographers, no recording devices, only the names of the members and department heads could be used in an article, and to be fair to other journalists, the stories would be dispensed to other print media before the attending journalists could release theirs.

Committee members sat on a raised platform in a wide semi-circle, and each had a name plate clearly displayed in front of their microphone. Winters and one of the men Robert saw talking to her outside were seated at a long table on the floor of the room facing the members. Stanton and Crisp were seated directly in back of Winters in the area designated for spectators. Owens and a women Robert had never seen sat three rows in back of Stanton and Crisp.

Robert followed Webster into a spectator row away from anyone else. The four journalists sat together on the back row. The room had four exits, each one guarded by Capitol police. The committee members began to arrive; they greeted each other. Robert thought it odd not one member acknowledged there was anyone else in the room; he started to question Webster about it but opted not to when one of the members at the center of the group leaned over and spoke into his microphone, "Check credentials." At this utterance Robert saw two of the policemen going from person to person. They started with the reporters, each journalist, who had already been through a metal detector just outside the door, was asked to stand as the officer examined them with a handheld wand. Each one's credentials studied closely for forgeries.

Robert was getting nervous. He started to turn to get a better look when Webster raised his arm and whispered, "Don't. Chill. Look stoic." One of the policemen circled around to the row just in back of Webster and Gray. Robert looked straight ahead but watched him approach from the periphery. The officer turned toward them when he got to the aisle and leaned in close to Webster. An African American man of about sixty, Robert guessed, but his robust shoulders compensated for his age, bidding one to behave in spite of his white hair.

"Congrats, Mr. Director, sir," he said with an enormous grin.

"I don't know, Charley. I guess time will tell. How's the new job?"

"Home by six, weekends off, good pay, no stress, better than being an agent. And, hell, Jerry, they don't give a damn how old I am." He winked and gave a thumbs-up, then moved on to Stanton and Crisp. Webster leaned over covering his mouth with his left hand. "I worked under him just out of Quantico, the best teacher I ever had. Retired a few years back, and got this cushy job."

"He didn't even check me."

"Nope. Guess we won't go to jail today."

A few minutes later, Charley approached the committee mem-

ber who ordered the check and reported. He nodded, and the four policemen stepped out of the room and closed the doors.

"We are ready to begin. If you'd take your seats, we will get started." The committee members quickly finished their side conversations and sat down.

"Let the record show it is September the twenty-sixth, the year of our Lord and Savior, Jesus Christ, two-thousand and seven. I am James Murphy, co-chairman of the House Permanent Select Committee on Intelligence." Murphy looked to his right then left as if counting to make sure a quorum was present. "Introductions, please." He pointed to the minority co-chairman. "Congressman, if you'd lead off."

Murphy studied the committee again during the introductions.

Robert leaned over. "What's all Murphy's rubbernecking about?"

"He's got a quorum; he's just making sure that most are from his side of the aisle."

"Oh."

Murphy's voice boomed out over the speaker system. "Let the record show that our guest today is Central Intelligence Director, Margaret Winters." He stopped long enough for the proper effect to settle in with the members. The sharp edge of distain in his tone was unmistakable, and he wanted everyone to know it. "Director Winters, who is the gentleman to your left?"

"Robert Bright—"

"And who is Robert Bright?" he interrupted.

"Mr. Bright is the agency's general counsel."

"Your attorney?" Murphy spat.

"No, sir. It is my understanding we'll be going over OMR, and to that end he's here to advise me on the efficacy of answering questions relatable to an ongoing mission."

"If you say so, Director." Murphy looked at the other members hoping to see heads nodding, confirming his insinuation. A few accommodated the majority co-chairman more out of fear of political reprisal than agreement with his personal dislike for Winters.

James Murphy began his monologue as Winters predicted, making reference to the present executive branch of government as officials with no regard for the US Constitution. He was generous with his unconstructive remarks about the CIA regarding past intelligence gathering and operational conduct. With each downgrading remark, Murphy seemed to gain momentum; his intention was to expose the CIA for what it was and discredit Margaret Winters in the process. The current president and his party would be embarrassed, and Murphy would gain the positive notoriety he needed during his assumptive conformation hearing.

"Director Winters, it has come to this committee's attention that you may have run some kind of operation out of your office without the president's knowledge." Murphy hesitated while he studied a document.

"Mr. Chairman, if I might—"

Murphy raised his hand. "One minute, Director Winters, I haven't finished."

"I'm sorry, Mr. Chairman."

"The most troubling concern, but certainly not the only one I have, is your attempt to incite unrest between different Middle Eastern cultural and religious factions. This debacle apparently put into play by you to cover another meager, but predictable attempt at collecting intelligence concerning Iran's nuclear intentions. How am I doing so far, Director Winters?" The question obviously rhetorical, Murphy cared less about her opinion. He pulled himself up on his elbows and peered over the top of his reading glasses, and from his elevated perch gazed down on the director like a buzzard eyeing two-day-old road kill.

"Yes, Chairman Murphy, some of what you've described is accurate, but I wouldn't characterize the ruse as an attempt to incite the factions, neither would I characterize the intelligence gathering as meager."

Murphy glanced quickly at the journalists hoping they were busy writing everything down. "Well, Director Winters, I have your

report of this so-called Moriah Ruse operation, I've read it thoroughly, and frankly I find it redundant." He stole another glance at
the reporters.

"I'm not sure I understand." Winters understood completely;
she wanted Murphy to play his hand first.

"This is the same information we've seen before. Frankly, Director, I can buy a copy of the *Washington Post* and read this." Murphy
leaned back in the tan-and-tufted leather executive chair, appearing
triumphant.

"The information you have there has been verified—"

"Director Winters," Murphy interrupted, certain Winters had
set one foot in the trap, "How? With satellite pictures run through
Photoshop, or better yet, maybe you know someone that knows
someone who has an uncle living near the nuke plant in question
that says, without a doubt, they're making bombs." Murphy threw
the report synopsis on the floor in front of Winters in a dramatic
show of scorn.

The minority co-chairman, Richard Cleveland, a man not
inclined toward theatrics, turned to Murphy. "Let's put some of our
concerns in the form of answerable questions and let the director
make a run at 'em. There's no need to badger Ms. Winters—"

Murphy didn't let him finish. He was on target, and nothing would stop him from exposing Winters and her crowd for the
incompetent people they were. "Director Winters, before we leave
here today, I want a full accounting of the two million you appear
to be laundering through some bank in Oman—"

Cleveland stood brazenfaced, looking down on him. "That's
enough, Mr. Murphy. Laundering implies a criminal act, and to
my knowledge, we aren't here as an investigative body, but fact-
finding only. Am I wrong, Mr. Murphy?" Before Murphy could
answer, Cleveland sat back down and addressed Winters. "Director
Winters, at least on my behalf, I would like to apologize for the
way things have gotten out of hand. As co-chair of this committee,
I want to welcome you here. We know you are a very busy person,

and we don't want to take up too much of your time, but in the interest of the committee's oversight responsibilities, we do have questions that need to be answered."

"Yes, sir."

Cleveland wrenched committee leadership away from Murphy audaciously; not that he meant it to seem defiant, it just happened that way. He knew there would be a price to pay, especially if Murphy successfully maneuvered his way into the secretary of defense position. He addressed the other members and asked if they had comments before the question and answer period began. Two repeated, in a more palatable manner, what Murphy said. Emphasizing the quality of past intelligence gathering was in question and curiosity about the two million was on their minds also.

Cleveland sipped water, took off his eyeglasses, and folded his hands on top of the committee desk. "Now, Director Winters, we all have the OMR synopsis in front of us." He smiled and added, "With the exception of Mr. Murphy."

Murphy shifted noisily in his chair, demonstrating his contempt for his Co-Chair, but said nothing. He knew it would look unprofessional to interrupt Cleveland at this point; he'd just have to wait his turn to ask questions. And as painful as that seemed, it was his only alternative.

Cleveland went on. "We've read the report and frankly I have to agree with Congressman Murphy: there is not much there we hadn't heard before from the agency. We also know that intelligence gathering is an inexact science, in that you have to rely on various forms of information, which then has to be analyzed. I don't see here where any analysis was done, and, correct me if I'm wrong, I have reliable information the directorate of intelligence within your own agency played no active role in OMR." He looked from side to side to see if any other members had something to add. "So, Director Winters, let's begin with that—how did you get this intelligence, and how do you know it is reliable?"

A commotion occurred at one of the doors. Everyone turned

to see Frank Ellison being allowed into the room. The journalists looked at one another, not knowing who the new arrival was, but all made note of his arrival. They'd get his name and agency affiliation later. The committee members appeared irritated, but only stared at Ellison; no one asked who he was or what he was doing there. Ellison sat on the back row near the journalists. The reporter nearest him scooted over and, with pad and pen in hand, said quietly, "Who are you, and who are you with?" Ellison leaned in closer; the young man poised his pen ready to write.

"None of your business." Ellison added a smile. Not giving a damn about the media gave him a sense of separation from the life he'd spent the last twenty-eight years living, and it felt good.

Murphy had taken the brief distraction to reconsider his approach; it was obvious his tactic was garnering Winters some sympathetic support. Before Cleveland could restate his question, Murphy moved in, a calm exterior, this time, portraying congressional comportment. "Director Winters, I believe the Congressman's questions were how did you get this intelligence and how do you know it is reliable?"

Before Winters could speak, Bright was standing. "May we approach the co-chairmen?"

Murphy shook his head. "Let me remind you, Mr. Bright, this isn't a court of law nor is it a hearing. And we have nothing to hide—"

Cleveland, smoldering from Murphy's earlier display of enmity toward Winters, cut him off. "I don't see any harm." And he motioned them forward.

Murphy choked back words he realized would work against him later and nodded, offering feigned approval of Cleveland's invitation.

"What's this about?" Murphy whispered while holding his hand over the microphone.

Bright leaned in over the desk. "Gentlemen, you have every right to expect Director Winters to answer your questions; however, she has the right to immunity from prosecution should any revelation made by her in this room be used against US interests here or abroad."

"She doesn't have that right if facts support the notion she's willfully committed a crime." Murphy shot back, removing his hand from the mic.

"Certainly not, Congressman. The immunity would apply only to information that had the potential of exposing tactics, strategies and assets pertinent to the security of America."

Cleveland turned to Murphy. "I don't see the harm in granting that privilege."

"I suppose not." Murphy turned to Bright. "What are your suggestions?"

"I will recommend to Director Winters that she answer each question in detail if you either ask the journalists to leave or you both sign an affidavit granting the immunity we've requested."

Cleveland motioned Winters in closer. "From your perspective, Director Winters, which of these two solutions would be best for the country? Not which is best for the committee, not which is best for me or Congressman Murphy, and not what's best for you personally or the CIA's reputation. My question is which solution is best for our country?"

"I understand, sir. There is no question, the only alternative, or solution, as you call it, is to ask the journalists to leave."

Murphy pushed back from the private conversation in an apparent act he hoped would be seen as disagreement by the journalists. He dropped his hand away from the mic again and grimace. "I would have bet the farm that's what you'd say, Director Winters."

Cleveland ignored his colleague's performance. "Yes, you're right, Director." He turned to Murphy. "Do you want to tell 'em, or do you—"

Murphy interrupted, pulled the mic close and clearing his throat said, "Journalists ... journalists, if I could have your attention please. I am sorry to have to do this, but I'm outnumbered, and this

is a democracy. The minority co-chairman and Director Winters, under advisement from her attorney, have asked that you leave." Murphy was satisfied to leave his remarks at that. He had scored a homerun with the reporters. Tomorrow's news would describe him as a man of the people, a lone advocate for common men and women against the secret society that powered oppressive government. He restrained a grin in favor of a frustrated scowl.

CHAPTER 64

The HPSCI proceedings had now taken an hour and forty minutes, and not one question had been answered. Murphy called for a fifteen-minute break, and Robert Gray followed Webster out of the room into the hall. He saw Crys talking with Limber Crisp not thirty feet away and without thinking started in her direction.

"Robert."

He heard Webster call his name sternly and turned.

"Where are you going?"

"Talk to Crys."

"No," Webster said quietly. "You're with me. You don't know Crys."

Gray realized his error and returned to where Webster was standing. He stood looking out the window trying to count people milling around on the Capitol steps, an exercise to distract him from thoughts of what he was witnessing. "You know, Webster, there are more people on the steps of this building, I'll bet, than's in my hometown."

Winters whispered to Bright again. The general counsel checked a law book and wrote her a short note. She read the note and whispered back, inducing a vigorous nod from Bright.

"I respectfully request permission to delay answering that question until later."

"How much later?" Murphy's patience was wearing thin. He wanted to move quickly into questions that would discredit her, but well aware Winters and her lawyer knew the dance steps, too, he chose the cautious path.

"Within the hour, sir."

Murphy gestured for her to continue.

"During the months following the State of the Union, I took it upon myself to develop a mission structure using what expertise I had. I included no one in that phase."

"Why?" Cleveland asked.

"Frankly, I didn't want to waste anyone's time. Everyone was busy, and I knew what needed to be done."

"If you want something done right, do it yourself philosophy, right, Director Winters?" Murphy chimed in.

"No, not at all. My reason will be made clear later."

Murphy threw up his hands. "Okay, you win. Continue."

Winters filled her glass with ice water from a pitcher provided by a legislative staffer and took a drink. "When I felt the structure was sound, I asked Tom Owens, director of operations, to go over it and look critically at what I was proposing. That was mid-July of this year. Within a week, he returned the mission proposal with his critique—"

Murphy interrupted. "And where was Mr. Paul in this mix?" As soon as he uttered the question, Congressman Murphy realized his mistake; he had played the first card, but it was too late to do anything about it. He checked his response quickly to make sure his body language wasn't screaming *tilt*.

His mistake, apparent to Winters, wasn't a surprise. The director, however, assumed Murphy would be smart enough not to tip his hat early. She was wrong though, and that delighted her. "The long-standing rule of thumb at the agency is the fewer people involved, the better. Planning a mission starts in a closed environment and opens up to others in stages depending upon that department's need to know. Mr. Paul did not yet have that need, Congressman."

Murphy didn't say anything, afraid his relationship with the director of intelligence would become obvious. A moment of uncomfortable quiet passed while Winters let him stew in his error.

"I made some necessary adjustments Mr. Owens suggested to the structure and began looking for something to embed the mission in. Something of such great importance the distraction would provide a cover for a very dangerous operation, but an operation that would once and for all, at least for the current period, tell us what Iran intends to do."

Winters intentionally tossed chum to the sharks, hoping the resulting feeding frenzy would catch Murphy off guard and play to his attack mode, and it worked.

Murphy couldn't help himself; blood was in the water. "So, Director Winters, you came up with this silly story about the ark of the covenant being discovered under a Muslim holy place and in the process"—his voice cracked under the strain of his tightening neck—"you single-handedly jeopardized lives of innocent people and nearly instigated a war."

Winters sat patiently while Murphy ranted. He finished, pounding the desk in righteous indignation, demanding answers, and wishing the journalist were present to see his performance.

"With all due respect, Congressman, I'm not sure where you got that information, but it's been spun to you inaccurately. If you'll allow, I can help the committee understand the truth."

"Well, Director, you and your agency are the spin champions, so let us hear your side. Before you say anything though, I want to remind the committee members we are the oversight element of government responsible to the people of America, and it is incumbent upon us to get to the bottom of this debacle I call Operation

CHAPTER 65

Diego Garcia, Chagros Archipelago, Indian Ocean, 2100 hours Zulu Time, the *Spirit of Mississippi,* a B-2 bomber known as the *Black Widow* rolled out of its hangar. The pilot and mission commander began their pre-flight check, and within ninety minutes the seventy-three-ton stealth bomber armed with two one-thousand-pound Joint Direct Attack Munitions disappeared unceremoniously into the night sky headed northwest.

The B-2 reached cruising altitude of forty-seven thousand feet, and the pilot leveled air speed off at four hundred knots. A woman's voice came over the headset earphones. "*Widow,* this is Justice."

The pilot responded. "Justice, we read you loud and clear."

"*Widow,* mission code confirmed at 2300 hours as a go. Do you read?"

"Affirmative, mission code confirmed at two-three-zero-zero hours."

The woman's voice softened. "Good luck, *Widow.*"

"Thanks, Justice, going to radio silence in five, four, three, two, one."

Director Winters' confident answer startled the majority co-chairman. "I believe I have all the proof the committee needs to share my assurance in the reliability of the intelligence collected—"

The minority co-chairman stopped her from going forward with proof. Richard Cleveland was a straight arrow, as ethical as any legislator on the hill, and his pet peeve was congressmen who played political gotcha games. He knew his co-chair partner was one of the best at the sport, and he'd sensed an air of subterfuge arising in Murphy's questioning.

"Director Winters, I'm as anxious as anyone to see this proof, but I have to warn you that I find it somewhat irregular your own subordinate, the director of intelligence, Mr. Paul, wasn't a part of the intelligence gathering and analysis." Cleveland raised his hands in a gesture of frustration. "Before showing us this proof, would you explain why the government spends billions on that department of the CIA and you ignore it." Several of the committee members nodded their agreement. It was a question on the minds of everyone except Murphy.

"I can give you my thoughts, unsupported right now with evidence. It is merely supposition on my part gained through my personal observations. You'll have to draw your own conclusions as to the worth of my theory."

"Okay, Director Winters, what's your theory?"

Murphy knew if he objected it would only worsen the situation, so he sat hoping her theory was wrong. His churning stomach told him otherwise.

Winters explained about the petty jealousies that arose when she was named director. The harder she worked at bridging the widening gap between the three directorates the more sabotage she encountered. Mistrust and deception were rampant within the agency. All of it coupled with Clinton's downsizing made the CIA's mission all the more difficult. Winters paused, thinking about what to say next. She whispered something to Bright; he nodded. She

folded her hands in front of her and laid them slowly on the table. "I have felt for the longest time that my friend and long-time associate Doug Paul was at the center of the disorganization. I think he has collaborated with other powerful people, including legislators, to unseat me in hopes of taking over the agency. After the State of the Union address, my assignment was obvious; to make matters worse, I had very little time to accomplish the task. The mission had to be done fast, it had to be done right, and I couldn't afford distractions."

"So you left him out of the loop?"

"I did."

Cleveland was jotting notes on a legal pad. "If this theory of yours is true, do you see legal action that may need to be taken?"

"Not at this point."

"You say Mr. Paul collaborated with legislators; that right?" His head was down while he scribbled.

"Yes."

"Would you care to elaborate?"

"Not at this time, Congressman."

Cleveland stopped writing and looked up. Winters could see his disappointment. "Mr. Chairmen," she addressed both congressmen. "I would prefer, for the moment, presenting the proof of our intelligence reliability, if that's all right."

Murphy nodded, maybe a little too vigorously. Cleveland noticed; for him it was just another confirmation his counterpart had ulterior purposes. He looked to his right and left checking to see if anyone objected, and no one did. "Be my guest, Director; show us the proof."

"Thank you," Winters said as she got to her feet. The general counsel stood also out of respect for the women and what they'd accomplished. "I would ask Crystal Stanton, Harper County, Oklahoma, Sheriff, and Limber Topanga Crisp, agent of the US Secret Service, to join me at the table." As they were making their way around the banister that separated the spectators from those being questioned, Winters turned toward FBI Director Jerry Webster. "If Director Webster would permit, I would also like for Special Agent Frank Ellison to join us." Webster nodded his approval as Ellison slumped in his seat, glaring at Winters.

Webster nudged the agent, and he too took a chair at the table. Winters sat back down when all three were seated and pulled the microphone close. "This, gentlemen, is what's left of team one. There was a team two poised in Oman as backup, but they were not needed; however, I would like to read their names into the record." Cleveland nodded. Winters read the list of names and what agency they were with. "I also want to mention two other names. Nadim Bin Faxhir, a Muslim Arab and legitimate businessman from Oman that was instrumental in getting our agents into Natanz, Iran." She noticed that every committee member had awakened from the drowsiness that followed long and complicated testimonials. They were all sitting on the edge of their chairs. "If it hadn't been for Mr. Faxhir, we would not have the information presented today. To that end, I've asked the Justice Department, and they have agreed to allow two million in drug-recovery money to be deposited in a bank as compensation for his services—"

A committee member interrupted. "Two million is a lot for a few weeks' work."

Winters was seething, not so much at being interrupted but because the congressman hadn't allowed her time to explain Faxhir's demise in a proper way. "Yes, Congressman, two million is a lot. We originally agreed to pay him fifty thousand dollars for his services, the other one million nine hundred and fifty thousand is for his wife and two children who are now without a breadwinner." Winters paused, hoping someone would ask why the family was without a head of household, but they all had picked up on the implication and weren't about to stick their necks out and confirm their stupidity. "Congressman, Nadim Bin Faxhir was beheaded, and his body left to decay in the mountains southwest of Natanz." The room grew eerily quiet, the only sound coming from Robert Gray coughing, trying to hide the moan that had arisen deep within him, an expression of grief he was unable to stifle. Robert was agonizingly aware that what he was about to hear had nothing to do with testifying against terrorists. In some way his fiancée had participated in an event of extreme danger and of extreme importance.

Winters and Stanton exchanged a brief and hushed conversation, then she returned to her microphone. "The other person I want to mention is Karush Talavi, an Iranian guard at the Natanz Nuclear Plant. Mr. Talavi was Iran's heavyweight wrestling entry in the 1998 Olympics. His family was given permission to attend, and their plan was to defect to the US, but because of a series of unfortunate circumstances, his parents and siblings were the only ones to make it to America. Talavi, his wife, and son did not make it. Since then Mr. Talavi has voluntarily passed information to the US pertinent to the plant near Natanz. In exchange for this information, the US government has provided a home, job training for his parents, and college education for his siblings."

"What happened to Mr. Talavi?" Cleveland asked.

"We're not sure. We know he was responsible for getting Stanton, Crisp, and Ellison out of the plant compound and provided them with equipment and intel to help them find their way out of Iran."

The House Permanent Select Committee on Intelligence members shifted nervously in their chairs. Some fired quick questions to one another and before either co-chair could get control of the rumbling, two members approached Murphy and Cleveland. After a two-minute animated conversation no one but members could hear, Cleveland turned his mic on and cleared his throat before speaking. "Director Winters, I think we've gotten the picture, but, just to make sure, let me reiterate."

"Yes, sir." She nodded.

"You are telling this committee you actually had people inside the nuke plant, and that's how you got this intelligence. And you are telling us those people are sitting with you now." Cleveland bent forward, past his microphone, as if it wasn't there. He took his glasses off and stared down at the new faces, eager to hear more.

"Yes, sir. These three people were inside, under horrendous conditions to collect actionable, accurate, and timely intelligence at the risk of being caught, tortured, and ultimately killed."

While Murphy remained silent, Cleveland took the lead. "Director Winters, I want to apologize for the cumbersome way our committee functions, I hope you and the others understand. It is nearly noon, and I'd rather break now for lunch before we proceed. Is that all right with you?"

"Yes, that's fine."

"Members, is that agreeable?"

Everyone nodded.

"We will reconvene at two p.m., and members, please be prepared to stay until all of the mission participants have had an opportunity to speak. Thank you, and we are adjourned."

Robert Gray watched his fiancée leave the committee room with Winters, his mind demanding answers to a mystery of enormous proportions. She'd participated in a mission with consequences he couldn't fathom. His intention at the moment was simply to hold Crys and tell her how deeply he loved her. With instinct overriding any of Webster's warnings, he bolted for the nearest aisle and headed for the exit. Webster called after him, but it was too late, Gray was hurrying through the door. By the time Webster got to the waiting area and looked out the window, he could see Stanton headed for Winters' SUV and Gray rushing in her direction. Webster stepped out the side door of the Capitol and pointed at Gray who was now taking the marble steps two at a time. Seemingly from out of nowhere, five agents closed in quickly and ushered Gray off to the left like herd dogs on a stray sheep. Seconds later Webster reached Gray surrounded by agents; he stepped inside the tight circle of suits and looked at Gray. "Okay, Robert, as you can see, I didn't trust you, and I can understand what you're thinking. I'm sorry this has been difficult for you, but, and I emphasize *but*, this is either done my way or not at all."

Gray nodded, his jaw locked tight, eyes down to prevent them from showing just how angry he was. He knew Webster was right but watching the proceedings for the last hour reminded him of a coyote pack circling a newborn calf, and all he could think about was saving her and eliminating the pack.

Webster told the agents they could re-disperse. After they were far enough away, the FBI director said, "Now you know you are being watched closely. I don't want to sound mean or insensitive, but you make another unauthorized move, and you'll spend time in a holding cell until we can send you home. Do you understand?"

Gray looked around, searching for his captors, but they had disappeared. "Yes, I understand. I just—"

"Hey, man, no need to explain. I would've done the same thing."

"Okay, what do we do now?"

"Eat and hurry back."

Richard Cleveland struck the gavel to get everyone's attention. "Take your seats. It's two p.m., and we've got important ground to cover." Minutes passed while the Capitol police made sure only authorized guests were present; they finally stepped out and took their sentry positions outside the closed doors.

"Director Winters, the committee has many questions, but we've elected to withhold them until after the team has completed their explanation. Does that meet with your approval?"

"It does, Mr. Chairman."

"Then, Director Winters, you have the floor."

Margaret Winters led the way; she covered the mission from its inception up to the point where Faxhir, Stanton, and Crisp set sail across the Gulf of Oman to Iran. The committee asked for details, and the two team members obliged, leaving nothing out. Winters displayed sat photos of the nuclear plant with numbered arrows superimposed, pointing to certain buildings. The numbers corresponding to locations where Crisp and Stanton said they saw evidence of the enrichment process as well as the manufacturing of engine parts infused with highly enriched uranium. Crisp detailed her escape through Shushtar posing as a widowed Muslim wanting to avenge the death of her husband. Winters broke in, apologizing to Crisp and the committee.

"Gentlemen, Agent Crisp is leaving a detail or two out of her story that must be told." Without looking at the agent, Winters gave a blow-by-blow account of the armory destruction and the insurgents' assassination plot against the US vice president. "Both of these events carried out exclusively by Limber Crisp."

The committee members were in shock. Some shook their heads while others stared at the group sitting with Winters. Utter amazement, a surreal moment fell over the assembly, no one said a word. The director of Central Intelligence paused, looking from one member to the next waiting on questions that did not arise. "Congressmen, Crystal Stanton and Frank Ellison will conclude with the account of their escape. Sheriff, if you'd begin with the night Talavi came to your room."

An hour later, the mission team and Winters concluded the briefing. Members of the House Permanent Select Committee on Intelligence began to stir from their frozen positions, no one had moved during the presentation. Cleveland called a fifteen-minute break to give members a chance to craft questions for the team, but just as everyone stood to stretch, a legislative aide came in pushing an audio/visual cabinet. The aide whispered something to the two co-chairmen, and Cleveland turned to his microphone and told those headed for the doors to be back in five minutes. "I'm sorry, folks; we've just been advised the president is making an announcement from the Oval Office in about eight minutes. Congressman Murphy and I have been told it is pertinent to our current discussion. So in seven minutes from now, the Capitol police will re-lock the doors and no one will be allowed in." People quickened their pace, most desperately needing to make a restroom call, and within five minutes everyone had returned. The aide finished connecting cables on the TV and turned it to a C-SPAN channel showing the president's empty chair behind his desk in the Oval Office; there was no sound, no talking heads, only the occasional rattle of off-camera equipment being set up. She moved the TV in front of both co-chairmen, and Cleveland asked her to turn it to the audience. "The committee will view from out there so that everyone in the room can see."

Five minutes later, the president sat down at his desk and began the announcement. "Fellow Americans..." During the following four-minute announcement, the president sighted irrefutable evidence Iran was enriching uranium far beyond what was necessary to operate a utility plant, and the only plausible explanation was for it to be used for weapons purposes. He also explained machinery parts manufactured at the plant were being made with HEU and then being shipped via the People's Republic of China for distribution to assembly plants in several countries including the US. He said sleeper cells in those countries collected the HEU parts and were now working on building a bomb. "A one-mega-ton bomb, strategically placed, could kill a hundred thousand citizens, cause one hundred billion dollars in immediate damages, and disrupt commerce for several years. As your president, I cannot allow that to happen; therefore, I authorized an air strike against the Iranian nuclear plant near Natanz. The strike took place early this morning, and we have verified target destruction using satellite photos. A Stealth Bomber delivered two one-thousand-pound JDAM, satellite-guided bombs hitting the targets precisely as planned. Very little collateral damage was expected, and according to an analysis of photo data, the electric generating portion of the plant sustained only minor damage and should be providing electricity to homes and communities within a week." The president paused, his stern expression diminishing as the subject turned personal. "In following weeks, you will see the evidence we have based our actions on; in the meantime, please trust that my decision to bomb the plant was a difficult one. We chose the early morning hour to make use of darkness, and we knew there would only be a skeleton crew at the plant monitoring the overnight rest phase. However, no matter how much you trust me or my administration, I know there will be anger and dissent among citizens of other countries as well as from our own, and I understand that. Propaganda is sure to arise from this air strike; please be patient. Information will be forthcoming that will shed light on the truth..."

The president concluded, and C-SPAN transferred its coverage to the senate floor and a debate on the economy. The aide disconnected the TV and wheeled it out of the committee room. Committee members quietly returned to their places. Knowledge of Operation Moriah Ruse was sufficient proof for the House Permanent Select Committee on Intelligence to agree with the president's decision in principle. However, some still clung to the theory of diplomacy regardless of what intelligence revealed. Their belief that military action should only follow a direct assault on the US or US allies had been the central debate issue since World War I, and most likely it would continue to be the crux of debate well into the future.

When everyone was seated, Cleveland officially reconvened the committee with a proposal. "Based upon the team's testimony, I recommend we issue a letter to the president supporting the preemptive strike on the nuclear plant in Iran. Debate?"

A short discussion followed, hardly a debate, and the most critical member of the committee remained surprisingly quiet. The majority took that as tacit agreement, and the recommendation was approved; Murphy abstained. Cleveland thanked Winters and her team for their service and reminded everyone of the strict classified nature of the proceedings. As soon as Cleveland announced adjournment, Webster leaned close to Stanton's fiancée. "Now you know. And here's the rest, plain and simple."

Robert Gray's eyes betrayed the reserved appearance he'd finally mastered. From a distance, he looked calm, even detached, but up close his eyes revealed just how shocked he was. He looked at Webster speechless.

"Listen to me while I repeat what I've said to you at least three times since we met."

Gray nodded, his pupils beginning to contract, the look of utter astonishment fading.

"If you ever say anything about what you've heard or where you've been, you might face serious federal charges. Do you understand?"

"Yes."

"I got you in here as a favor to Crys, and if you do let something slip, I will be fired and face charges too. Do you understand?"

"Yes."

"And, Robert, there is a good chance Crys will too. Do you understand?"

"Yes."

"You will leave with me, just as you came. You will not wave, look at, blow a kiss to, or give thumbs-up to Crys if we happen to meet outside in public. Do you understand?"

"I do; I really do. I don't want anything more to happen to Crys; she's been through enough."

"Good. Now let's get something to eat, and I'll take you back to the hotel. A single ticket back to Oklahoma will be delivered to you tonight. It's an early morning flight out of Reagan; be on that plane. When Crys finishes up here, in the next day or two, we'll make sure she gets home safe and sound. Okay?"

"Yeah, okay. Hey, Jerry, thanks for getting me in." Robert was still seated; he looked down and straightened his tie before going on. "The way I am, always have been, I gotta know what's going on with people I'm close to. You know what I mean, so I don't think it's something I've done or said."

"I'm with you on that. If my wife is sad or mad, I immediately think it's my fault."

"Exactly, and if I thought Crys was struggling with something, well, like you, I'd think it'd be me that caused it."

"Women."

"Yeah, women." Robert stood. "I'm hungry. Where can we get a good rare steak?"

CHAPTER 66

The director of Central Intelligence waited in the parking lot near the Capitol exit door she knew Congressman Murphy would come through on the way to his car. His arrogant attitude had withered during the committee meeting, and she thought the time was right to capitalize on his vulnerable state of mind. Her three-vehicle security detail sat in a row fifty feet from Murphy's car. One of Winters' assistants who had been watching the congressman's movements since the committee adjourned notified her that he was on his way out. Five minutes later Murphy came out of the building and headed toward his car; Winters watched as he approached. He looked like a defeated man with his head bowed and shoulders slumping. Murphy's eyes were down as he cut in and out of the parked cars on his way to his designated spot, he didn't notice her waiting. He pressed a button on his security key fob, and the trunk of his car opened. As he tossed his briefcase in, Winters approached. Her abrupt appearance startled Murphy, and he dropped his keys.

"I'm sorry; I didn't mean to sneak up on you," Winters said.

"Oh, I thought that's how you did business, Director Winters." Murphy hissed as he picked up his keys.

She ignored his retort and stepped closer to be eye to eye with the congressman. Her tone remained smooth, quiet, but unmistakably frank. "Congressman Murphy, I know how you've been getting advanced intel, and I know the motivation. You want the secretary of defense job, and Paul wants mine." She gave the congressman an opportunity to say something on impulse. He looked away, loosening his tie then at the pavement.

"What in the hell do you want from me, Winters?"

"What I want, Congressman, is what's good for the country, and having you as the next secretary of defense isn't. You and your friend Paul have turned out to be opportunistic egotists; you've both sold out to ambition. You both want the power and prestige of the office but ignore the responsibility."

Murphy pulled a handkerchief from his back pocket to wipe sweat from his burning eyes. His pale skin exhibiting various shades of crimson as the color crept up from under his collar, he said, "So, Winters, what are you saying?"

"Simple. If your party man wins in November, keep your hat out of the ring."

"And—"

"Don't even say it, Congressman."

Murphy was livid, feeling the kind of anger that comes bound tight in frustration because there isn't anything that can be done about it. He slammed the trunk lid shut, got into his car, and sped out of the lot, leaving Winters standing—but standing in control. She gave Murphy time to contact Paul about the committee-meeting outcome and their private chat before she spoke to her one-time protégé. The next morning she called the director of intelligence in for a closed-door, off-the-record talk.

"You've talked to Congressman Murphy by now, I'm assuming," Winters said after Stimmon left them to their privacy and shut the door.

"I have."

"And?"

"Personally I don't care what happens to Murphy; I'm still going for the director's job that you're going to lose soon."

Winters pulled a single white page from her lap drawer and held it up so Paul could see the subject. "Sorry, Doug, I'm not losing my job, this is a letter of resignation dated for the end of the month and to take effect as soon as a replacement has been confirmed." She pulled another document out of her desk and handed it to Paul. He studied the page of bullet points and handed it back. "No, Doug, that's your copy. I thought you might want to show it to your attorney in case you want to fight this in court."

"Even if you can prove any of this, it's not illegal. It has always been just between Murphy and me; remember, Margaret, he is the chair of the hips committee."

"I believe actually he is the co-chair. So how often did you share with Cleveland?" Winters knew the answer. "You're right; what you did may not be illegal, but do you think for a minute whoever becomes president is going to want you and Murphy on his team? I think not." Winters pulled a third document from the drawer and handed it to Paul.

"A letter of resignation? Margaret, you have to be kidding. I'm not signing this." Paul's statement was defiant but weak; he knew Winters would get her way.

"Look it over, let it settle in, show it to your attorney along with the list of points, and get his advice. Or sign it and leave the agency for unspecified reasons, and move on to the next chapter in your life. I would imagine you could exchange the headaches and the government paycheck for a lot less stress and a bigger salary with your expertise."

Paul looked at the resignation letter then at the listed points; he set his coffee cup on Winters' desk and left her office.

"You'll see what I mean; it's narrow. By the way, I forgot to ask, are you claustrophobic?"

"No."

"Good. The others are at the end of the narrow corridor working."

"How close are they to getting through?"

"No way to tell just yet, maybe fifty centimeters."

"Where are we, approximately?" Bethel asked.

"Remember the drawing I showed you of Solomon's Temple?"

"Yeah."

"The holy of holies?"

"Yeah."

"We're about ten meters to the west of that location and twenty meters east of the existing Western Wall. We're another six or eight meters from the surface." Ramirez's light flickered and disappeared.

Bethel searched the corridor for his friend, but there was no sign of him. "Carlos?" he yelled.

"Yes, Lee, I'm here around the corner, the narrow part I told you about."

"Okay, I see your light now. I see what you mean by narrow."

The overhead lighting stopped where the wider passageway and the narrow one converged. The two men were totally dependent on their flashlights now, edging themselves sideways along a path no wider than a large box of cereal.

"One thing's for sure, Carlos."

"Yeah?"

"The temple priests didn't cart the ark of the covenant through here."

"No, this is the back door. The main entrance to the underground chambers would have been on the east side, closer to where the Dome of the Rock sits now. There is no way we would have gotten permission to enter from there."

"But you did get permission, didn't you?"

"I told you back at the cabin, remember."

"Something about Arabs, Israelis, and our State Department working a secret deal."

"When the secretary of state was in Athens working out the parameters concerning the rumor about the tablets being authentic, an assistant was covertly working a deal for a joint excavation of the chamber. The agreement that was eventually hammered out called for breeching the chamber, a one-hour look-see, reseal the chamber, and get out. Nothing is to be taken or disturbed in any way, and absolutely no photographs."

"I still don't understand why I'm here."

They could hear chipping and drilling nearby. Ramirez stopped and pointed his light to the floor. The stale air mixed with the smell of quarry dust was growing strong. He handed Bethel a dust mask. "Two of the men are Israeli, both professors of antiquities and experts in biblical history. The other two are Muslim, one from Iraq and one living here in Jerusalem. Both are museum curators who hold PhDs in archaeology. The fifth man is the US diplomat that brokered the agreement. They asked me to participate; I asked them if I could bring my own expert, and they agreed. So, here it is in brief, there are eight people who know this is going on—"

"Eight?"

"The seven of us down here in the dark, and the eighth is the US Secretary of State." Ramirez slipped his mask on and pointed toward the sound. "Ready?"

Bethel put his mask on and nodded. Ramirez's light beam reflected off the thick dust surrounding the nearby worksite. They followed the corridor as it made a gentle curve back north then another short climb over what appeared to be three rock steps each about thirty centimeters high. The five men gave no indication Ramirez and Bethel had arrived; they were on their knees watching as one man drilled and another hammered away at the loose rock. Faces couldn't be seen, but it was evident all five had jobs to do. The man drilling stopped long enough to change out a low battery pack. Another grabbed it stuffing it into a small satchel containing other

depleted batteries, and without saying anything, headed down the passageway to the charger.

"Can we help?" Ramirez said.

One of the men shifted his body in the confined space so he could see Ramirez, "No, we're about through. We stuck a probe between these two stones. Anytime now."

Dr. Ramirez had called Lee Bethel forty-eight hours earlier to tell him the expedition was getting close—tempting his friend one last time. Ramirez tossed his last enticement on the table telling him the agreed-upon veil of silence was about to fall, never to be raised, at least during his lifetime. Bethel boarded a plane that afternoon, and twenty-one hours later, he checked into the King David Hotel in Jerusalem exhausted. Ramirez met him in the lobby, and they had dinner together. "I'm glad you're here, Lee. I hesitate to say this, but I feel strongly we're on the verge of the most important archaeological discovery of all time."

"And why the hesitation?" Bethel asked.

"I don't want to jinx it."

"I'd never take you as the superstitious kind."

"I'm not, but I want this discovery so bad I can taste it." Carlos smiled nervously, ashamed he'd allowed such an unscientific thought to push reason to the side. "Just covering all the bases, so to speak."

"Point taken, Carlos. Now, what's next?"

"I'll pick you up at seven a.m., and we'll go straight to the site. The others will already be working; hopefully we'll be inside the chamber by mid-afternoon. Be ready."

The men shook hands, and Ramirez left the hotel. Bethel showered and went straight to bed hoping he would fall asleep soon. That state of altered consciousness where rest revives the body and renews brain function never came, only flashes of excitement that kept his mind spinning and his eyes open.

Less than a half-hour later, the man returned with a fresh set of recharged batteries. The driller dropped the exhausted pack and inserted a fresh one and returned to his work. A thin man, covered in gray dust speaking Arabic, pulled two heavy sacks of stone debris from the opening and moved them out of the way. The space where the seven men were grew tighter, the smell of a hot drill bit working against the stone, and the dust made the area seem even smaller. Suddenly the man drilling backed out of the small hole breathing deeply.

"I've broken through," he said, gasping for air through the mask. The others got quiet waiting for more information. "Get your hammers and chisels; we'll work in fifteen-minute shifts until we've made the opening large enough to crawl through." He pointed at the man who'd just returned with the fresh batteries. "You first." Then he pointed at Bethel. "Find a hammer; here is my chisel. When his fifteen minutes are up, you go."

The other participants had already cast lots to see who would enter the chamber first. Ramirez, Bethel, and the diplomat were last, and the decision of their order was left for them to decide.

By six p.m. all seven men were standing in the chamber directly below where the holy of holies was once located, their flashlights darting from place to place, up and down the stone walls and across the ceiling. The chamber looked perfectly square with the walls as high as they were long and wide. All of the walls were bare, no carvings of any kind, the same with the ceiling. The floor was dirt and sand mixture. A large flat stone sat in the middle of the room, Bethel guessed it to be three meters long, two wide, and one meter high, but there was nothing on it. The room was empty. Everyone in the chamber kept his thoughts private, each disappointed. They had hoped to see a once-powerful relic of a past culture. On the other hand relieved, knowing full well that if it had been there the signed secrecy agreement would become worthless.

After a shower later that night, both men met in the restaurant at the King David to put some closure on a hunt that prompted questions and fueled their curiosity even more.

"You as disappointed as I am?" Lee asked.

"That requires a complicated answer, Lee." Ramirez held the menu up to the brass lamp hanging over their table. "What are you having?

"Salmon, the wine they suggest with the name I can't pronounce, and a salad."

"Beaujolais, pronounced bo-zho-la. Good choice, I'll have that too."

The waiter came soon and left with their order, and when he was some distance away, Ramirez said, "The answer to your question has to be *yes* and *no*."

"Why?" Lee's frustration was difficult for him to hide, and he didn't have the energy to conceal it anyway.

"Yes, disappointed I didn't get to see the most sought after artifact of all time, of course. No because the outcome was unknowable."

"That sounds like double-talk, what do you mean unknowable?"

"In most cases involving discoveries—and Lee, I know you've dealt with this—after a discovery is made, it can be put on display. Historians and scientists can study it and verify legends or the development of a culture and the fall of a society, but not so with the ark of the covenant. It means as much today as it did four-thousand years ago. It has current influence—"

Lee interrupted, "And it's the influence that is at issue here."

"Right! We don't know who it will influence most—the Muslims or Jews, and we don't know what that influence will prompt them to do."

"Maybe nothing?"

The waiter brought the salmon, uncorked the wine, and left their table. Neither man had eaten since breakfast, which elevated food consumption to the number one task. The clatter of forks and knives striking porcelain china was the only sound at the table other than an occasional groan of satisfaction. Twenty minutes later the food and Beaujolais were consumed and Ramirez tried to recall their last words.

"Influence, yes, Lee, influence, and I guarantee you it will prompt one or both to do something."

"So, Carlos, you're saying that right now the world is safer because we didn't find the ark?"

Ramirez motioned for the waiter. "I'm having a desert wine, Lee, how about you?"

"One, then off to bed. Got to be in Tel Aviv by four p.m. tomorrow to catch my flight home."

"Anxious?"

Lee peered into his glass of Merlot as if it were a crystal ball and smiled. "That requires a complicated answer, Carlos."

Ramirez laughed, "I know, Lee, *yes* and *no,* right?"

"But you love me the most, right?" he said.

"Of course, now get out, so I can finish dressing."

"Can I watch?"

"Get out," she said pushing him toward the door.

The wedding was held at the home of Robert's parents. A small gathering of mostly out of town guests celebrated the informal but highly anticipated occasion. There were no balloons, doves, white lace, or bouquets. No gifts, no songs, or organ music. Robert's dad served as best man, Maude Bingham the maid of honor, and Jerry Webster gave the bride away. Rosalind Henry, a longtime friend of the family and local district judge, performed the civil ceremony.

The newlyweds stood together near the dining room entrance, and following Helen Gray's command, a congratulatory line formed. "After you've kissed the bride, please go on to the dining room, fill your plates from the buffet and take a seat anywhere you please." The first person in line was Frank Ellison. He stepped close to the woman he'd loved and lost, taking her hands in his, Ellison leaned forward and kissed her on both cheeks, but didn't say a word to her. He looked at Robert and whispered. "I know I don't need to say this, but just the same, I am. Please take good care of her; she's a jewel."

"I will; that's a promise. And, Frank…"

"Yeah."

"Thanks for saving her life."

"Entirely my pleasure, Mr. Gray. Now step aside, I see food."

Later that afternoon, Ellison checked his rental car in and caught a shuttle to the airport terminal. The wedding was fun; seeing everyone together in a setting filled with joy instead of danger was especially gratifying. Frank had somehow gotten by the intense feeling of loss at not being the one to marry Crys. He'd moved on; it was his time to enjoy life. His retirement papers were approved, and he had turned in all the FBI paraphernalia. The cabin in the woods was waiting for him. Frank boarded the plane in Oklahoma City bound for DC, and before taking his seat, he pulled a brochure from his carry-on bag. Twenty minutes later, the plane was airborne. He reached up and pushed the light button and opened the glossy four-page ad. The youngster seated next to him pointed to a picture in the brochure. "My dad has one like that."

"He does."

"Yep, he fishes every weekend."

"You go with him?"

"Yep." The boy looked down and fumbled with the buckle on the restraint belt. "Yep, when I get to stay with him."

Frank could hear the sadness in his voice. He knew the sound; he'd been there himself. "Mom and Dad don't live together?"

"Nope, they're divorced."

"Oh, that's bad."

"Yep." Tears came with no sound, not even a sniffle.

"What's your name?"

"Brent Allan Stokes."

"Nice to meet ya, Brent. Mine's Frank."

"Nice to meet you." The boy searched his ten-year-old social skills for more to say. "What do you do?"

"Nothing now, that's why I'm looking at these boats, trying to figure out which is best. Got any advice?"

"That'n." With no hesitation he pointed to the one like his dad's.

"Well then, Brent, if you think it's the best, that's the one I'm getting."

The boy smiled.

Frank folded the brochure and put it in his coat pocket, and in doing so felt the leather edge of his ID. He pulled the well-worn wallet out and held it in his hand, turning it over and over as he thought about Brent Allan Stokes. "Hey, Brent."

"Yeah."

"You want to be friends?"

"Sure, but Dad says to not talk with strangers."

"That's good advice, Brent, but you've been talking to me." Ellison watched the boy struggle with the predicament he'd gotten himself in. "Why?"

"You seem nice," Brent whispered as if to conceal his comment from his dad.

"A lot of people seem nice, Brent, especially people who aren't sometimes."

"What do you mean?"

"It's hard to explain."

"Have I been bad?"

"Of course not. You seem like a nice kid; I just don't want anything to happen to you." Frank opened his ID wallet and took out a card with his name embossed over the official seal of the FBI. Below his name in bold letters were the words *Special Agent.* He scratched out the obsolete phone numbers and wrote a post office box number, town, and zip code on the back and handed the card to the boy. "Put that in your pocket and show it to your folks."

"Okay."

"Here is something else I want you to have. Put it in a special place with the card I gave you." Frank unfastened his badge from the wallet and handed it to Brent.

"Wow." He looked up at Frank with an expression that made Ellison glad he was seated next to the kid.

"Wow. For me?"

"Yep."

The following week Ellison backed the boat trailer through the clearing next to his cabin and down the incline to the water's edge. He carefully edged the new fully-equipped bass boat—the one Brent Allan Stokes recommended—into the water next to a small pier built by the previous cabin owner. He tied it off on one of the support pilings and stepped back to admire what he'd worked so long and hard to own. He looked at the three-room log cabin, the lake, and back at the boat. There was only one thing missing, something he couldn't buy even if he had the money.

A chilly gust of wind cut through the pines and skidded quickly across the cove, rocking the bass boat. Frank didn't notice the wind; he had a largemouth on the line giving him a real battle. Fish and fisherman sparred several minutes before the bass was alongside the boat exhausted. Frank's routine allowed a fresh catch for his evening meal, and the rest he released. He weighed the bass, carefully removed the lure, and gently set him free. With shorter winter days, Frank's time on the lake had dwindled to a few afternoon hours. It was four p.m., and by the time he crossed the lake to the cabin, the sun would be disappearing behind the high pine-covered ridgeline to the west.

After the wedding, Frank cut what was left of his hair off to barely visible stubble, and as some men do to compensate, he grew a beard. He wore a bright orange stocking cap most of the time now, the cap to keep his head warm and the color to warn area hunters he wasn't Sasquatch. With the cap pulled over his ears, Frank sped northeast, and as he rounded a rocky peninsula and into the mouth of the cove where his cabin was, he spotted something unusual. He killed the engine and reached under his seat for the binoculars. The distance from where he was to the cabin was an eighth of a mile, but the trees surrounding his property shrouded the cabin in shadows, obscuring a clear view. The only thing he could see was the silhouette of something that wasn't there earlier in the day. He reached under his jacket to make sure his Beretta was there then moved the boat forward as close to the west bank as possible using his trolling motor, stopping periodically to refocus the binoculars.

By the time he was within a hundred yards of his pier, he could make out the top of a car parked next to the cabin. He hadn't invited anyone to his place, and as far as he could remember, he'd never told a soul the location of his hideaway. Whoever it was had no business being there, and that privacy infringement brought out the FBI in Frank Ellison.

Crossing the cove would expose him; he'd be a sitting duck for anyone wanting to take him out, and as far as he knew, there were still a few around that would with fervor. He threw his orange cap under the boat dash and pulled the weapon from its holster. The range was too far to count on accuracy, but he could still pepper the area with enough rounds to make an assailant take cover and hopefully give him time to find shelter in the woods. Ellison maneuvered the boat to shore under an overhanging willow tree and took another look into the shadows with the binoculars. He holstered the gun and readjusted the focus; alarm gave way to excitement as he began spelling aloud a message beamed across the cove by flashlight. w-h-y a-r-e y-o-u h-i-d-i-n-g i-n t-r-e-e-s? The message was repeated again, this time it was signed.

Ellison didn't want to appear eager; he started the big Evinrude and moved the throttle forward slowly. The boat glided over the water at just over idle speed. By the time he tied off at the dock, Margaret Winters was standing on the pier, a brown paper bag at her side. He hadn't seen her since Crys' wedding—a tough day for him. Frank had not socialized much that day, the way he felt seeing Crys married didn't contribute much toward that warm and fuzzy feeling everyone else seemed to have. He was invited, so he went, he said his piece and closed the door on something he couldn't nor wouldn't change. Frank did remember one thing about that wedding day, something he'd quickly dismissed, but it had somehow invaded his peaceful contemplation time while fishing. The attraction began while watching a ballgame with Winters; it couldn't be mutual, he remembered telling himself. He'd been through enough. And another heartbreak, he was afraid, would just send him over the edge, so he shut those feelings off before they had a chance of tormenting him. But there she was standing on the pier, smiling and even more beautiful than he'd remembered. "Margaret Winters—"

"Maggie, please," she corrected. Her smile wasn't just warm, it was embracing.

"Maggie, how the hell did you find me?" He held up his hand, shaking his head realizing the foolishness of his question. "Never mind, stupid question, for a second I forgot I was talking to the top spook."

"Not for long."

"What?"

"Resigned effective as soon as the new president appoints and the committee approves."

"Owens?"

"It'd better be Owens. He's the only reasonable choice, and if someone else gets the job, then there's some skullduggery going on."

Frank finished tying the boat up and began unloading gear. "And what if there is?"

"Skullduggery?"

"Yeah."

"I've got friends in low places that'd be delighted to pay off their debt."

"Remind me never to get crossways with you." He chuckled.

"Hey, changing the subject, I see you've dubbed your boat with a unique name." Maggie pointed to the forward hull where *BAS Boat* had been professionally painted. "Here all along I thought that bass was spelled *b-a-s-s*."

"Just a little play on words, something to remind me how good I have it in spite of shit happening."

"What do the letters stand for?"

"Someone I met recently."

"A woman?" she asked cautiously.

"A ten-year-old boy by the name of Brent Allan Stokes; the kid reminded me of me when I was his age." Frank slung his fishing gear over his shoulder and pointed to the cabin. "Come in; I'll show you around." His heart pounding. "I don't want to sound inhospitable, but what are you doing here?"

"Just decided I needed a rest; thought I'd try fishing."

"Here?"

"Either here or somewhere else. You got any recommendations?"

"Nope, here is as good as it gets."

"Where is the nearest motel?"

Ellison realized he was being played, but it was okay, he was enjoying every minute of it. "What's in the sack?"

Winters pulled the contents halfway out of the bag so he could see.

"Hmm, Bud Light. A great choice, Ms. Winters."

She took the tackle box from his overburdened hand. "If you say so."